MUTANT
CITY

About the author

Steve Feasey lives in Hertfordshire with his wife and kids. He didn't learn much at school except how to get into trouble and played truant as often as he could to avoid a successful academic career — but he was always a voracious reader. He started writing fiction in his thirties, inspired by his own favourite writers — Stephen King, Elmore Leonard and Charles Dickens. His first book, Changeling, was shortlisted for the Waterstones Prize and became a successful series. Mutant City is his first book for Bloomsbury and will be followed by Mutant Rising in 2015.

ABOUT THE AUTHOR

Steve Feasey lives in Hertfordshire with his family. He didn't learn much at school except how to get into fights and chat up girls – he wasn't particularly successful at either – but he was always a voracious reader. He started writing fiction in his thirties, inspired by his own favourite writers: Stephen King, Elmore Leonard and Charles Dickens. His first book, Changeling, was shortlisted for the Waterstones Prize and became a successful series. Mutant City is his first book for Bloomsbury and will be followed by Mutant Rising in 2015.

MUTANT CITY

STEVE FEASEY

BLOOMSBURY

LONDON   NEW DELHI   NEW YORK   SYDNEY

Bloomsbury Publishing, London, New Delhi, New York and Sydney

First published in Great Britain in May 2014 by Bloomsbury Publishing Plc
50 Bedford Square, London WC1B 3DP

Bloomsbury is a registered trademark of Bloomsbury Publishing Plc

www.bloomsbury.com
www.mutantcitybook.com

A CIP catalogue record for this book is available from the British Library

ISBN 978 1 4088 4303 1

Typeset by Hewer Text UK Ltd, Edinburgh
Printed and bound in Great Britain by CPI Group (UK) Ltd, Croydon CR0 4YY

1 3 5 7 9 10 8 6 4 2

This book is for all the 'freaks' out there.
You know who you are. SF

BEFORE

The Farm

The raiding party comprised only seven individuals: six mutants and the 'Pure' insider who'd planned the incursion. They hurried down the corridor that led to the research facility, stepping over the uniformed bodies of the guards that lay on the floor. The small canisters of powerful nerve gas they'd used to incapacitate those in charge of this place – pumping it in through the air-conditioning system – had worked better than any of them had expected, and they now stood before a huge steel door, sweating behind their awkward gas masks.

The man closest to the door slid a key card into a small metal box on the wall. When he tapped in today's security code and held his thumb over the scanner, he was rewarded with the noise of automated locks disengaging.

The seven stepped through this door, squeezing into a

decontamination chamber on the other side. From here, they were able to pass through a second door and enter the top-secret facility beyond.

The air supply in the lab came from a separate system to that in the rest of the facility, and they could finally remove their masks and look around them properly. Steel benches crammed with high-tech equipment lined the walls, but their eyes were immediately drawn to the huge glass tank that took up most of the centre of the room. Inside, suspended in a murky yellow liquid to keep it preserved, were the remains of a grotesque humanoid figure. Long dead now, it was almost unrecognisable as a man; its limbs and body were bent and contorted, as if they had been incorrectly attached by some sick and twisted creator. A huge, deformed head with large bulging eyes stared sightlessly back at them through the glass.

'What is that thing?' the woman named Maw asked.

'The mutant they found in the Blacklands,' Silas answered. As the insider responsible for getting them all into this place, he had seen the preserving tank many times. Nonetheless, he was still horrified by it. 'That poor, unfortunate wretch is the reason we're all here today.'

A noise from behind a door set into the far wall silenced them. It was the unmistakable sound of a small child crying out.

'Let's get a move on,' said Silas. 'We don't have much time before the effect of the gas wears off.'

Another keypad, another door. This time, as it swung open, they halted on the threshold to take in what lay beyond.

The nursery was a harshly lit, featureless room containing three aluminium cots and, at the far end, two beds. Beside these were small wheeled trolleys, vials, syringes and other medical paraphernalia neatly arranged on each one. There were two cameras mounted in opposite corners of the room. Motion-activated, they now swung towards the door and the intruders, the whine of their servo-motors just recognisable over the hum of the air-con. The men who usually monitored the images from these cameras would not be raising any alarms. Like the rest of the workers on the facility, they were out cold.

The children, none of whom was asleep despite the late hour, stared back at the strangers, almost as if they had been expecting them. There were three in the cots, all around two years old, maybe a little more. The other two were older. One, an albino, appeared to be about six; the other was perhaps four years older. Unlike the toddlers, these two were secured into their beds by leather straps around their wrists and ankles. Silas hurried over to one of these beds, motioning Maw towards the other. He quickly undid the restraints and helped the albino boy to stand up. Already tall and lanky for his age, the young mutant's skin was the colour of milk. He looked back at the man through eyes of the palest blue imaginable.

'Jax,' the man said, nodding at the youngster.

'I knew you could do it, Silas,' the boy replied. He spoke in a clipped and calm manner that seemed at odds with his age and the situation.

Jax stepped over to the nearest cot, reaching inside to lift the little girl out and balancing her on his hip so he might stare into her face for a moment. 'They've come for us, Anya. They've come for us all.' As he looked at her, tears welled up in his eyes and slid down his pale cheeks. As if in response to this show of emotion, the infant in his arms transformed into a spitting-and-hissing wild thing; a furless cat-like creature that pulled back its lips to bare its teeth at the newcomers.

'No, Anya. These are our friends.'

It was the gentlest of remonstrations, but the animal quickly became a girl again, burying her face into his chest as if embarrassed by her outburst.

The young albino shrugged apologetically. 'They have already been through so much, and they're only babies.' He looked about him at the other children, shaking his head at what he saw. 'And the men who ran this place called *us* monsters.'

'Where are the scientists?' Silas asked.

Jax gave him a sly grin. 'Those metal helmets they wore? The ones to keep me from using my powers on them? Well, it seems as if they went missing just about the time that the alarm sounded. The scientists had a terrifying vision. Apparently they were under the impression that a giant snake-headed monster had broken into this facility. They fled via the emergency escape tunnel.'

'A snake-headed monster?'

The pale child's grin intensified, and he shrugged again.

The woman, Maw, having undone the eldest boy's restraints, knelt by his side, her hand resting on his arm. The boy lay in the bed watching everything going on around him. If Jax was tall for his age, this youngster was *huge* for his. A great blockhead stared back at his rescuer, a hint of a smile touching the corners of his mouth. 'Brick!' he said in a loud voice.

Maw reached out to flatten some stray hairs that stood up on the boy's head. In response, the youngster reached up and took her hand in his, pressing it to his face. 'Brick,' the boy said again.

'Why does he keep saying that?' she asked, without turning away from the child.

'Brick was one of the first experiments,' Silas explained. 'His mental faculties were impaired by the things they did

to him. One of the guards said he was "as thick as a brick".'
He shook his head, the corners of his mouth turning down
at the memory. 'He would torment the boy over and over
with that expression, until eventually the name stuck.'

'How could such cruelty be allowed?'

The look Jax gave her suggested the guards' taunts were
the least of it.

'You've already met Anya,' Silas said, gesturing towards
the girl in Jax's arms. He nodded to the other cots. 'The
little boy is called Rush. The girl next to him is Flea.'

'Who named them?' Maw asked.

'I did,' Jax said. 'Before that, they were simply known
by their case numbers. Many of the scientists still insist on
referring to us in that way. I suppose they're frightened of
humanising us.'

'So who named you?'

He looked at the man by his side and smiled warmly.
'Silas did.'

There was a moment while the members of the raiding
party took this in.

One of them, a man called Josuf, reached inside Rush's
cot and lifted him into his arms. 'They're just kids. What
kind of person builds a place like this?'

Silas turned to him. 'As Jax said – a monster. A monster
who likes to pretend he's a god.'

'A madman.'

'That too.'

'There's no place anywhere, not even on a messed-up planet like Scorched Earth, for a horror factory like this one.'

'Then it's a good job we're here, isn't it?' Silas said. 'Come on, we've got to get out of here. We still have a lot to do tonight. Take the children back to the safe house where we rendezvoused. I'll join you there as soon as I'm finished.'

Silas watched the children and their new carers depart until only he, Jax and the woman who was to escort the boy to safety were left. When she reached out to take his hand, Jax shook his head. 'I'll stay and help Silas,' he said.

'That's not what we agreed,' Silas said.

'I'm not going without you.' Again it was hard to reconcile the boy's tender age with the way he spoke and acted.

The woman hesitated, not knowing what to do for the best.

After a few moments, Silas sighed. 'Let him stay,' he said to her. 'Go with the others. I'll bring Jax.'

The woman gone, Silas and Jax stood in that terrible place, looking about them in silence. Eventually Silas turned to the albino boy. 'You're sure you can wipe their memories?' he asked.

'Brick will be difficult, if not impossible. He's older and things are . . . complicated inside his head. But he won't give Maw too many problems.'

'And the little ones?'

Jax nodded. 'Trust me – I'll erase every last trace of this place from their minds. They'll be able to live normal lives.'

'Normal?'

'As normal as possible.'

'What about their powers?'

'Separating them will help. The powers we have are enhanced when the five of us are together. In addition, I should be able to suppress the areas of their minds associated with their gifts. That will help for their early years, but as they get older, there's a good chance those "bizarre abilities" will re-emerge. It's in all of our natures to be what we really are, Silas. You'll need to keep a close eye on them, even if they are sent away.'

'And what about you?'

'I can't exactly wipe my own memory, can I?'

'I guess not.'

There was another pause before Jax said, 'I'll stay with you. If you'll have me.'

The boy's proposal was unexpected. Silas had planned that Jax too would be sent off to a remote location, to live in one of the safe houses he'd set up.

'That won't be possible. Even with this place gone, you're hardly difficult to spot.'

'You know I can make anyone see me however I want them to, Silas.' As if to demonstrate this, the boy transformed into a replica of the man himself, so that Silas was looking at his own twin and hearing his own voice speak to him inside his head. *Even though this is only a trick of the mind, I think you'd agree it's a pretty good disguise.* His doppelgänger disappeared as quickly as it had appeared and a grinning albino boy was standing before him once again.

Silas blinked, an uneasy expression on his face. 'Don't do that again. It's . . . weird.'

'I'm sorry. I was just trying to demonstrate to you that I would not be a liability to have around.'

His rescuer considered this. 'There would have to be rules if you were to come and live with me. No more paranormal mind tricks unless they are absolutely called for. And the first time I find you rummaging around inside my head, you're out, OK?'

'Rummaging around in your head?'

'I know you can tune into my thoughts, Jax.'

'I wouldn't do that to you. I respect you too much.'

Silas blew out his cheeks. 'I can't believe I'm going to do this,' he said under his breath, 'but, all right. You can come with me.'

'Thank you.'

Silas looked about him at the room where the children had been imprisoned. 'What do you say we erase this hell-hole from the face of the earth?'

Jax didn't hesitate. 'Nothing would give me greater pleasure.'

With that, the two set off in the direction of the cold fusion reactor deep in the bowels of the building, both determined that in a short while the place referred to as the Farm would utterly cease to exist.

THIRTEEN YEARS LATER

Rush

A low, rumbling sound registered with Rush despite the fact he was fast asleep and dreaming. It was the same dream he always had. He was in a large white space. He was very small, but knew what was expected of him. Around him, set into the walls and ceiling at various points, were small, dark apertures, like black eyes staring out at him. In one wall was a mirror, and he somehow knew that the men who ran the place were behind it, looking in on him. There was a series of hisses followed by *phlump!* sounds as, suddenly, one after another, wooden balls flew at him from every direction. Just as the objects were about to strike, they were deflected, as if he and the projectiles were magnets of the same pole, repulsing each other at the last moment. He had the vague impression of a man's voice – a man hidden behind the mirrored surface – but not of the words he was saying. All he knew was that the man was pleased Rush hadn't been hit, and Rush was pleased he had made the man feel this way.

A door opened in the wall and a woman dressed all in white entered. The woman would take him back to the room where the others were kept. It was always the same woman in the dream.

But there was something different this time. She stopped before him, but instead of reaching down to pick him up, she spoke. The woman in white never spoke in the dream, and it was clear the voice wasn't hers; it was the voice of a young man, as if someone was using this dream phantom to speak to him.

They're coming for you, Rush. You have to escape NOW. You must make your way to the mutant ghetto near City Four. Cross the Wastelands and find the Tranter Trading Post. There's something you need to collect there.

Rush opened his eyes and turned his head in the direction of the window beside his bed. The rumbling had stopped abruptly. Strangely, it was this sudden lack of noise that had finally wrenched him from his sleep. Night had not yet given way to day, but the colour and quality of the light outside told him it would not be long before dawn broke. Getting to his knees on the small wooden pallet with the straw-stuffed mattress on top, he peered outside at the official-looking vehicle that had come to a halt outside their farmhouse, its engine making loud ticking sounds as it cooled.

Josuf appeared at the doorway to Rush's room, hastily pulling on a holed and misshapen woollen jumper as he looked fearfully towards the window. His hair was sticking up and he ran a hand over his beard in a manner that made Rush nervous. They could both clearly hear the voices outside now. Josuf spoke with quiet urgency. 'Get your clothes on, Rush. Get them on and get ready. It's probably nothing. But just in case . . .'

'But –'

'Do it. Now.' He turned away from the boy and walked back along the narrow hallway in the direction of the front door.

As he tugged his trousers on, Rush stole another glance through the window just as men began to disembark from the vehicle. The first out looked down at an electronic device in his hands, swiping the glowing screen with his finger before nodding back at two more men, each of whom Rush could now see was carrying a rifle of some kind. Rush leaned forward until his forehead almost touched the windowpane, squinting to get a better look at the weapons.

He heard the front door open, and the man he thought of as a father spoke: 'Can I help you? Who are you people?'

'Agency for the Regulation of Mutants. Get everyone in the house outside.'

Rush's blood ran cold. The ARM was a relatively new organisation set up under the direction of President Melk. The men and women who served in its units were notorious for their brutality and there had already been a number of deaths during the breaking up of 'illegal mutant rallies'. It was especially worrying that they were out here; the ARM crews usually stayed close to the cities, and to the mutant slums that had sprung up beyond their walls.

'It's rather late. Couldn't this wait until –'

'When I want your opinion, Mute, I'll ask for it. All members of this household out front now. You've got two minutes to comply.' The man glanced down at his omnipad. The light shining up from below cast deep shadows over his face.

'What makes you think there's anyone else here?'

'The people on the neighbouring smallholding told us that there's a young boy living here. Approximately fifteen years of age?'

'He's asleep.'

'Then you have –' the man consulted his watch – 'about one minute fifty seconds to wake him up and get him the hell out here.' He stopped, his abrupt tone softening a little. 'We just need a small blood sample from you both.

Nothing more than a prick of the finger. We'll run it through our machine and be on our way.'

'Right.' Josuf gestured back towards the house. 'I'll, er . . . I'll go and get him.' As he turned and walked towards the door he lifted his hand, accidentally knocking the metal triangle that hung beside the door and making a loud clanging sound. He grabbed the thing to quieten it again, turning and nodding his apologies to the armed men.

The triangle was the signal. Rush hurried from his room, making his way down the hallway and into the kitchen. There, disguised to look like a part of the wall, was a secret panel. He pulled it back on its hinges, crouched down and peered inside. The space seemed much smaller than he remembered. It was the 'safe place' Josuf had shown him when he was still small. In those days, his guardian had spoken often about what to do if a 'situation' occurred, but it had been a long time since the pair had even thought about such a thing or conducted the 'emergency drill' that had been so commonplace back then. Nevertheless, the boy remembered the things they'd agreed; he shuffled inside, pulling the panel back into place behind him. Cobwebs stuck to his face and hair; he blew them away as best he could while listening out for the sounds of the house on the other side. If ever he heard the signal, he was to come here and wait until Josuf arrived.

Rush tensed as the panel slid open, but was relieved to see Josuf's face. 'You remembered,' the man said with a sad smile.

'Of course I remembered. Get in.'

He was perplexed when Josuf shook his head. 'You have to go, Rush.' He reached over the boy's shoulder and pushed at another section of wall that fell away, clattering noisily down a set of stone steps that appeared to lead behind and beneath the farmhouse. A damp, earthy smell filled the small hiding space.

Rush stared at the opening before turning back. 'How long has that been there?' he asked.

'Long enough. Listen. You have to take the tunnel and run. Don't stop, Rush. Don't stop until you're past the orchard and into the woods on the other side. Make your way towards City Four and –'

'That's what the voice in my dream said.' The vision of the woman speaking in a voice that was not her own returned.

'What?'

'I had that weird dream again – the one about the things trying to hit me. Only this time it was different.' He frowned, remembering. 'In my dream it's a woman that comes to get me. She never usually speaks, but this time she did . . . in a man's voice.'

'What did the voice say?'

'It told me to collect something from the Tranter Trading Post, then go to the mutant ghetto at City Four.'

Despite the danger they were clearly in, Josuf shook his head and allowed himself a brief smile. 'Jax,' he said.

'Who?'

'Never mind that now, you have to go. Get to City Four. Find Silas . . . and Jax. You won't remember them, but they will know you.'

'What's going on? What about you?'

'I'm going to hold them back as long as I can.'

'But –'

'I knew men might come looking for you one day, Rush. It's part of the risk I was willing to take when I promised to protect you, and I'll be damned if I won't do just that, now I'm called upon to do so!' He stopped. Reaching out, he placed his hands on the boy's shoulders, taking in the teenager's face in the dim light. 'You've been like a son to me, Rush. The son I always –'

There was a loud bang from somewhere in the house. Josuf shoved the boy towards the opening. 'There's a chain at the bottom of the steps. It hangs down from the roof – you can't miss it. Reach up and pull it down hard. Then get to the end of the tunnel as fast as you can.'

'TIME'S UP, MUTE!' Josuf half turned at the sound of the soldier's voice. 'We're coming in to get our blood!'

'What's going to happen, Josuf?'

'I'm going to keep my promise.'

The two looked at each other for a moment longer. 'I wish you *had* been my father,' Rush said as tears slid down his cheeks.

'Thank you, son. Thank you.' The man who had been Rush's guardian for the past thirteen years shoved him through the opening and closed the panel behind him.

The tunnel was a dark, rat-filled space. With one hand on the cold mud wall to his right, Rush half stumbled, half fell down the steps leading to the long escape route away from the farmhouse. He had no idea how Josuf could have made such a thing, or how long it must have taken him. He could hear the usual residents scurrying out of his way as he stepped off the bottom step. Remembering Josuf's instructions, he groped around overhead, reaching up and blindly seeking out the chain in the blackness. When his fingers finally brushed the cold metal links, he grabbed hold and pulled down with all his might, jumping involuntarily as a heavy iron grille dropped down to block off the stairs behind him. He stared at the thing, knowing it not only cut off any chance for him to return via the stairs, but also the possibility of Josuf's joining him in the tunnel. He had little choice but to do as he'd been told. He was about to start out into the dark tunnel, but froze when he heard the muffled sounds of shouting somewhere beyond the stone steps. He didn't want to be down here on his own. It felt like cowardice to be running away like this when he should be up there, helping. But the only way back was to get to the end of the tunnel and turn round. Feeling for the wall again, Rush stumbled blindly ahead into the blackness.

After what could only have been a few minutes – it felt like much longer – Rush made out a small glimmer seeping down into the darkness from above. He looked up at the dim ring of light describing the edges of what must be a small, covered hole in the ground. His heart sank. There was no way he could get up to it without help. The thought of being stuck down here chilled him, until he realised that as tall as Josuf was, he would not have been able to reach it either. He took a step backwards to get a better look and nearly tripped over the wooden ladder on the floor behind him. Quickly grabbing the thing, he thrust the leading edge upward.

As the sole of his foot touched the third rung he heard the loud crack of what could only be a shot being fired.

His spine turned to ice and his stomach lurched. Then,

full of rage and fear, Rush threw himself at the wooden lattice structure above. The earth on top of it had formed a seal around the edges, so he had to slam his shoulder into it to lift it up and out of the way.

He found himself at the edge of the orchard, where he stood getting his breath and his bearings. Spinning round, he looked back down the slope in the direction of the house he'd grown up in. There was a strange calm as the rest of the world slowly woke up. Then the second shot rang out.

Despite everything Josuf had said, Rush began to run back towards the house, slowing only a fraction as he saw the men coming out. When one of them spotted him, a shout went up and they headed for their vehicle.

Then Josuf was at the door, holding a heavy-looking metallic tube in his right hand. The front of his jumper, the jumper he'd been pulling on as he came into Rush's room, was a bloody, wet mess. Josuf staggered towards the vehicle as its engine started up, and raised the arm holding the tube above his head. Rush gasped as he watched the personnel carrier move off, heading at speed straight for his guardian, who did nothing to get out of its way. As the vehicle ploughed into Josuf there was an almighty explosion, the force of which knocked Rush backwards off his feet, the air above him transformed into a rolling wave of heat.

Ears still ringing, the teenager lay on his back for a moment trying to comprehend what he'd just witnessed. The sky above him was thick with life, as if every bird in the world had taken flight, all cawing and screeching to each other at the same time.

Gingerly getting back to his feet, Rush stared down the hill at the mangled wreckage of the ARM vehicle and the even more mangled figures within it. Where Josuf had stood only moments before was nothing but a dark red-and-black smudge.

Rush dropped down on to his hands and knees and vomited into the grass.

When the mutant boy finally turned his back on the horrific tableau outside the farmhouse and made his way through the orchard, he was in a dazed and confused state, still not quite able to believe what he'd witnessed. Because of him, the man he'd come to think of as his father was dead, killed by the ARM while trying to protect him.

For a while after the incident, Rush had sat on the grass, holding his mud-and-tear-streaked face in his hands as he tried to figure out what to do. How could this have happened? What had the men, supposedly on a routine check, really wanted? Part of him wanted to stay at the place Josuf and he had called home. But Josuf had told him to go. Not to do so would mean his guardian had died in vain. It was this realisation that finally forced Rush to pull himself together and set off away from the only home he'd ever known.

City Four, the capital, the biggest of the Six Cities, was far away to the north. Rush knew it was the heart of government, of corruption. And mutants were not allowed within its wall. So why was Rush, a mutant, supposed to go there? He refused to allow himself to dwell on the enormity of the task ahead of him. Josuf had taught him to hunt and forage for food, and he was perfectly capable of concealing himself and making his own shelter when he needed to bed down for the night, but even so, the thought of making such a long trip on his own was daunting. Without really knowing where he was going, the mutant boy set off to find Silas and the mysterious Jax, who was able to speak to people in their dreams.

Melk

The sound of Principal Zander Melk's footsteps seemed unnaturally loud to him as he hurried along the corridor towards his father's hospital room. The urgent summons by the president had taken him by surprise, his father's carers conveying the older man's desire to speak to his son as 'a matter of urgency'.

He paused at the door, peering in through the small viewing window to take in the sallow-skinned figure atop the sheets, connected via an array of tubes and wires to a multitude of machines about the bed. It was unusual to see anyone so ill inside the cities' walls, but the thing eating away at his father from the inside was something the old man had created himself, one of his experiments intended to wreak havoc on the mutants. It was a derivation of the Rot disease that now afflicted so many Mutes, but this strain appeared to have no cure. It was difficult to escape the irony: a disease designed to harm Mutes had itself mutated and infected its maker via a tiny tear in his hazchem suit; the old man well and truly hoist with his own petard. The only saving grace for those caring for him was that, unlike its deadly cousin, his father's version of Rot was not contagious.

'Father?' Zander said as he stepped inside.

Just moving his head to look in the direction of his son's voice seemed to take a huge effort. For Zander Melk it was impossible to reconcile the wizened figure before him with that of the powerful oligarch who had done so much for the Principia and the Six Cities that had been built in the aftermath of the Last War.

Propped up on pillows, the incumbent president nodded at his son. Until recently he'd managed to keep his illness a secret; blood transfusions and a whole host of medications made it just about possible for him to maintain appearances. But his opponents, particularly that Cowper man, had begun to suspect things weren't right. And rumours spread quickly in a place like City Four. Like sharks sniffing blood, they'd begun to circle in the political waters, waiting for the right moment to attack. So he'd pulled the rug from under them, called an emergency election in which he intended to use his power and influence to install his son to power. If he was honest, he had grave doubts about Zander's ability to carry off the role. He lacked the . . . mettle to make the harsh decisions Melk knew were needed to put a stop to this mutant rights nonsense. Still, if everything went as planned, the situation would be temporary at best.

Melk Senior reached up and removed the transparent mask from his face, the hiss of pumped oxygen escaping as he did so. 'Close the door,' he said, then fluttered his fingers in the direction of the chair beside his bed.

'How do you feel?' Zander asked as he sat down.

'I'm dying. How do you think I feel?'

'The doctors say that there's still –'

'The doctors can't cure this. *I* couldn't cure this, and I created the damn thing! I was too clever for my own good, and look where it's got me.' He took a gulp of oxygen and lowered the mask again. 'I wanted to speak to you before it's too late. There's something you need to know.'

'What's that?' Zander inwardly groaned. No doubt his father was about to give him another lecture on what he was doing wrong and how he should be running things. The last time they'd spoken the old man had told him he was too liberal, pouring scorn on his campaign, and saying he needed to continue with the current hard-line policies when it came to the 'mutant problem'.

The old man looked across at his son, an all too familiar sneer forming on one side of his mouth as he did so. 'Don't worry, Junior, I didn't ask you here to use my last breath to tell you how much I love you.'

'Why doesn't that surprise me?'

The frail creature in the bed tried to laugh, but what came out instead was an ugly, wet coughing sound that spoke of lungs filled with more than just air. 'See? That's the man I made and brought up. You need to work on that attitude some more. That hardness is in the Melk genes. That's why we got to be where we are.'

Zander waited. Maybe it would have been better to trust his initial instinct and ignore the invitation to come here. The pair had never shared much love between them.

'I need to tell you about the Farm.'

'The what?'

'It was a place I set up about twenty years ago. A research institute, if you like.'

'Like the labs at Bio-Gen?' Zander asked, referring to the vast genetic-modification empire his grandfather and father had built up, first here, in City Four, but subsequently in all six megalopolises. It was the reason City Four had risen to become the most powerful of the cities, quickly becoming the capital, where the ruling body, the Principia, was based. The other cities were each given over to specialist industries: manufacturing of electronic goods and vehicles; food and livestock (especially genetically modified crops and animals); arms and defence; mining and power production. But the empire was run from C4, the city the Melks had always lived in, the city they practically owned.

'No, not quite like them.'

Zander didn't like the way his father said that. 'Why haven't I ever heard it mentioned before?'

'Because officially it never existed. It was a facility where I tried to uncover secrets, secrets that nobody else wanted to look into.' He gave a vague wave of his hand. 'The Farm was established so I might look into mutant anomalies.'

'Anomalies?'

'Aberrations. Mutations so extreme that they defy scientific explanation.' He paused to wet his dry, cracked lips.

Zander was beginning to wonder if the old man's ramblings might be simply a result of the pain-controlling medication he was on. He glanced back towards the door, weighing up whether he should call one of the nursing staff.

The old man continued. 'I'd heard rumours about mutants from the most extreme environments who had psychic powers and other weird abilities.'

'They're just old wives' tales. Something that mothers tell their children to get them to sleep at night – "Behave or the mutant bogeymen will get you".'

The old man held up a finger. He reached out and retrieved the mask, holding it to his face and sucking in more oxygen before continuing. 'I thought so too at first. But as scientists we owe it to ourselves to investigate such things, so I set about trying to find a mutant who showed signs of having a special gift. And I found one.' He let out a harsh bark of a laugh which was quickly followed by another round of coughing. 'Boy, did I find one.' After a slight shake of his head he continued. 'My men set out into the Blacklands, where the ravages of the Last War have created a landscape so inhospitable that for a while it was thought nothing could live there. But things *do* live there: horrible and grotesque things that you would hardly think of as human. One of these was brought back from that place. How they got it back with the things they experienced while it was in their custody is a miracle, but they managed somehow, although the cost was high in terms of the lives and minds lost. The freak was taken to the Farm to be picked apart, like a wristwatch, so I could see if I might be able to work out what made it tick. It didn't survive, but I succeeded in isolating the mutated genes of interest.'

'What did you hope to achieve?'

His father stared at him for a few moments. 'What do we do at Bio-Gen, son? Hmm?'

'How do you mean?'

'What do we offer to the citizens of the Six Cities?' He paused, waiting for an answer that didn't come. 'Hope, that's what. We offer them flawless, disease-free, intelligent, athletic human beings that are ordered up like food from a restaurant menu. You want a baby with green eyes and jet-black hair? No problem. You want him or her to be tall and strong so that they might fulfil *your* dreams of playing in the InterCity Games? Sure, why not? You want a child with musical abilities, with dextrous fingers and wide hands to easily span those octaves? A concert pianist? Hey, whatever you want, you're paying! We can do all that.' There was the maniacal glint in his eye that his son knew so well. 'But what if we could offer more? What if we could make them *more than human*?'

'We are forbidden from mixing our DNA with that of the mutants.'

'It was all the same DNA, before they became freaks!'

'But it's *not* any more. We made certain of that. We refined and reprogrammed our own genome to remove the defects and disease. We did that precisely so we might offer the hope you just described.'

'Ha!' Another bout of hacking coughs followed the old man's exclamation, this one longer than the last. 'You make it sound as if we were on a mission to save humanity! We did it for money. We did it *because we could*!'

'Tainting our DNA with mutant genes? That's the most illegal thing you could possibly do.' Zander's mind was a blur as he tried to take all this in. 'Is that what you were doing at this Farm?'

'We tried to create perfection: a superhuman being, if you like. We used artificial wombs and implanted single-cell fetuses with the DNA material I'd collected.'

'Where did you get the fetuses?' Zander couldn't stop himself asking questions to which he really did not want to hear the answers; his father had already admitted to some of the most serious crimes imaginable. If anyone found out about this, the Melk name would be destroyed and his whole presidential campaign would be over. When the old man shrugged, he could hardly contain his anger.

'*Where?*'

'I took them out of stock.'

Rush

It was the third day of his journey and the sun was beginning to make its way towards the horizon. It'd be dark again soon. Tired and dirty, and more than a little hungry, Rush was walking along the side of an old dirt track, his feet dragging in the dust. He paused to look up at a bird sitting on a bough of a tree – a strange creature with a long proboscis where its beak might have been – when he heard the noise of a wagon approaching from behind. Scurrying into the nearest bush, he peered out from the dense foliage to see the large, harg-drawn vehicle come round the bend. He kept perfectly still, knowing he could not be seen, but his heart sped up when the vehicle came to a halt beside him.

There was a moment or two of silence, eventually broken by a man's voice. 'What you doing hiding in that

35

bush, boy? You planning on jumping out and attacking me, like one of those bandits from the Wastes?'

There was little point hiding any longer, although how the man could possibly have known he was there was a mystery. Rush stood up and looked at the driver of the wagon for the first time.

'Tink!'

'I thought it might be you,' the wagon driver said, a sad look on his face. 'At least, I hoped it would be you.'

The man reached down, offering the youngster a hand so he could climb up on the jockey-box alongside him. Side by side, they sat in silence for a while, just looking ahead.

'I came by your place – what was left of it – yesterday. I was going to pay you and Josuf a visit, maybe trade some merchandise for a few barrels of that fine cider he makes.' The old man sighed and shook his head. 'How much did you see?'

'Everything. Those men . . .' He couldn't say the words.

Rush had known Tinker all his life; the trader visited their smallholding at least three or four times a year as he travelled from place to place carrying news and bartering goods. The man had an uncanny knack of having just the right thing on the back of his wagon whenever he pulled in at a place. Rush had no idea how old the man was; his eyes looked youthful and were quick to smile, but the thick, drooping moustache that framed his mouth was almost white. On his head he had a large, battered flat-brimmed hat, and he took this off now, wiping the sweat off his forehead with the back of his hand.

'You don't have to talk, son.'

'They killed him.' Rush spat the words out, turning away so the man would not see the tears that welled up and ran down his cheeks.

Tink nodded and replaced the hat. He remained quiet, looking off in the other direction and giving the boy as long as he needed to get himself back together again.

'He told me to get away. Told me to run. I was in the orchard, and Josuf . . . There was an explosion. He –'

'All right, boy. What matters is that you're safe. For now, at least.' He sighed. 'But more men will be coming – men looking for you.'

'So they came because of me?'

'Uh-huh.' Tink nodded, thinking things through in his head. 'They can't have been certain you were there, but they will be now. You can't go back.'

'I'm not going back. I know where I have to go.'

'Oh? And where's that?'

'City Four. Before he died, Josuf told me to go there. I have to find somebody.'

'A man called Silas.'

'You know him?'

'We've met.'

Tink raised his head and stared off into the distance again, his bushy eyebrows knitted together. 'And so it begins.'

'What, Tink? What begins?'

The old man waved the question away and shook his head. 'City Four is a heck of a long way from here. I'd take you there, but I have to go east first. Somebody, somebody else like you, might also be in trouble.' He shook his head. 'The ARM will probably be patrolling the usual routes in the hope of finding you. Sticking to the smaller tracks and pathways like this one will help, but it's still risky. If they spot me, they'll want to search the wagon. I'll be damned if I know how I'm going to hide you.'

'I can't go east. I have to cross the Wastes.'

'Josuf told you to do that?' The expression on his face told Rush exactly what Tink thought of that idea.

'No.'

Tink gave him an odd look. 'So who told you to cross the Wastes?'

Rush didn't want to say he'd been told to do so in a dream; he knew precisely how that might sound. But when he shrugged, he was surprised at how quickly Tink let it go, pressing him no further.

'The Wastes,' the merchant said, more to himself than to

the boy beside him. 'Maybe it's not such a mad idea. At least the soldiers won't follow you.' Something else occurred to him. 'Any particular route you were thinking of taking?'

Rush shook his head, but as he did so he remembered something else from the dream he'd had that night. 'I thought I'd head out to the . . .' he racked his mind for the name, '. . . Tranter. That's it. The Tranter Trading Post.'

Tink narrowed his eyes. He clearly knew of the place. 'I see . . .'

Another thought struck Rush. 'How did you know I was hiding? You couldn't have seen me.'

'Oh, you know old Tink. I got a feeling for these things. Like I always know what the people on the next leg of my trip might be hankering for. Call it a sixth sense.' The old man eyed the boy carefully. Then he looked about him at their surroundings. 'I was aiming to stop for a bite to eat now. This looks like as good a place as any to rest my old harg up.' He leaned forward and gently patted the animal's rump, the tentacles on the sides of its face briefly waggling in response. He steered the wagon across the track into a small clearing. 'You're welcome to join me if you like.' He climbed down and unhitched the animal, leading it over to a place where it could graze.

Tink and Rush ate sitting on the ground a little way ahead of the wagon so they could see anything coming down the track. They chose not to light a fire and risk drawing attention to themselves; besides, the large waxing moon that hung in the sky bathed the world in an eerie silver hue that was easy to see by. Wrapped in blankets, the pair sat in silence. The food was delicious: small crispy crackers, cheese and strips of salty dried meat. When they'd finished, Tink leaned back on his elbows and took a small clay pipe from the pocket of his shirt. Stuffing what looked to Rush like dried brown leaves into the bowl, he lit it with a match and drew the smoke into his mouth, letting out a sigh as he exhaled.

'Filthy habit,' he said to the boy, nodding down at the pipe.

He noticed the boy looking back towards the wagon.

'Go see if there's anything that takes your fancy.'

'I don't have any money.'

The old man waved this away and took another puff on his little pipe. 'Go and take a look anyway.' The boy was almost halfway across to the wagon when the man shouted out to him again. 'Mind yourself with that thing tied up round the back.'

Intrigued, Rush went round behind the vehicle. There, on a short chain, was the strangest animal he'd ever laid eyes on. It had a vaguely dog-like appearance: a muscular, squat body atop short legs that ended in black clawed paws. The front of the animal's face was turned up, like that of a pug or a bulldog, but the slightly bulging eyes were like a lizard's, with vertical slits for pupils. Each reptilian eye also appeared to have a third, transparent eyelid that closed a fraction earlier than the outermost ones. The chimera effect was completed by a combination of scales and wiry fur that covered the beast from head to toe.

'What is it?' he called over to Tink.

'That . . .' The man pointed towards the wagon with the tip of his pipe. 'That is what is known in the trade as a deal gone wrong.'

'How do you mean?'

'It's a rogwan. At least that's what the man who sold it to me called it. I purchased it at a place on the edge of the Blacklands. You know about the Blacklands, Rush?'

'No.'

Tink got to his feet and wandered over to the boy, tapping the bowl of his pipe out against the side of his leg.

'Away to the south, about ten days' journey from here, is the start of a place about as hostile as you could imagine. Whatever happened there in the Last War has scarred the earth for ever, so all that's left is a landscape of black glassy rock as far as the eye can see. Despite that, things live there. Hell, *people* live there! The scariest, weirdest people you ever laid eyes on. I'm not talking about mutants with odd-coloured eyes or hair, or an extra finger and toe.' He puffed out his cheeks. 'These people are as horribly altered as the landscape they live in. I saw one man with two heads! Yeah, you heard me, two heads. One big one, and one smaller one that stuck out of his shoulder at an odd angle.' He lifted a shoulder and put his head to one side to demonstrate. Straightening up, he frowned at the memory.

'The rogwan?' Rush prompted, when it was clear the merchant had forgotten what they'd been talking about.

'What? Oh, yeah. Well, I know a man who owns a travelling zoo. He asked me to see if I could acquire him some new exhibits, so I bought that thing. Turns out the zoo owner hasn't got any money. Now old Tink is stuck with it! The damn thing eats like a harg!' He regarded his pipe for a moment, as if contemplating whether to refill it, but he put it back in his coat pocket.

'She looks sad, tied up like that.'

'She?'

Rush nodded. 'It's a she.'

'Well, that's where *she* is going to stay until I can find a home for her. Have you seen the teeth on that thing?'

As if on cue, the rogwan gave a big yawn, showing off its razor-sharp fangs and long black tongue.

'What's her name?'

'Name?' The old man chuckled and stroked his moustache. 'You don't give a thing a name unless you intend to keep it, and I ain't keeping *that*.'

Rush reached out towards the creature.

'Don't touch it! It'll take your hand off faster than you can –' Tink cried out and made a grab for the boy, stopping when he saw the youngster reach out and roughly pat the animal's head. 'I'll be damned,' he said, staring from the boy to the animal and back again.

'I'm good with animals,' Rush explained. 'There was a harg at our place that wouldn't let anyone ride him but me.' He nodded down at the rogwan. 'She's not dangerous.'

Tink approached the animal, but stopped when it growled and narrowed its eyes at him. He mumbled something under his breath and looked again at the pair, and then up ahead into the darkness.

'Like I said, Rush. I'm heading east. But just over two days from here is a point on the edge of the Wastes. City Four lies due north of there, across the Chisel mountain range. The journey won't be easy, and I wouldn't attempt it myself. But if you're determined to go, I'm happy to give you a ride as far as I can.'

'I'd like that,' Rush nodded.

'OK. Well, I suggest we climb back on board the wagon and get moving, young sir. We can see well enough, and travelling overnight will give us a good head start on anyone sent out to your old place.'

Silas

Jax and Silas sat across from each other at one of the tables in the refectory. The children who attended the orphanage they ran were all in bed, so the pair had the place to themselves. The building had an odd feel to it at night. The rooms, usually filled with the raucous noise of youngsters, seemed more than merely empty; it was as if their essence was missing.

'Are you sure we're doing the right thing by bringing them all here?' Jax asked. 'Straight into the lion's den.'

'I seem to remember it being your idea.'

'Still . . .'

'If we leave them out there, even if we move them around, they'll eventually be discovered. You said yourself that they're finding it harder and harder not to utilise their gifts. That in itself will draw attention to them. And now he knows they're alive, Melk won't stop until he has them. He'll offer a bounty next. People will happily turn them in.'

'That's all true. But for precisely the same reasons, we won't be able to hide them here for long.' Jax nudged a cup in front of him with a long white finger.

'Maybe we won't have to,' said Silas. 'Things are changing: inside and outside the walls.' He gave the teenager a guarded smile. 'Perhaps we are on the verge of a new order.'

'Mutants and the Pure living together in perfect harmony?' The albino raised an eyebrow. 'Come on, Silas, you can't really believe that.'

'I'm not sure what I believe any more. All I know is that whatever is going to happen between the Mute communities and the Six Cities, you and the other children are going to play a key role in it. We've got an opportunity to turn this world around for the betterment of all. If nothing else, revealing these children will topple the Melks from power. That alone has to be a good thing.'

'It could have the opposite effect. It could make them even more powerful.'

'I hope for all our sakes that will not be the case.'

Zander

Zander Melk stared at the wizened figure of his father in disbelief. The fetuses held at Bio-Gen were the next-generation city dwellers. They were precious, perhaps the most precious thing in the Six Cities, and the security that surrounded them legendary. If anyone ever found out that his father had taken them for experimental purposes . . .

The hiss of the oxygen seemed louder than ever as Zander held his breath, waiting for the sick man to continue. 'So you stole fetuses and took them to your illegal secret lab to experiment on them with mutant DNA.' A harsh, bitter laugh escaped him. 'I'm almost terrified to ask, but what next?'

'The first batches weren't entirely successful. We rushed in, too eager to see what we might be able to do. Most of those earliest attempts were horribly deformed creatures;

the cocktail of DNA material coupled with deficiencies in the artificial womb system meant they were not . . . viable. Only two survived: a huge kid with strange powers of healing was the first, and a few years after him we were able to produce an albino boy with psychic abilities. Albinos and giants . . .' He shook his head. 'Not exactly what I was going for.' The president smiled, remembering. 'Brick.'

'What?'

'That was his name, the first Mute, with the ability to heal.' He nodded at the banks of machines surrounding him. 'Guess I could do with him now, eh?'

'You said *first* batches?'

'Maybe I should have given up then, but I didn't. How could I? The scientists working there – all handpicked men – refined the process, and a few years later we tried again with more success. Four children were created. Three survived and these went into the next phase of the process. These three –' he smiled sheepishly, remembering – 'they looked perfect. If you saw them walking in one of the cities, you'd never know they were . . . different. They were subjected to an epigenetic programme that would allow them to hone the powers I had given them. One perfect shape-shifter; one telekinetic; one who moved faster than time. From birth they were placed in extreme conditions: specially constructed cells with stimuli designed to force them to use their gifts in order simply to stay alive.' His eyes shone as a humourless smile contorted his bony face. 'Even at the age of two, they were extraordinary. It's impossible to say what they might have become because they were taken away. The Farm was destroyed.'

'How?'

'There was an accident – a problem with the cold fusion reactor. When I got to the site there was nothing left but a huge hole in the ground that went down as far as the eye could see. The devastation extended five or six miles in every direction. The entire forest around the facility was laid low by the force of the explosion. All my research notes, the files, the computers, the equipment – gone. The children had gone too.' He shook his head and sighed. 'I told myself it was for the best, that the project was doomed. And at least all the evidence had gone with them.'

Zander narrowed his eyes at his father. 'Why do I know nothing about this? Why have you chosen to tell me this now, when I'm standing for election? You said there would be no hindrance to my becoming president. What would happen if anyone found out what you'd done?'

'That's *why* I'm telling you. Like I said, I assumed they were all dead: destroyed along with the Farm. Then I received this.' He nudged an omnipad that was on the bed at his side and the screen came instantly to life.

Zander picked it up and looked at the image. It was a picture of an illegal gathering of Mutes somewhere in one of the slums. A small section of the image had been highlighted and this magnified as soon as he tapped it, the new image focused on three individuals in the crowd. 'Who are they?'

'The tall, pale one calls himself Jax now. That's my albino mutant. Isn't he a handsome young fellow?' He lifted the oxygen mask to his face and greedily gulped at the air. 'The older man is called Silas. Brilliant mind. He convinced me to give him a job at the Farm.'

'How can you be sure it's him?'

'I'd bet my life on it.' He smiled weakly at the joke. 'Besides, how could I forget what my own brother looked like.'

The son stared at his father, lost for words. 'Did you say *brother*? You have a . . . I have an uncle?'

'No. You and I have a treacherous snake for a relation. A snake I should have stepped on and killed when we were growing up.'

'And you didn't think I should know about this . . . uncle?'

The old man gave him another of those infuriating shrugs. 'What was there to know? I thought he was dead.'

Once again, Zander struggled to suppress his ire. 'Who's the third man?'

'He's the engineer who installed the cold fusion reactor. His name is Thorn. The picture you're looking at is a little over six months old, but a short while ago our men managed to relocate him and bring him in. They used a number of methods, each more persuasive than the last, until he eventually started talking. He told them that my "extraordinary" children had survived. The albino apparently wiped their memories and suppressed their powers so they wouldn't be conspicuous. Then they were sent out to the furthest corners of Scorched Earth to start new lives. They're out there, son, and you have to find them.'

'Why? Why would we rake something like this up? They haven't been a problem till now – maybe they're better simply left alone.'

His father sighed. 'That picture – it's from a Mute protest march. I don't need to tell you how these mutant "rallies" are gathering momentum. The freaks are demanding rights – rights they've been denied for a long time now. There's trouble coming.'

'And what does that have to do with these kids you created?'

'The mutants outnumber us by about twenty to one. We can't simply wipe them out – that kind of thing just isn't allowed these days. The Last War put paid to that. But there might be another way.'

The man in the bed was hardly the same one Zander had seen when he'd first entered; his father seemed reenergised somehow.

'Imagine if we were able to use these mutant uprisings to repeal the anti-cloning laws. We'd argue that it's the only way to raise an army in time. Now, try to imagine a clone army of my beautiful freak kids. We wouldn't need a nuke; we'd have walking, breathing death machines!'

'They were *that* powerful?'

'They could have been, if I'd been allowed to carry on with my work.'

'And that's the only reason you want them found, is it? As a deterrent against any mutant uprising?'

His father narrowed his eyes at him. 'I can't pull the wool over your eyes, can I, son?'

'Somebody once told me there was more to be learned from what somebody doesn't say than from the words they want you to hear.'

Melk Senior nodded, smiling ruefully back. 'The healer Mute – the one who called himself Brick. I need him. He's my only chance of survival. I've already sent a large number of ARM units out to try and find any of these kids based on the information we extracted from our engineer friend. One of those units had an "unfortunate accident" involving an explosive device. The whole thing is getting . . . messy. I want you to oversee the operation from now on and find them.'

Zander stood up, the anger and frustration clear to see on his face. 'You just can't stop, can you? Even here, like this, you can't stop interfering.' He headed for the door.

Melk watched him leave. He knew full well his son would carry out his instructions; he always did. The boy was weak, a disappointment in every way. President? Ha! No, he was a pawn, a means to an end. Because there was only going to be one president of the Principia while Melk was still breathing, and if the mutant hybrids had survived, he might be able to keep doing exactly that.

Rush

At dusk the day after they'd met, Tink's wagon slipped down into a deep rut and broke two spokes. Swearing as he reined the harg to a halt, Tink jumped down to inspect the damage, swearing even more when he saw what had happened and cursing himself for not having had the wheel replaced when he'd last had the opportunity. 'I knew the thing was on its way out,' he admitted to Rush. Luckily there was a spare tied up beneath the wagon bed, so they pulled off to one side, unhitching the harg so it could graze while they set about replacing the wheel. It was hard work – the heat of the day had not yet dwindled – but Rush was glad of something practical to do. Sitting atop the wagon next to Tink, he'd had too much time to think. And every time he did so, the terrible scene of his guardian's death played out over and over in his head.

When the work was finished, the two of them agreed they would stay put and make camp. Rush cleared the ground so they could make a fire, while Tink began putting up an old, battered tent that was little more than a thick tarpaulin stretched over two poles.

It was as the old man was finishing this that Rush looked up to see a large lop-eared creature emerge from its burrow and sneak out into the murky half-light. Inching closer, Rush straightened up, carefully putting his hand into his trouser pocket and feeling for the stone he always kept there. He curled his fingers around the object. Without taking his eye off the creature, he slowly pulled his arm back and whipped it forward again, releasing the stone.

There was a dull *thunk!* as the stone connected with the creature's skull. The animal twitched once and then lay perfectly still.

'Nice shot,' Tink said.

Rush turned round to see the old man appraising him. He shrugged and gestured towards the hare. 'Lucky, I guess.'

'Luck, you say?' There was a moment when Tink looked as if he was about to say something else, but it passed and he went back to pushing the last of the tent pegs into the ground.

They ate the roasted game for dinner.

* * *

To describe the roaring, rasping sound that came out of Tink's mouth when he was asleep as merely 'snoring' was derisory. The noise had started almost as soon as the man's head had touched the ground, making it impossible for Rush to doze off. Sleep clearly came easily to Tink. Rush nudged him to see if he might stop, and he did, for all of three seconds, after which the angry bear noises began again in earnest. Realising there would be no sleep for him inside the tent, Rush gathered up his blanket and crawled out through the opening.

The moon, framed by countless stars, hung in the sky. He stood, staring up at the nightscape, in awe at the size and beauty of it all. It was said that after the Last War the skies were filled with black clouds that blocked the sun out for weeks on end, killing most of the vegetation and almost all the animals that fed on it. Thankfully the clouds had cleared a long time ago and Scorched Earth could see, and be seen by, the distant galaxies once more.

It wasn't especially cold, so Rush wandered over to the wagon, reasoning with himself that if he could make himself comfortable beneath the vehicle it would provide him with some shelter if it should rain. As he approached the wooden truck he heard the *hurghing* sound of the rogwan, followed by the noise of its feet padding back and forth. Clearly the creature was finding it as difficult to sleep as he was. Coming closer, Rush saw the animal walking round and round in tight little circles, eyeing the bushes beside it.

'You need to go, don't you?' he said. He hadn't asked Tink how he usually arranged for this to happen, but clearly the animal had no wish to foul the area where it would have to sleep. He glanced at the tent and wondered if he should wake its occupant.

The rogwan made another plaintive noise, this one almost like a sigh.

'Oh, what the hell.' Rush reached forward and undid the karabiner that attached the chain to a metal ring on the back of the flatbed. The rogwan watched him. When he led the animal over to the bushes so it could do its business, he half expected it to make a dash for freedom; it was easily powerful enough to break free of the grip he had on the leash, but it surprised him by allowing itself to be led there and back again without a fuss.

Dog-tired, Rush crawled beneath the wagon. Pulling the blanket around himself, he looked up to see those bulging lizard eyes staring at him. He'd forgotten to secure the chain back on to the ring. The rogwan *hurghed*. Despite everything Tink had told him about the animal, Rush did not seem to feel in any danger. Quite the opposite, in fact.

'You want to join me?' Rush asked, moving aside and lifting up his blanket. He smiled to himself as the rogwan curled up next to him.

Rush woke up early the next morning, chained up the rogwan again, started a fire and had the coffee brewing by the time Tink put his head outside the tent flap. The old man crawled out, screwing his eyes up against the early morning light until he could finally stand and stretch. 'Sleep well?' he asked, nodding in the boy's direction.

'Not too bad once I got away from you and your snoring.'

'I don't snore.'

'Loud enough to wake the dead.' Rush held out a cup of coffee which Tink gratefully accepted.

They breakfasted on eggs and hard black bread that Tink fried in the same pan. Afterwards, Tink called Rush over, having taken something from the back of the wagon. He held it out for the boy to see. It was as long as the man was tall, and appeared to be little more than two lengths of leather cord, one with a loop at the end. Between these, in the centre and joining the two lengths together, was a small diamond-shaped patch of soft leather.

'What is it?' Rush asked.

'You never seen a sling?' Tink blew out his cheeks and shook his head. 'I'd have bet a tooth you'd have had one of these down on that ranch of yours.' He grinned at the youngster. 'When I saw you throw that stone at the hare last night, I remembered I had me one of these in the back somewhere. This'll let you throw a stone as far as a bow can shoot an arrow. It's like an extension to your arm. I seen people take birds out of the sky with one of these things!'

Rush looked dubiously at the device.

'Don't take my word for it – give it a go!'

For the next hour or so Rush practised with the weapon until he'd perfected the technique of swinging it up and round his head and letting go of the non-looped end at just the right moment so the stone flew out at incredible speed. While he did this, Tink broke camp, and it wasn't long before the two were back on the road again, Tink telling the boy everything he knew about the Wastes and how to stay alive there.

There were no further incidents on the road, and as night fell they pulled in on the edge of the Wastes, some-where due south of City Four. This time there was no fire. Tink wouldn't risk anything that might bring them to the attention of one of the marauding mutant gangs that roamed there. 'This is a bad place,' he explained to Rush for the umpteenth time. 'Sure you won't come with me? You're good company, and you seem to have a way with that creature.'

The boy considered this for a moment, then shook his head. 'No. I think we both know that my route lies that way.' He hoped he sounded braver than he actually felt.

Tink accepted this, getting to his feet and moving in the direction of his wagon. 'You have the tent tonight,' he said. 'Apparently I snore, and I want you to have a good night's sleep before you set off on your own.'

Rush tried to argue, but the old man insisted, telling him it would not be the first time he'd slept up on his truck.

When Rush woke the next day, Tink and the wagon were gone. He wasn't entirely surprised.

Just inside the opening of the tent was a canvas rucksack. On top was a handwritten note.

Rush,

I'm not big on goodbyes, so I hope you'll forgive me for taking off like this. I have left you and your travelling companion a few 'necessities' to help you on your way. When I'm finished doing what I have to, I'll swing on by to City Four and look you up.

Your friend,
Old Tink

Travelling companion? Bleary-eyed, Rush crawled out of the tent and saw the rogwan sitting outside waiting for him.

He smiled at the creature, receiving a *hurgh* and a black tongue to the face in response.

'Well, if we're going to travel together, I guess I need to give you a name.' He looked at the rogwan, trying to work out what kind of name you gave a beast that looked like that.

'Dotty,' he said, frowning. He had no idea why that particular name had occurred to him. 'How do you like that for a name?'

The rogwan blinked and waggled her rear end on the ground.

'OK. Dotty it is then.'

He stood and stretched, looking out over the lands simply known as the Wastes. If everything Tink had told him was true, he'd do well to cross it in one piece. But at least now he wouldn't have to do so alone.

Tia

'It's not possible, Tia.'

'Why?' The girl looked across at her father and thought how tired he looked; the strain of the election he was fighting against Zander Melk and the ongoing war of words with the Principia over mutant rights was beginning to etch itself on his once handsome face.

'You know why. Melk and the Principia have ordered a curfew prohibiting any Citizen from being beyond city walls after nine o'clock.'

'At exactly the time the ARM has been charged with terrorising the inhabitants of Muteville.' She inwardly winced at her own use of the name given to the mutant ghetto out there, but it seemed to have stuck in recent times. 'The curfew isn't in place to *protect* our people, it's to stop them discovering what's happening right under their own noses.'

'Do you think the people of City Four are really that obtuse?'

'What do you mean?'

'I mean that many of our fine Citizens are already all too aware of what's happening out there, but as long as they don't have to see it –'

'All the more reason for me to report from beyond the wall. To *show* them what's going on so it can be stopped before it's too late.'

'You assume they want it to stop.'

'Then it's our duty to make them want that, Dad. You know that as well as I do.'

Her father shook his head. 'It's simply too risky. I can't afford to give you a cameraman and a soundman, only for you all to end up in jail.'

The teenager looked at her father, annoyed at his refusal. She, more than anyone, knew that Towsin Cowper, owner of a large and powerful media empire, could afford to do pretty much anything he chose to. And one of the things he chose to do was stand up to the powers that be and report on the mutant plight, even if doing so had cost him. Friends and associates had turned their backs on him, preferring, like so many others, to close their ears and eyes to what was happening outside the cities' walls. Ignoring these people and their warnings, Cowper had gone ahead anyway, using his wealth and influence to highlight the mutants' predicament and to campaign on their behalf. Most of what he said and did fell on deaf ears, but he didn't care. Wrong was wrong, and what was happening out there was definitely wrong. He'd been pleased to discover his philanthropy had rubbed off on his daughter. Tia had become a reporter, and she too had already made a number of news pieces on the subject. But now she was asking for something else entirely and, as her father, he couldn't allow her to put herself in the type of danger she was describing.

'You're forbidding me to go?'

'It's not that. As I've just explained, I can't afford to give you –'

'I don't need a crew,' she said with a look he knew all too well. It was the grim look of determination her mother had often displayed when she'd been alive. The girl reminded him of Regan in so many ways. Like her mother, she was beautiful in an elegant, effortless way that needed none of the modifications so popular in a city where people changed their eye colour, body shape and facial appearance at a whim. 'I can do it all on a small handheld cam. I'll be able to set it up on a tripod for my broadcast pieces, and use it to film the ARM crews as they go through the ghettos. I've met some people out there – good people who will keep me safe.'

Cowper sighed. His daughter and he clearly had very different ideas of the meaning of 'safe'. 'You're forgetting the most important thing, Tia: your chip.'

At birth, every citizen had a small chip implanted into their thigh bone. Without it, each door you passed through identified you as not having one, and therefore as a non-Citizen. It was a way of keeping out those who didn't belong inside the walls. It was also a convenient way for the Principia and security forces to keep tabs on those who did.

'I had it removed.'

Cowper stared at his daughter in disbelief, momentarily lost for words. The penalty for having your CivisChip removed was death – that was *if* you could find anyone crazy enough to perform the operation, which also carried the same sentence.

When he spoke again his voice was small, the words faltering. 'You did what?'

'The money I earned from the last three broadcasts? I used it to have my chip taken out.'

'Where is it?'

'In Buffy.'

Her father stared at the small marmoset monkey sitting on his daughter's shoulder. The animal cocked its head and returned the look. There were bio-labs in the city that specialised in growing clone replications of animals that had become extinct following the Last War. Tia had brought the little creature home about six months ago, and the two of them had hardly been apart since then.

The comms unit on his desk beeped as the image of the smiling face of a business associate appeared. Cowper waved a hand across the screen, blocking the call.

Although outwardly he appeared perfectly calm, his heartbeat was racing as he tried to figure out various ways he could get this mess sorted and keep his daughter safely out of the clutches of the City Security Police.

'It has to be transplanted into another living creature,' Tia explained. 'The guy who performed the surgery suggested putting it in Buffy. He said he'd had success with transplanting the device into monkeys before.'

'And what will happen to the marmoset once you get to Muteville?'

'I'll let her go. In fact, it was Buffy who gave me the idea during the last broadcast. She escaped while we were out in the ghetto. I thought she'd been killed – you know how short of food they are out there – but when we returned she was sitting in my bedroom waiting for me.'

'She got back inside? Without you?'

Tia looked across at the monkey. 'You're a very clever girl, aren't you?'

Cowper couldn't work out how this might have happened. The security gates were rigorously manned and monitored, with automatic scanning devices to stop anything getting in or out unnoticed. The animal should at least have been captured. In fact, he was surprised it hadn't been killed.

'How?'

'Marv – the camera operator I was with – saw her. She climbed up one of the long steel cables that support the mast above the west wall. All the way up, clinging on underneath like that, hand over hand. He said it took her about seven minutes to get to the top. If she's done it once, she can do it again. My chip will be back here, but I'll be out there. They'll never know.'

'They'll know. There won't be a log of you coming in through the gate. That'll set alarm bells ringing.'

His daughter gave him a long look. 'I thought you might know someone who could help with that.'

Cowper was about to say something when another thought struck him. 'How will *you* get back in? Afterwards, I mean. I doubt very much that you've managed to train your simian friend to go back in the other direction at your beck and call. So how were you planning to return?'

Tia shook her head, avoiding meeting his eye. 'I don't know. I hadn't really thought that far ahead. The most important thing to me right now is that I get myself embedded with the Mute population and start to put together the story of what's really happening out there. I'll shoot for a few weeks, edit it all together and then find a way back inside so that you can show it.'

His daughter's choice of words struck him. 'Embedded? War reporters are described as being "embedded", Tia.'

'You don't think war's been declared on the mutants, Daddy?'

That stopped him. He looked across at her. When had his little girl grown up into the beautiful, intelligent young woman he saw before him now? He was reminded of Regan again. The two were even more alike than he'd thought.

'When I said I wanted to be a reporter, you said you'd do everything you could to help me. Reporters report on injustices, Daddy. That's what they do. If that means they have to bend the rules and perhaps put themselves in danger sometimes, then that's the price they have to pay.'

'I can't talk you out of this, can I?'

She shook her head.

He sighed and waved the screen of the comms unit back to life.

'Who are you calling?' Tia asked, concerned.

'A friend. Somebody who can tell us straight if this monkey-brained idea of yours could actually work.'

Brick

Rush sat on his haunches, perfectly still, behind a large mangled wreck of concrete that might have once been a building of some kind before this world was almost annihilated all those years ago. What was left of the structure was now covered in foul-smelling chokeweed, but the mutant boy hardly noticed the stench as he held the spyglass up to his face, taking in the terrible scene in the distance. Dotty made a *hurghing* sound beside him, and he blindly reached out with one hand, placing it upon the stocky little creature's back, urging her to be quiet. She trembled beneath his touch, but not from fear; in the week or so they'd been in the Wastes, Rush had come to realise the rogwan was almost fearless. No, Dotty was merely responding to the horror and revulsion the boy felt at what he was witnessing through Tink's telescope.

The mutant marauders had almost finished the sacking of what had once been a trading outpost of perhaps thirty or forty people. From the description Tink had given him, he knew it had to be the Tranter Trading Post he'd been sent to find in his dream; it was also clear that he'd arrived too late. Whatever he had been supposed to discover here would be gone now; the place's former inhabitants were all either killed or captured, the buildings ransacked and razed to the ground. Of the former inhabitants, the dead were the lucky ones. Those still alive had been forced into three large cages that sat atop wagons drawn by massive horned creatures. These gargantuan beasts chewed the cud as they stood harnessed, seemingly oblivious to the death and destruction their masters had meted out all about them.

Although too far away to make them out, Rush could imagine the despair on the faces of the unfortunate captives. Close up, they'd witnessed the terrible brutality that Rush had thankfully only caught glimpses of, sickening scenes that had left him feeling hollowed out and wretched. The attackers were one of the new breed of cannibal gangs that roamed these lands, and Rush knew it was pure luck he too had not become one of their victims.

Last night, cresting a low hill, he'd spotted the small settlement off in the distance. He stopped, observing the place and weighing up his options. He'd already been travelling for a long time, sticking to his plan of moving under the cover of darkness, and the stretch between him and the little colony looked bleak and barren, with little or no concealment. Nevertheless, he was getting desperate for food and water, having long since eaten all the dried meat Tink had left him. Despite Dotty bringing him back the odd morsel from some of her hunts, Rush was dreadfully hungry and getting weaker by the day. It was a toss-up whether to cross the desolate landscape separating him from the trading post in the dark, or wait until the morning, and his decision had undoubtedly saved his and the rogwan's lives. He'd made his camp in the shelter of the ruins he was now in, eschewing a fire and huddling down with his blanket around him. He'd eventually fallen asleep, not coming to again until just before sunset, when the attack came.

They had taken their time, the mutant marauders. They easily outnumbered the traders, whom they killed at will, often toying with their prey, prolonging their agony and suffering. Eventually, bored, they set about dispatching the people of the settlement in horrifying ways, laughing and shouting as they went about the murderous business. Now, with the sun long past its zenith and making its way towards the horizon, they looked as if they were preparing to move out.

Dotty growled softly, and this time Rush took the small brass telescope from his eye and looked down at her, glad for an excuse to drag his focus away from the stomach-turning events that were finally coming to an end in the distance. The rogwan stared back at him, her squat, compact body rigid. Her dark tongue flicked out and her lips peeled back to reveal the razor-sharp black teeth that lined her gums. He'd learned that there was another set behind the first; these curved backwards slightly to hold on to prey larger than herself, and she stretched her mouth wide enough for them to be seen too. Shuffling around on her short legs, she bumped her head against his leg before turning to look in the direction of the outpost.

'I know,' Rush said, reaching out and placing his hand on her again. He could feel how tense the muscles were beneath the rogwan's scales and rough fur. 'But if we go down there now, we're as good as dead too. We've got to wait, Dotty. We've got to wait until the bad people have gone.' He shook his head and sighed, hating himself for what felt like cowardice. 'I don't like it either, girl, but we don't have any choice.' Her long tongue flashed out again, the rough surface rasping his skin. He guessed that, like him, Dotty was thinking about the poor unfortunates in those cages. Tink had told him there were rumours that ranches had been set up somewhere in the Wastes, ranches where humans were bred as food. He shuddered and hoped the people who'd been taken captive were not going to end up as livestock.

'Just wait, girl. That's all we can do,' he said, reluctantly putting the spyglass back up to his face.

Only after Rush had witnessed the last vehicle in the caravan of death roll out of sight over the horizon did he and Dotty emerge from their hiding place and make their way across the plain to what was left of the outpost.

The landscape was every bit as bleak and hostile as he'd imagined, and the searingly hot day had given way to a bitterly cold night. What little that did grow here was the same dreary and oppressive grey colour as the earth it emerged from, and Rush remembered Tink's description of the Blacklands. Both places were a testament to the time when man had made a concerted effort to wipe himself off the face of the planet, scarring the terrain for ever.

Rush and Dotty were almost upon the ravaged settlement now. Neither had any real wish to go into the place, but without the water he hoped to find among the ruins, Rush knew they were in big trouble. As they reached the outskirts, the smell of death hit them, the rogwan's reaction being to blow a blast of air out of her nostrils and make low rumbling noises that perfectly echoed Rush's own unease.

So when they found that the stone well at the edge of the settlement had not been destroyed or deliberately contaminated, he almost cried out in joy. The water had a strong metallic tang to it, but to Rush it tasted divine. His thirst slaked, he left Dotty with her head in the bucket he'd drawn up for her and reluctantly went off to explore – he needed to find food and somewhere to sleep before the temperatures plummeted further.

Standing in what might have once been the centre of the settlement, he turned about him, taking it in. Whatever he'd been sent here to find was either gone or destroyed.

A big half-moon hung low in the cloudless sky, its light transforming the world into an eerie silver-and-black monochrome of harsh, sinister shadows. He tried to ignore the dark patches on the ground, some of which were still wet. Greasy-looking trails of the same darker colour led away from these patches, where something had been dragged off. What had once been a community of hard-working traders was now a ruin, and he wandered through the rusted metal, broken timbers and tattered plastic sheeting that had once housed the people of this place. A howl in the distance made his heart jolt, and he stood stiff and rigid, staring off in the direction of the noise. It went unanswered. Eventually he allowed himself to breathe again. The last thing he needed now was for a pack of werfen to turn up.

Something moved in the air overhead, and moments later the first of the winged carrion creatures arrived, swiftly followed by others, drawn there by some silent signal. Within minutes the skies were full of great bats and birds and strange amalgams of the two. He turned to look as a group of the ugly creatures landed, folding leathery or feathered wings along their backs and hopping about clumsily in search of the cannibals' leftovers.

The stone that left Rush's sling shot out, bullet-like, making a sharp *crack!* when it connected with the skull of the nearest creature. The clagbat gave a brief cry and flopped down on to its side, where it lay perfectly still. The other creatures about it scattered momentarily but quickly returned, not bothering to move too far away even when Rush walked over and picked the carcass up. Clagbat wasn't particularly good to eat, but it was better than anything else on offer, and he and Dotty had made do with a lot worse. The rogwan was among the scavengers too now, chasing them back and forth and making that low, irritated sound. Rush frowned. Dotty didn't usually waste her energy on such creatures, but this time she seemed intent on keeping them away from one particular wreck of a building. He hurried over to her, and when she saw him approach she ran about in a small circle, came a short distance towards him, then returned to the wreckage.

'What is it, girl, hmm? What have you found? Is it food?' Rush stepped forward. Despite the protests his under-nourished body made, he began to pull back planks of wood and sheets of canvas, throwing the debris off into the shadows all about. A cold wind blew, and he shivered as it rapidly cooled the sweat on his head and neck. After about ten minutes he finally stopped. There was nothing there. The only thing he found were two tubes sticking out of the dry earth, their tops curved over and down. Dotty was sitting looking up at him expectantly, head cocked to one side. He was about to berate the rogwan for wasting his time and effort, when he heard a noise. He stopped and stood motionless, unaware that his carriage and bearing mirrored those of his four-legged companion. Then he caught it again. There was something below the ground where he stood. He glanced at those tubes again, frowning. When he stamped his foot, his heart quickened; the sound was all wrong. Quickly getting to his hands and knees, he clawed at the canvas sheeting he'd assumed was simply a floor covering, pulling and tearing at it until he revealed a door flush with the ground. There was no sign of a handle, so Rush cast about him for something he could use to open it. Dotty began *hurghing* again.

'All right! I can see what it is,' he said, speaking half to himself, half to the rogwan. 'You know, it would have been a lot easier if you'd helped a bit with the digging and shifting, instead of sitting there like some lazy dollop!'

He needed to be able to see. He hated the idea, but he was going to have to use his torch; the light would shine out like a beacon in the darkness, signalling his position to anyone who might be about. If any member of the cannibal gang had hung back from the rest of the group and happened to look in his direction, they'd know there was someone still here. But there was nothing else for it. He dug about in the hide rucksack Tink had given him and came up with the device. He wound the little handle on the side a few times before flicking the switch, covering the cracked, yellow lens at the front with his fingers to muffle the glow as much as possible.

Down on all fours, he forced his fingertips into a small gap along one edge of the hatch door. Gritting his teeth, he sucked in a huge breath and heaved upward with all his might until he finally managed to pull the thing up before letting it crash to the ground on the other side. He shone his torch down on the person curled up in the pit down there. He'd expected to find a small child hidden away in the bolt-hole. Instead it was the biggest person Rush had ever laid eyes on.

The great, hulking figure knelt, face down, in the underground pit. His hands, fingers interlaced, were clasped behind his head as he rocked back and forth a little, mumbling the same phrases over and over again to himself: 'Stay-in-the-hole. Don't-come-out-till-Ma-tells-you-it's-safe. Stay-in-the-hole. Don't-come-out-till-Ma-tells-you-it's-safe. Stay-in-the-hole. Don't-come-out-till-Ma-tells-you-it's-safe.' His voice was incredibly deep, like two vast boulders grinding against each other.

'Hello?'

'Stay-in-the-hole. Don't-come-out . . .' The man continued to intone the words.

'Hello?' Louder this time. Rush looked about him at the once inhabited little settlement. Whoever 'Ma' was, she wasn't coming back to tell the giant *anything*. He turned his attention back to the hole.

'What's your name?' he asked. 'You can come out now. They've all gone.'

A pause in the mantra, then the instructions were repeated in full one last time before they stopped altogether. Rush was about to say something else when that rumbling bass voice came from the hole again.

'Brick.'

'What?'

'Brick. Sounds like "stick", but with a *b*.' The big man sounded out the letter: '*Buh*.' He paused, a frown momentarily creasing his brow. 'And a *ruh*. Buh, ruh, ick.'

Rush frowned. Despite his size, Brick clearly wasn't very bright. When Rush spoke again, he did so as if he were talking to somebody much younger in years.

'Why don't you come out of there? The bad people have gone now.'

'Not allowed to. Not safe.' Brick shifted a little, but remained huddled over his knees, hands still firmly clamped to the front of his face. 'Is it dark?' he asked.

'Of course it is. It's night-time.'

A long, low moan drifted up out of the hole. 'The dark. The bad people came with it. Ma knows Brick hates the dark, but she still put him in the hole. "For safety," she said. Brick gonna stay here till the dark gone. Then Ma will come back.'

Rush was about to say something else when another long, ululating howl drifted out of the night. This one seemed closer. He stood perfectly still, scanning the shadows out in the distance. The werf that had called wouldn't be alone. The creatures hunted in packs and loved to attack at night, when their keen eyesight and sense of smell helped them to locate their prey. They were being drawn to this place by the smell of the blood, just as the voltores and clagbats had been, but unlike the winged beasts, the werfen would attack the living too, especially if their prey were few in number. Dotty also stiffened and stared out into the shadows.

'You can't stay there,' Rush said, looking down into the hole again, his anxiety levels rising.

'Not safe in the dark!'

Rush looked at the little plastic light in his hand. Tink's generosity had astounded Rush. The light, like the spyglass the trader had left him, was an antique. He hated the idea that it might get damaged or broken, but it was the only thing he could think of that might help right now. He gave the little handle on the side a few more twists and the bulb glowed brighter in response. 'Here, Brick. I have something for you.' He jumped down into the pit and pushed the device next to the man's head, bathing it in light. The giant turned round to look directly into the bulb, gratefully grasping the torch with both hands. He made a soft mewling sound. Rush guessed Brick to be about twenty years of age, maybe a little more. Despite this, he doubted the big guy could look after himself if left out here alone.

'That's better, isn't it? Light whenever you want it.'

The werf's call was answered. This time the sound was definitely nearer. The animals were surrounding the place, preparing to attack from all sides. Rush straightened up and peered over the top of the hole. Despite his weariness, he knew he had to get away. He'd have one last go at getting Brick out, and if that didn't work he'd have no choice but to abandon him. He'd have to lie to the gentle giant.

'Ma's not coming back, Brick.' That much at least was true. 'She had to go away with the bad people. She didn't want to go, and before she was taken away she said to tell you that you had to come out of there. She told me to let you know that it was OK to leave the hole now. She said to tell you that you're a good boy and that she loves you and that she's sorry she didn't get a chance to say goodbye.'

He stopped and waited, hoping his choice of words might ring true in some way.

'It's Maw, not Ma.'

'What?'

'You said Ma. It's Maw. Sounds like four, but spelt with a *muh*.'

'Right. Maw. I must have misheard her.'

'Brick.' The big man said in that loud sobbing moan again before slowly rising to his feet. Standing, he was even bigger than Rush had first thought. 'Maw said that? Safe to get out?'

Rush gave him a shrug.

Just then the torchlight began to dim and Brick's face transformed into a stricken mask of panic.

'No, no! It's fine, look.' Rush hurried across and showed the big guy how to turn the little handle to reinvigorate the light. Having done so, Brick jammed the thing against his nose so the light shone straight into his eyes. His breathing slowly returned to normal. 'No more dark?'

'No more dark.' Rush said. 'Any time you want to, you can give the little whirly thing a spin or two and have all the light you need.' He stared up at the hulking figure, knowing in that instant that he'd acquired a new travelling companion. The thought didn't fill him with joy. Rush and Dotty had survived a week in the Wastes because of their ability to disappear whenever there was danger, hiding and waiting until it had passed. How they were going to do that with this hulking giant in tow was beyond him. And this thing with the dark was a problem. Whenever in doubt about their safety, Rush would go through the night without a fire or a light. But the alternative was to leave Brick here. Leave him to the werfen, the cannibals and the dark he feared so much. Rush sighed. 'Before she left, Maw also said you were to come with us.'

'Us?'

Rush gave a short low whistle through his teeth, and the rogwan came hurrying over from where she'd been snuffling among the debris.

Rush nodded at the creature. 'This is Dotty. She found you under the ground.'

When he saw the creature, the big man's tear-streaked face broke into a broad smile. He moved his arm and was about to reach out and pet the animal when Rush stopped him.

'I wouldn't do that if I were you. I'm not sure how she'll react.'

With a crestfallen look, Brick withdrew the hand. 'She's pretty,' he said.

Rush looked across at the little creature, who was at that moment sitting on the ground with one leg lifted in the air, her head craned around so she might lick her own rear end. Despite his growing love for the animal, he thought Dotty might well be the ugliest thing he had ever laid eyes on. 'Yeah . . . I guess.'

When the big guy finally climbed out of the hole, he momentarily lowered the light and took in the devastation all about him.

'Everyone gone,' he said, nodding to himself. 'Brick all alone.'

'Rush,' the boy said, holding out a hand. 'That's my name. It sounds like "hush", but it's spelt with a *ruh*. And you're not alone, Brick. You have Dotty and me now.'

Having moved what he hoped was a safe distance away from the devastated settlement and the werfen, in a little hollow surrounded by boulders, Rush threw caution to the wind and lit a fire. He spitted the clagbat and roasted it over the flames, sharing the meat with Brick. Dotty had gone out hunting in the darkness and waddled back after a short time with a bellyful of some poor unfortunate creature. She flopped down next to the fire and fell asleep instantly, farting loudly in her slumber in a way that, despite his ordeal, made Brick laugh. The big man ate an enormous amount, and moaned when Rush told him he couldn't eat the portion of meat he planned to smoke for the next leg of their journey.

As they sat by the little fire, Brick humming tunelessly and staring into the flames as he rocked back and forth, Rush explained that he was heading for City Four and the mutant township that had grown up outside its wall.

The humming stopped. '"Go to City Four" – that's what the voice said,' Brick muttered, nodding to himself.

Rush froze. 'What did you say?' he asked, but the giant simply stared at the fire as if hypnotised. *He simply repeated what I said*, he told himself, eyeing the man through the flames. There was little doubt in his head that the big guy 'wasn't all there', and that travelling with him would be burdensome. Not to mention that if he always ate as much as he had tonight, he would be a nightmare to feed in a landscape where food was difficult to come by, even with Rush's unique skills. Nevertheless, Rush couldn't abandon him. The voice in his dream had told him to collect something at the trading post. Was Brick that something? Unquestionably, somebody had gone to great lengths to hide him, even if doing so had cost them their own life. The thought reminded him of Josuf and his own sacrifice to save his young charge.

'So what do you think about coming along with me and Dotty?' He nodded back in the direction of the ransacked settlement. 'You can't really go back there, can you?'

'Brick's Maw might come back.'

The horrific scenes he'd witnessed through his spyglass replayed in Rush's head. He took in the big man's face and sadly shook his head. 'She's not coming back.'

'Rush sure?'

He nodded. 'I'm sorry.'

The big man's shoulders began to heave as he silently wept.

They sat like that for a long time, Rush allowing himself to grieve too in a way he hadn't before. Eventually Brick let out a long sigh. He straightened himself and nodded his huge head up and down as if he'd come to a decision. 'OK. Brick and Rush.'

Rush held out a hand. 'Rush and Brick.' His hand disappeared all the way up to the wrist, but the handshake was surprisingly gentle.

'Brick tired,' the big man said. And with that, he lay down on his side, closed his eyes and, like Dotty, fell fast asleep.

Rush watched the pair for a few moments before hunkering down and pulling his collar up around him to stave off some of the cold. After a few minutes he realised he'd neglected to feed the fire before settling down. It would almost certainly die without more fuel, but he'd got comfortable and the wood he'd found earlier was a little too far away for him to reach. He sighed and closed his eyes, concentrating on the logs until he *connected* with them, feeling them with his mind as surely as if he was touching them with his hands.

He hadn't done this for a long time, and never with anyone as close by as Brick was. Josuf had told him from a young age he wasn't to use his gift. The stone throwing was one thing – he could always put that down to luck if anyone saw him do it – but this was something altogether different. The firewood shifted a little, as if disturbed by an animal or something unseen beneath it. Then three pieces rose up, wavered in the air for a second, before slowly moving over the fire and dropping gently down into the flames.

Rush smiled to himself as he closed his eyes. It had felt good. It had felt . . . right.

Rush

Forced to travel by day because of Brick's refusal to do so in the dark, the two of them should have been easy targets for bandits or anyone else intent on attacking them.

How they avoided being seen in those first few days – walking across desolate scrubland with no cover as they headed for the distant mountain range – was a mystery to Rush. Travelling like this went against everything he'd done up until now, and despite their luck at not being spotted, he found himself doubting if he'd done the right thing by persuading Brick to hook up with him. As the days went on and their good fortune continued, Rush, a natural pessimist, became convinced that bad juju of some kind was merely building up, and the longer they went on undetected, the worse it would be when Lady Fortune finally turned her back on them.

Sure enough, on the third day their luck nearly failed them. The sun had almost dipped below the horizon; spiky shadows reached out across the ground, like long dusky fingers trying to hold on to what remained of the day. Rush, failing to notice the hole a burrowing animal had made, stepped into it and fell. The loud shriek he let out brought Brick hurrying over, asking the teenager over and over what had happened. Hissing through gritted teeth against the waves of pain, Rush was unable to answer at first, and when he did, he was short with the big guy, telling him to back off and leave him alone. Brick made camp, bringing covers over to Rush and telling him everything was going to be all right. But lying wrapped in the rough blanket, Rush knew how far from the truth this was. The slightest movement of his ankle sent waves of agony shooting through him, and there was no doubt in his mind that the bone was broken. That being the case, he would almost certainly die out here. Shivering beneath the thin covers, and trying to block out the pain, he eventually fell asleep.

The next morning, Rush woke to discover his ankle was fine. He flexed his foot, stunned to discover no hint of pain. Getting to his feet, he tentatively tested it a few times, and then stood fully upright, leaning so it bore all his weight. There was nothing to suggest he'd injured it in any way the previous day. He gawped stupidly down at the limb, shaking his head in astonishment.

'Better?' Brick asked.

'Wh . . . ? Er, yeah. Better.'

'Good.'

They set off in the direction of the mountains again, Rush in the lead and the humming Brick bringing up the rear. Walking like this, the younger mutant didn't notice how the big man now had a distinct limp. It didn't last long, and by the time they stopped again to rest, there was no sign anything had ever been wrong.

They carried on for two more uneventful days. Five days in total had passed since they'd set out from the outpost, and now the pair had finally reached the foothills of the mountain range they were headed towards. The vast rope of mountains stretched out as far as the eye could see in both directions, as if the earth had spewed up a natural barrier to stop travellers from reaching whatever might lie on the other side. From way off, the two had selected a particular peak as the one they would cross; it was lower than those around it, and unlike its neighbours, there was no indomitable-looking summit reaching up into the clouds. Instead, it appeared as if the uppermost part of their mountain had been neatly sliced off with a knife. 'Like the top of an egg!' Brick had said.

If Rush had had a sense of impending doom before, it was positively crushing now the mountains loomed ominously over them. He took to stopping every few minutes to scan the ridges and bluffs with his telescope, looking for signs of movement or the flash of reflected sun on a spyglass pointed back in their direction. When Brick asked him what he was looking at, or bugged him to let him have a go with the telescope, Rush would snap back at him or simply ignore him altogether. When they struck camp at night the forebodings of danger were so bad that he was unable to sleep, imagining that whatever might have been watching them all day would use the cover of darkness to creep down and cut their throats. This lack of sleep did nothing to improve his mood, and neither did Brick's constant tuneless humming, which was slowly beginning to drive him mad.

The morning they were to begin their ascent proper – the low foothills finally giving way to tougher, rockier terrain that they were forced to scramble over – Rush opened his eyes to the sight of Brick grinning at him from across the ashes of the previous night's fire.

'Morning,' the big guy said, poking a stick into the grey-and-black mess. Having consumed all their dried meat, and failing to find anything to hunt in this desolate waste-land, there was no food for them to break their fast.

Rush ignored him, rubbing his eyes and getting up to stretch his legs and back. He looked up and groaned at the thought of starting such a climb on an empty stomach. It didn't look too bad from down here, but there were a couple of areas higher up where he thought they might need the aid of the rope they'd brought along from the ruins of Brick's former home.

'Where's Dotty?'

The big man shrugged. 'Hunting?'

Rush scanned the landscape – a gloomy vista of tumbled, broken rock with the odd tussock of stiletto-grass here and there. It was unusual for her to leave them so early in the morning; she normally hunted at night. At least she would be starting the day with a full stomach. Who knew? Perhaps, after she'd gorged herself, she might bring some-thing back for the two of them, though he wasn't going to hold his breath on that one.

Brick's humming started again, punctuated this time by a *tap-tap-tap* of the stick on a rock.

Rush fought the urge to tell the big man to shut up, and angrily began shoving their things in the knapsack. It occurred to him that maybe he *should* have left Brick back there in the hole. Maybe, in the long run, that would have been the best thing – for both of them. He'd asked himself time and again why such a big man had been shoved in the bolt-hole when he could have been better used to defend the place. And every time he came up with the same answer: because whoever had put him there must have known he was of no use in a crisis. That, no matter how big he was, he couldn't be relied upon to help when danger struck.

Rush shook his head. Like it or not, he was stuck with the big guy. 'Let's go,' he said, setting off without so much as a backward look.

'Are we nearly at the top yet?' Brick asked for what seemed like the hundredth time that fateful morning.

'No.'

'Brick hungry.'

'Rush hungry too.' He winced. He was even beginning to talk like the dummy now. 'Just shut up about food, will you?' Except for some foul-tasting norgworms they'd managed to dig up and cook into a soup, neither of them had had anything to eat in nearly forty-eight hours.

They were on a narrow rutted path that might have been made by animals of some kind. Rush was hoping they were mountain goats, and he salivated at the idea of killing and cooking one.

'Rush grumpy today.'

'Yeah? Well, Brick's being a pain in the arse today. And if he wants to –'

He came to halt. The route they'd been following disappeared up ahead, falling off the side of the mountain in what must have been a landslide. Now there was nothing but a sheer wall of rock that, even with the rope, would be impossible to climb. Rush swore under his breath and looked helplessly around him. Frustration gave way to despair and he was about to announce that they would have to turn back and pick another mountain when he saw the cascade of trailers hanging over a darker patch of the rock face. He walked over to it, pulling the curtain of plant matter aside to reveal a narrow fissure that could have been formed at the same time the mountain fractured and the path was lost. What was left was a high, thin corridor just wide enough for a person to go through. The light didn't penetrate beyond the entrance, but when he shouted into the void, he could hear how far his voice travelled. He was suddenly aware of Brick standing by his side.

'We're going to have to see where this leads,' Rush said, nodding into the gloomy passageway. 'Of course, it might not go anywhere. If that's the case, we'll have to turn back. But having come this far, I don't think we can leave without checking it out.'

'Dark in there.'

'We've got the torch.'

'Still dark.'

The boy rounded on the hulking figure next to him, his top lip drawn back in a snarl. 'Well, I'm sorry about that! But take a look about you, Brick. There's no other way for us right now. We either see where that leads –' he jabbed a finger in the direction of the opening – 'or we go back the way we came, where we know there's no food, kiss good-bye to the time we've already spent getting *this* far and try another mountain that we *hope* doesn't have any dark places on it!'

Brick stared at his feet. 'Your lip looks funny when you get angry,' he mumbled.

Rush took a deep breath, calming himself. 'Look. I'll take the torch and go ahead first. The way my luck is running, it'll be a dead end. But if it *does* go somewhere that looks promising, I'll come back and we'll go through together. How does that sound?'

He was answered with a shrug.

He held out his hand. 'Torch.'

Brick dug around in his pocket and came out with it, putting it in the boy's hand.

'Look at me,' Rush said, suddenly feeling a little guilty for having shouted at the big guy. 'I won't be long. Stay here and wait. See if you can spot Dotty. I know she'll find us, she always does, but I'd rather have her back with us when we go through.'

'Be careful,' Brick said. He added something else, but Rush was no longer paying attention. Something about 'bad things coming out of the dark'.

Rush soon left the daylight behind. If he turned to look back, he could still just about make out the figure of Brick standing close to the entrance, but ahead the inky darkness was complete. The little cone of light thrown out by the torch didn't penetrate far, but it was enough to show Rush that the fissure carried on deep into the heart of the mountain. The floor of the passageway soon began to get steeper and, despite the fact that this quickly blocked off any sight of the light behind him, he was grateful that the incline meant he was heading up and not down. He came across pinch points where he had to turn sideways to get through, as well as sections where the cleft opened up. Water intermittently dripped from above so he was soon soaked to the skin. At one of the sections where the passage became wider Rush realised that the mountain above him might not be as solid as he'd hoped. Rocks and rubble littered the floor, making the going underfoot different here: muddier than the hard surface he'd been walking on until now. He shivered, trying not to think too much about the vast mass of rock above him. He swung the torch up, but it hardly made any impression on the darkness overhead. Shining it towards the floor illuminated tracks. His heart quickened and he crouched down to inspect them more closely. Cloven-hoofed animals had passed this way. Mountain goats perhaps, or maybe sheep? The animals had used this pathway in the past, and that meant it led somewhere.

He had no idea how long he'd been walking – it probably seemed much longer than it really was – but there was a smell and it was getting stronger. An eggy, foul stink that made his empty stomach clench. He stopped for a second when the light from the torch began to dim again. As he was about to wind the handle to recharge the dynamo inside, he sensed a very faint light up ahead. He frowned, thinking he must have imagined it, but it was there all right. Somewhere up ahead was the tiniest hint of daylight. He switched the torch off and carefully carried on in the direction of the glow, putting a hand out to use the wall beside him as a guide.

He stood in the entrance to a cave. A small break in the rock high up in the roof away to his left allowed in a shaft of light which fell at an angle on to the huge lake dominating the subterranean space. The surface of the water shimmered in the darkness as hundreds of jet-black droplets rained down from overhead. But neither the lake nor the narrow shore that surrounded it held much interest for Rush: he only had eyes for that small hole in the cavern roof, a hole that might be their way back out to the mountain again.

Rush nodded to himself. Turning, he left the cave behind him and hurried back in the direction he'd come, switching Tink's torch back on as he went.

Usually so cautious, Rush's pleasure at discovering a possible way out, and his eagerness to let Brick know, meant he didn't bother to investigate the cavern properly. If he had, he would have spotted the stark white animal bones scattered around the stony shoreline: bones of the same animals that had made the tracks in the passageway. Bones of the last creatures to visit that place.

Zander

Zander Melk stood looking down on to the world below from his top-floor office at the ridiculously high Bio-Gen Tower complex his father had had built. The place was a symbol of power and wealth, and loomed over the buildings around it. 'Look at me,' it said. 'I can do anything.' Zander reflected that it was precisely this attitude his father had adopted throughout his life. As CEO of the biggest and most powerful genetic-modification and robotic-enhancement corporation in City Four, his father had achieved an almost god-like status among the city dwellers whom he helped achieve 'perfection', and the man had delighted in the adoration and adulation. But the old man's time had come to an end. It was Zander's turn now, and he was determined to do things differently; his father's harsh policies regarding the Mutes were no longer what the Citizens needed. Zander could sense the winds of change, and *he* should have been the man to funnel them in the right direction. Now that was at risk.

The younger Melk's elevation to president should have been a shoo-in. His father's power and influence should have meant there was little standing between Zander and power. Each city elected ten principals to represent them, and these in turn elected one of their number to head the Principia, the body governing the Six Cities, as its president. There was only one man in the election against him, and the maverick media tycoon Towsin Cowper was hardly the most popular member of the assembly. If his father considered Zander to be liberal, he saw Cowper as someone who wanted to open the doors to each of the Six Cities and invite the freak hordes to come in and make themselves at home. But his father's revelations had thrown an enormous spanner into the works, threatening to destroy Zander's political aspirations for good. *What had the old fool been thinking?* There were strict rules governing the interaction of Pures and Mutes. Anyone wishing to visit the mutant slums outside the Six Cities' walls had to apply for a day pass, and no mutant could set foot within any of the cities. And yet his father had deliberately created a number of . . . he struggled to find a suitable word . . . hybrids! If news of his father's deeds escaped, the consequences didn't bear thinking about.

Now it was left to Zander to clean up the mess. Just as it was up to him to try to find a new way to deal with the 'mutant problem'.

The tower that these offices topped was one of only a handful of buildings tall enough to give a view over the city wall at the sprawling squalor beyond them. Even though the ghetto slums where the freaks lived were on the other side of immense steel bulwarks, the mere thought of the teeming masses out there was enough to make Zander's skin crawl.

The Principia, under the control of his father, had secretly hoped that deprivation and disease would be enough to see an end to their irksome neighbours. They should have known better. The Mutes had survived the apocalypse, and survived it 'topside'. They were resilient; he had to give them that. And they bred, oh boy, did they breed! He grimaced at this last thought, unable to imagine a city dweller's child being produced in *that* manner. Extracorporeal pregnancy had been the norm for many years now – children were grown in the laboratories of facilities such as Bio-Gen, in synthetic wombs to ensure they were *exactly* what their parents wanted, with no defects of any kind. Defects and deformities had no place inside the cities' walls. Outside, it seemed that little but abnormality prevailed.

They bred like rats, and their numbers grew and grew, and as this accretion went on unchecked, so the sizes of the slums expanded, creeping ever nearer to the cities like a cancer metastatically spreads towards healthy organs.

Their own space, that's what they needed. It was Zander's plan, should he get into power, to set up reservations; land far away from the cities, designated for Mutes. He would incentivise the slum dwellers to move there, and possibly have to resort to other tactics to remove those who would not do so willingly. When he'd proposed the idea to his father, the old man had dismissed it out of hand, telling him, 'Out of sight does not mean out of mind, boy.' But it could work, he was sure of it.

He turned away from the window, catching sight of the large metal plaque bolted to the wall behind his father's desk. This was the original, though there were countless copies. Scratched and warped, with a big number four on it, it had been part of the door of Ark #4, one of six vast underground facilities set up as havens for those people who would build the new world following the Last War. It was from these arks that the Six Cities emerged, constructed above the vast subterranean complexes where the 'Ark Children' had lived for more than forty years while the world above burned and died. One of these bygone pioneers had been his great-great-grandfather, Zebediah Melk. When, in their thousands, Zebediah and the other Ark inhabitants finally emerged into the sunlight again, they were surprised to find they were not the only survivors. Others had endured. Despite being bombarded by atomic, biological and chemical fallout, those left to die topside had not been wiped out. But they *had* been changed. The Mutes his ancestors encountered were far more freakish than anything around today. In fact, the vast majority of mutants looked almost normal these days. Sure, there was the odd 'lizard skin' or 'web hand' around, but not so many. Nonetheless, their DNA was screwed, and he agreed with the decree by the Ark Children – who after all were charged with creating the new world – that the two groups should never merge. The old expression 'You can't grow perfect corn if you start with bad seed' was as true now as it had ever been.

The mutant settlements were the only way to go – ship them out and let them have the 'rights' they were demanding in their rallies. Mutant rights? Who'd ever heard of anything so ridiculous? His plan could work. But first he had to be elected as president, and that meant erasing all trace of his father's stupid mutant hybrids.

Anya

The wagon jostled along the path, throwing those on board around like rag dolls. The way through the mountainous region where Anya and her guardian, Kerin, lived was arduous and slow, but by taking a more direct route, off the recognised tracks and lanes, it was agreed they could make better time and avoid any ARM units that might be in the locality. This decision, however, meant Kerin would have to stay behind.

Anya's guardian had lost a leg a few years back, and it was agreed that the trip would be too much for her.

Tink got the impression that neither the teenage girl nor the woman charged with caring for her were particularly upset by this decision. Their relationship had broken down somewhat over the last couple of years, and although there were tears shed by both parties prior to the departure, he was pretty sure they were both a little relieved to have some time apart.

They'd been lucky with their timing. As they made their way through the foothills of the mountain that had been Anya's home for the last thirteen years, they'd spotted an armoured vehicle high on a pass above them, climbing towards the cabin they'd left behind.

'She'll be fine,' Tink said when he saw the worried look on the girl's face. 'It's you they're after, not Kerin. Once they realise you're gone, they'll leave her alone.' He hoped so anyway. They'd agreed Kerin would tell the ARM that the pair had left, but say they'd gone over the mountains, in exactly the opposite direction to the one they'd taken. He thought the men might accept her explanation: that way *was* the best direction if you were trying to escape. Tink and Anya waited beneath the cover of the trees until they were sure the men were gone. Urging his harg forward, Tink, with Anya sitting on the jockey-box by his side, set off, determined to put as much distance between them and the men as possible.

A few hours later, when the pair found themselves in a patchy forest of evergreens, Tink brought up the subject of Anya and Kerin's relationship, asking what had gone wrong.

'She doesn't like me changing,' the teenager answered.

'You know, when I shift into other forms? She says I shouldn't do it.'

'You can understand her concerns. If you were seen –'

'Tink, we live in a cabin in the middle of nowhere. Our nearest neighbour is more than ten miles away. All last year we didn't see another soul until you came by just before the winter. Nobody.' She gave a little shake of her head. 'It's easy to get a bit of "cabin fever" up there. You know, go a bit gaga –' she made a twirling motion with a finger at her temple – 'so I've been going out. Taking another form and getting away for a while.' She paused. 'It's been causing arguments.'

He nodded, but he knew there was more to it than simply what Anya was telling him. While they were alone, Kerin had spoken to Tink, explaining that the youngster struggled to transform back into her human form after she'd been out on these trips. She described how recently, after going out to investigate strange sounds in an outhouse where they kept their winter fuel, Kerin had opened the door to discover a nightmarish chimera. The creature was bluish black, with bright yellow eyes and closely meshed scales, so its skin looked like that of a snake. In form the beast itself looked more leopard-like. Long black canines hung from its upper jaw, and from the look of the blood on the creature's front, they had been employed lately to good effect. The creature let out a tortured screech, its back arching high over legs held out stiffly before it.

'Breathe, Anya, breathe and concentrate,' the woman urged.

The creature hissed back at her. Racked with spasms, it contorted wildly again and threw itself to the ground.

And then, quite suddenly, the girl appeared in the cat-snake's place, her hair stuck to her sweat-drenched face as she gasped for air.

Kerin, not wishing to have another row, had just shaken her head, turned her back on the girl and returned to their cabin.

Tink was still thinking about all this when he was suddenly struck with a vision. A gasp escaped him and he pulled the harg to a halt. Sitting perfectly still with his head angled slightly to one side, he kept his eyes shut as if he was listening for something only he could hear. Finally, with a sigh, he opened his eyes again.

'What is it?' Anya asked.

'The road up ahead. The one we have to take? I think we could be in danger if we go that way.' He shook his head. 'I don't know what that danger might be though. If it's the ARM, we need to change our plans again.'

'And if it's not?'

'I'm not sure we have too many choices. We might have to face off whoever – or whatever – it is.'

'Is this one of your famous hunches?'

'Something like that, yes.'

'So why don't I go and check it out?'

'What?'

'You know, shift into something else and take a look.'

'I don't want you to put yourself in danger, and I don't –'

'Wait here so I can find you again,' the teenager said. With that, she stood up on the jockey-box.

'No, Anya, wait –'

But he was too late. She jumped up into the air. Mid-leap, the pale, dark-haired girl transformed into a truly hideous creature that beat its wings and launched into the sky.

Part-human, part-bat, but *all* ugly, the hideous pink-skinned beast had a humanoid torso with short frog-like legs curled up behind it. Its vast wings, also pale pink in colour, were translucent, so not only were the long thin bones stretching the membrane visible, but also the veins and arteries therein. The head was the pug-faced shape of a bat, but the large, blue, almond-shaped eyes that stared out from the face were decidedly human. When it turned to look down at him, the long, sharp teeth that lined its wide grin chittering, Tink couldn't help but shudder. He watched the diabolical-looking creature as it rose up over the trees and disappeared from sight.

The bat-beast soared back into view and stayed itself over the wagon with two massive downstrokes of its wings before dropping down on to the flatbed, its clawed hind legs scrabbling on the wooden surface for purchase.

Turning in his seat, Tink could see how ungainly and awkward the thing was now it was grounded. Twisting and writhing, it let out a screech that he was sure meant it was in pain.

'Is there anything I can do?' he asked. Although it was difficult to read the expression on the creature's face, the way its eyes rolled wildly in its head suggested it was in agony.

It may only have been a few minutes – it seemed much longer – but eventually, accompanied by one last terrible scream, Anya transformed back into her human self. She lay on her side, panting, finally looking over in Tink's direction and giving him a shaky grin.

Wrapping a blanket around herself, she sat up. 'You can see City Four from up there. It's enormous. Bigger than I'd ever have guessed. It's all towers and tall buildings and glass and metal.'

Despite his fears for her, Tink couldn't help but smile back.

'You were right,' she went on, standing up and coming to join him again. 'But it's worse than you first thought. About eight or nine miles behind us – not far from the point where we forded the river – there's an ARM vehicle. I think the water has done something to their engine; a couple of the men were looking inside it. I'm guessing they have the means to fix it, and once they have, they'll be headed this way.'

Tink sighed.

'Up ahead, about two miles, maybe a little more, along this track there's a group of armed men. They're up to no good. I think they've already ambushed some travellers – they've got them in a cart like this one, tied up in the back.'

'Caught between the devil and the deep blue sea, eh?' Tink said. He glanced behind them, the look on his face making it clear what he thought posed the greatest danger to them. 'How many men did you see up ahead?'

'Three, but I guess there could be more.'

'It looks as if we have little choice but to push on and hope we can get past these ambushers without too much trouble.'

He gave the reins a resigned flick, setting the harg off. 'I'm sorry, Anya. I shouldn't have let you do that. Kerin told me that you had been having trouble returning to your human form.'

She frowned and gave a little shrug.

'When we get to where we're going, I think there's somebody who can help you, someone who might help you control your gift.'

'The person who spoke to me in my dream and told me you were coming?'

'Yup. His name is Jax. Like you, he's . . . different.'

'What are we going to do about the men up ahead?'

'I'm not sure just yet. It depends on how many of them there are. I hate to say it, but there's a chance you might have to call upon your powers again before this trip is over.'

'That's OK. But if I *do* get stuck in the body of something like that bat-thing, I'm relying on you to tell everyone I wasn't always that ugly.'

Rush

The promise that it wasn't too far, coupled with another one that he could stop and hold the torch to his face whenever he wanted to, was just about enough to coax Brick inside the bowels of the mountain. He came along behind Rush, who pointed the dim beam of light almost straight down at his own feet, giving the big man something to fix his eyes upon. Even so, Brick was a gibbering wreck as they made their way along the claustrophobic fissure.

Rush kept up a running commentary, talking about anything and everything to try to distract the big guy from thinking too much about their situation. When they passed the point where the little rockslide had occurred, he knew they were almost at their destination.

'Smell that?' he said.

'Bad eggs!' Brick shouted, his voice unnaturally loud in the confined space. 'Or Dotty's farts!'

Despite everything, Rush couldn't help but smile. 'More like *your* farts after eating that norgworm soup the other day!'

'Ha! Brick!'

Rush took a big sniff and screwed his face up. 'Yep, definitely one of yours. We're here,' he concluded as they reached the entrance to the cave. He pointed out the gap in the roof. The light coming in was not as bright as it had been before, and they could just make out purple beard-like trails of lichen hanging down from the edges of the hole. 'That's where we're going to try to get through.'

They moved deeper into the cavern, Rush letting the light play over the far wall beneath the opening.

'Look,' Brick said, pointing to a ledge about halfway up. Thankfully it was suspended over solid ground, not hanging out over the lake.

Rush said a silent prayer of gratitude. Maybe their luck *was* holding out after all. As he swung the beam back down again, the light fell across an elongated skull lying on the shore among the multitude of yellow and grey pebbles. He shone the torch around some more, casting the light over the other skulls and bones littering the place. Among them were smaller, rounder ones – skulls that looked decidedly human.

'Brick,' he said in a small voice, 'turn around. We need to turn and go back the way –'

He didn't finish the sentence because the ground in front of him erupted.

The monstrous thing that sprang from the sulphurous soil on the lake shore resembled a giant salamander. Wet earth and stones rained from its leathery skin as it rose up on two legs, towering over Rush and Brick. A huge orange frill – a fan of leathery stretched skin – opened out behind the monster's head, and four prominent eyes blinked all at once as they took in their prey. The creature opened its mouth – a mouth lined with transparent, needle-like teeth – impossibly wide and issued a long shriek in Rush's direction before spitting a greenish liquid into his face that burned his skin and instantly blinded him. He staggered backwards, and would have fallen had a snake-like tongue not shot out from the creature's mouth and wrapped itself around his neck. He let out a strangled gasp as the living lasso yanked him forward, forcing him to stumble over the uneven ground. All he could think of was that vast, gaping maw and those glassy teeth sinking into his flesh. He could see nothing.

And that would have been that, had it not been for Brick.

The hulk of a man – whom Rush had expected to be of no use when danger finally reared its ugly head – moved with incredible speed, bellowing his own name like a battle cry. He dashed forward and grabbed hold of the long prehensile tongue about halfway between the creature and its intended prey. Using both hands and all his weight, he heaved downwards. There was a screech followed by a stifled gagging sound as the monster's head was jerked down. The creature dropped on to all fours, causing Rush to lose his balance and his footing. He hit the stony ground hard, the air knocked out of his lungs by the impact.

The little torch had dropped from Rush's hand as he'd been attacked, and he prayed it had not broken, leaving his defender as blind as he now was. There was another terrifying shriek from the monster, and he felt the living noose around his neck first loosen, then fall away altogether. Still blind, he scrambled backwards, scraping his hands and elbows on the harsh, skittering stones. Somewhere off to his left he heard another strange sound, like rock being torn apart, swiftly followed by the noise of the creature moving quickly in the same direction. There was a meaty *whump!* like something hard and heavy being slammed into flesh, and a screech that told him the salamander-thing had been hurt.

More scuffling sounds followed, rocks and stones scraping and rubbing against each other as if the two combatants were slowly circling each other, waiting for the right moment to attack. Then a sudden flurry of noise, during which Rush's heart almost stopped when he heard Brick shout out in pain.

'Brick? Brick, are you all right?'

There was a grunt, followed by two more loud thumping sounds, like someone hitting a side of beef with a large hammer.

'Brick!' Rush called out. Helpless, he heard more grunts and groans. Something large, or perhaps two large things, crashed to the ground, and he imagined he felt the earth shake with the force of it. He held his breath, listening to the two combatants, who were clearly locked together in a deadly wrestling match only one of them would survive.

He was about to call out again when, quite suddenly, the struggle stopped. The silence that followed, broken only by the *plink!* of water droplets hitting the surface of the lake, was terrifying.

'Brick?' Rush cried out into the darkness again. In his mind he imagined the huge black-and-orange creature making its way slowly towards him, toying with its sightless prey before it dealt the last, lethal blow.

A noise close by made him whirl around, lashing out into the darkness.

'Rush OK?' a voice asked. It was Brick.

Rush's heart thumped at the sound of his friend's voice. Brick's breathing was ragged and laboured, and although he'd uttered only two words, it was clear to Rush the big guy was in serious pain. 'I'm not sure,' he replied. 'Are you?'

'The bad thing tried to hurt Rush.'

'Where is it now?'

'Dead.' A sob escaped the big man. 'Brick didn't want to kill it, but it tried to hurt you.'

Rush held out a hand. There were more scraping sounds as Brick crawled over to him. He felt Brick's hand fold around his own. It was covered in a slightly tacky fluid that could only be blood. He wondered whose it was.

Trying not to let his panic show, Rush did his best to control his voice. 'I can't see, Brick. That thing blinded me. Now listen carefully. Can you get the water from my bag for me? I need to wash this muck out of my eyes.' Brick grunted, but instead of moving away and trying to locate Rush's bag, he sidled up closer to the boy.

'Brick? I need –'

'Shhh, hold still.'

'The water, Brick!' he shouted. 'Please. I have to get this stuff out of my eyes as soon as I can! It might be my only chance to see again!'

Brick stayed, leaning in close enough for Rush to feel

the man's warm breath on his face. 'Poison,' he said. 'Hold still.'

'Brick?' Rush felt his companion's hands reach out and take him by the head, the fleshy part of his palms beneath his thumbs pressing into Rush's eyes. 'What are you doing? Stop that, you dummy! I need the w–'

When he later thought about what happened next, the only way he could describe it to himself was like a flash of light so intense it took his breath away. A searing heat exploded in and around his eyes, filling him with an excruciating mixture of pain and exultation. He cried out – a harsh bark that was half laugh, half scream. Just when he thought he couldn't possibly take any more, he flew backwards away from the big mutant as if he'd been shoved by an invisible force.

He blinked his eyes and opened them. He could see. The gloomy cave, the tiny droplets falling from the roof, the lake, the stony shore – he took it all in in an instant. His saviour was sprawled on his back opposite him, as if the same invisible power had sent him flying too.

Rush hurried over, taking in the extent of Brick's own injuries for the first time. There was a low moan from the big guy. 'Brick, are you OK? What just happened?'

'I took it away.'

'Took what away?'

'The hurt. Brick took away the hurt that the monster put on Rush.'

Rush gasped as he looked at Brick's face. The big guy's eyes were completely black – twin globes devoid of all colour. The flesh around them was purple and inflamed, and the veins beneath the skin bulged darkly as if filled with black fluid. Rush lifted his hand and waved it front of Brick's face. There was no response.

'Brick, what's wrong with your eyes?'

'The hurt is there now.'

'You're blind? You're blind because of what you did for me?'

A hint of a smile briefly touched Brick's face. 'Not for long,' he said.

Jax

Silas looked across at the albino whom he'd watched grow from a stern young boy into an even sterner young man. As always, the youngster, now eighteen years of age, was dressed in black, the clothing accentuating his pallor and austere appearance. The interior of the room was dark; dirty curtains were pulled across the window to keep out the afternoon light. Jax preferred to avoid the sunlight that so easily burned his unpigmented skin. From somewhere outside came the incongruous sound of children playing, their high-pitched screams and laughter penetrating the thin walls. Jax sighed, small frown lines creasing his usually smooth white forehead.

'They're all on their way,' he said.

'Is it possible for you to work out who's the nearest?'

'Of course.' He paused, concentrating again. 'Flea and

Lana are only about a day away. Anya is with Tink and should be here shortly after that.' A ghost of a smile crossed his lips. 'Rush and Brick found each other and are still together. They are a little further away than the others, but closer than when I last reached out to them.' He opened his eyes and stared back at the man he'd lived with all this time.

'You seem excited at the prospect of seeing them all,' Silas said.

The albino nodded. 'Of course I am. Besides you, they are the closest thing to family I have. They are like brothers and sisters I've been estranged from.'

Silas was surprised at Jax's choice of words. He'd never heard the young man refer to the others in this way before. 'Hardly brothers and sisters. You have no idea where the embryos Melk used to create all of you were from.'

'What difference does that make? Like them, I share a syringe for a father and a test tube for a mother.' He stopped, realising how his words might have hurt his guardian's feelings. 'I am sorry, Silas. I didn't mean that you were not . . .'

'That's all right, Jax.'

'I just want them all to get here safely.'

'I'm sure they will.'

Jax nodded. 'I must lie down now. Locating others across such distances leaves me very tired.'

'Of course.' Silas stood up and went to the door. 'We are doing the right thing, aren't we? Bringing them here like this.'

'They all deserve to know the truth, Silas. We agreed that if they were ever discovered, this was the best way forward. Why should they hide any longer? Why shouldn't they come to understand the true nature of their powers and abilities?'

'Their arrival will cause problems. Things will become very difficult for all of us.'

'Things are already difficult for us, Silas. Maybe the arrival of the others will make it easier. Maybe it signals a new era for the mutants – one that doesn't involve oppression, discrimination and tyranny.'

'Maybe.' Silas nodded to his ward and left, closing the door behind him and pausing on the other side. *Or maybe it signals an altogether different era: one in which those inside the walls finally rid themselves of those beyond them.*

Rush

Through the gap in the roof they could see it was now dark outside. Brick sat on a boulder by the side of the lake, winding the handle of the dynamo. His vision had returned, and he'd taken to jamming the torch into his face again to soak up the light from the bulb. The injuries he'd received seemed to bother him far less than one would expect. He'd been bitten about the head, shoulders and hands, many of the wounds deep and bloody. A piece of his left ear was missing and what was left was only just attached, hanging down at an odd angle like a lump of bloody gristle. His leg was hurt too, and the way he was holding it, ramrod straight, out in front of him, and wincing and looking down at it occasionally, suggested to Rush that this might be the thing causing his friend the most pain.

'How are you feeling?' Rush asked.

Brick glanced up from the light and surprised Rush by offering him a big grin. He shook his head as if to tell the youngster not to worry. 'Brick heal real fast.'

Despite the extent of his wounds, the big guy didn't complain once as Rush administered to him, not even when the youngster stitched the ear back on using a needle and thread he found in his bag and doing his best not to botch the job in the gloom. Too exhausted to move far from the lake, they camped next to it. Huddling in close to each other for warmth and to share the light, they no longer noticed the hydrogen sulphide stink as they feasted on the raw flesh of their erstwhile adversary. It had a rubbery, fishy flavour that wasn't too bad after the first couple of mouthfuls. It was when Rush was butchering the carcass that he was able to fully take in the size of the creature. As big as Brick was, he had no idea how the man had managed to overcome it until he saw the large stalagmite, one end caked in blood, that lay on the shore not far from the monster's dead body. He realised it was *this* he'd heard being torn from the ground moments before the creature's tongue released his neck.

'Thank you for saving my life, Brick,' he said after they'd eaten. The words sounded inadequate. He shook his head, ashamed at himself for the way he'd behaved towards the man during their short time together. 'I'm sorry I've been grouchy with you for the last few days.'

As he said this, he remembered his ankle, and the miraculous recovery he'd experienced in his sleep. Brick had clearly healed him then too.

'Rush and Brick.' The big guy said, looking earnestly back. 'Friends.'

The big man's simple statement only heightened Rush's shame. Tears welled up, and he turned his face away. Brick had been willing to lay down his own life to protect him, and Rush knew that from now on he wouldn't hesitate to do the same.

He rubbed at his eyes with his palms and smiled back at the big guy. 'Friends.' He nodded and held out a hand.

Brick took it in his own, but rather than shake it, he pulled the youngster in, wrapping him up in a hug, despite his pain.

'Brick tired,' the big man said as he released him. 'Always makes Brick tired to take the hurt away.'

'You should sleep.' He noted how the big man looked around warily. 'It's all right, I'm right here. It's safe now. I'll keep watch.'

Brick nodded his big head and lay down, closing his eyes. The deep gentle snores that quickly followed were proof of the exhaustion he'd been fighting.

Rush sighed and moved in closer to his friend for warmth. The light from the torch in his hand slowly began to dim, and he too was on the verge of falling asleep when he heard a noise somewhere overhead. Glancing up in the direction of the small opening in the roof, he could just make out a handful of stars in the sky beyond. He kept still and then he heard it again. It was the sound of men talking. Getting up slowly so as not to wake Brick, Rush crept beneath the hole and listened.

'We should just kill it. Look at the mess that thing made of Bo's leg.'

'Are you mad? Sure, the critter's mean, but that's what we want, isn't it? Besides, Bo's a damn fool, getting near it like that. Now it's in the noose it don't pose us no risk.'

There was an unmistakable *hurghing* sound that caused one of the men to curse and order the animal responsible to 'shut the hell up'.

Rush, his heart thumping, held his breath.

'No, we stick to the plan. We take that animal to Logtown and pitch it against those pig-dog things they're so keen on.'

'I dunno . . .'

'That's right. You don't know. That's why *I* do the thinking for us. And right now I'm thinking that critter will make one hell of a fighter, and those mill folk'll go mad for the chance to see it go up against their boarnogs. The critter is as strong as it is ugly. And did you see those teeth? Tomorrow night is fight night. We bet everything we have on it, we'll clean up!'

'If you're sure . . .'

'Sure I'm sure. You doubting me? Hmm?' There was a grunt when no answer came back. 'Now we'll make camp. I'm not going any further tonight.'

Rush listened as the men moved off and he couldn't hear them any longer.

There was no doubt in his mind that they were mountain men of some kind, and that they'd captured Dotty. He had no idea what Logtown or boarnogs were, but one thing he knew for sure: he and Brick had to get Dotty free before these men made her fight for their pleasure.

Full of anguish, but knowing he could do nothing before first light, he walked back to the recumbent Brick and settled down by his side. His life had been turned inside out since that night when he'd woken to the sound of armed men arriving at the farmhouse – when everything he'd come to love and count upon had been taken away from him. But out of that terrible nightmare he'd found first Dotty and then Brick. They were all he had now, and he was damned if he wouldn't do everything he could to keep them safe. He listened to the steady plinking of water falling from the roof, his mind a swirl of emotions as he tried to formulate a plan.

Despite his belief that sleep would prove impossible, Rush found he'd dropped off at some point during the night. He opened his eyes to see Brick was already up and about. The big mutant stood, his back to him, throwing stones into the black waters of the underground lake. Rush watched as his friend bent down to fetch more pebbles; the damaged leg was still clearly bothering him, but Rush could have sworn the cuts and lacerations on his face and hands were much smaller than he remembered from the night before. The only other wound that still looked bad was the ear. Purple and horribly swollen, Rush feared it might be infected.

Brick, finally aware that he was being watched, turned around and nodded back in his direction. The flesh around his eyes was still a little puffy, but nothing more.

'You weren't kidding when you said you were a quick healer, were you?' Rush said, approaching the man to get a better look.

A big, lopsided grin was the only response. Rush leaned forward and stared at the bloody gap where one of Brick's teeth had been knocked out. There was a hint of white poking out from the gory mess of gum. 'Are you growing a new tooth, Brick?'

The big guy shrugged and jammed his tongue into the gap. He looked mildly surprised at what he discovered there, but he quickly lost interest and went back to throwing the stones.

Rush shook his head. As fascinating as Brick's rejuvenating powers were, he had other things to think about. He was convinced now that Brick *had* been the thing he was supposed to discover at the trading post, and Maw, like Josuf, had done everything in her power to protect her charge. For better or worse he and Brick were somehow linked. They had to get to City Four and find out what the hell all this was about. But first they had to rescue Dotty.

He nodded to the rocky ledge they'd spotted the previous day. 'Do you think your leg is strong enough to get up there, Brick?'

'What about Dotty?' Brick asked, looking back at the cavern entrance as if expecting to see the rogwan standing there.

'She's already up above us somewhere.' Rush paused and then explained. 'I heard something in the night – some men talking up there.' He gestured towards the hole. 'They've got her.'

'Bad men?'

'I think so, yes.'

Brick gave a sigh. Without another word he set about climbing the overhang.

The way up to the rocky shelf wasn't too arduous; Rush and Brick helped each other, and pretty soon they were standing side by side directly beneath the gap in the roof, staring up at a perfectly blue sky beyond. Although it was only about five metres overhead, getting through the hole was going to be harder than Rush had first realised. They needed a way of getting the rope up there. In the end they settled on the stalagmite Brick had ripped out to kill the salamander. Rush went back down and, with some effort, managed to drag the thing to underneath the ledge, where he tied the rope Brick lowered to him around it.

Brick pulled the long cone of rock up first, then sent the rope back down so he could do the same for Rush.

Rush's idea was for Brick to throw the stalagmite, rope still attached, up through the hole and for them to gently pull it back so as to wedge it in place. Rush would then climb the rope and, once topside, secure it to something more substantial so Brick could follow. Easy, he scoffed when Brick gave him a doubtful look. *Yeah, right*, he said to himself. *Easy.* Easy *if* Brick had the strength to hoist the thing up there in the first place; *if* it didn't come crashing down on top of them when they pulled on it; *if* it would wedge at all; *if* it would hold Rush's weight and *if* the rope was long enough. There was a whole host of other things that could go wrong, but with no other options they simply had to give it a go.

'Brick'll miss,' the giant said as he assessed the opening above their heads. 'Brick a bad shot.'

'You won't miss,' Rush assured him. 'Not this time.'

128

'How'd you know?'

'Trust me.'

Brick proved himself up to the task of hoisting the heavy cone up towards the hole. Holding it in two hands, he leaned forward, setting his legs wide. He swung the piece of stone back and forth a couple of times, increasing the swing each time until he finally gave an enormous grunt and heaved the thing upward. He'd been right about his aim though. He *would* have missed. Not by much, but enough for the stalagmite to catch an edge and come crashing down on them. But as the long cone of rock soared, Rush reached out with his mind, concentrating with all his will until he and the rocky thing were one. Like this, he guided it to one side so it sailed cleanly through and out into the open air beyond. The two of them gently pulled the rope to drag it back towards the hole, and when it lodged itself at the first attempt they shook hands and clapped each other on the back. After a few experimental tugs, Rush spat on his hands and set about climbing the rope. With every hand-over-hand grip he took the air got fresher and fresher, until he gave a cry of joy and scrambled over the lip into the sunshine, flopping on to his back and pulling in lungful after lungful of sweet mountain air. As soon as he could, he crawled back over to the edge of the hole and peered inside, giving Brick a grin and a thumbs-up.

'Let's get you out of there, shall we?'

Tia

Tia and her father, having revealed their scheme, were waiting to hear what Eleanor thought the chances were of its being successful. Six foot tall, with honed muscles, even when seated the ebony-skinned woman was imposing. Of course, as the former head of C4's CSP – the City Security Police – she'd needed to be, but Tia thought she also managed to look not just elegant but beautiful. She'd noticed the look her father had given Eleanor when he'd introduced them, and couldn't help but wonder just how close a friendship the two shared.

'What day did your little monkey friend get back into the city?' Eleanor asked. She gestured towards the marmoset sitting on Tia's shoulder, but her eyes never left the girl's.

'Thursday, I think.'

'You think?'

'Thursday. Definitely Thursday.'

'What time?' The questions were fired out, no doubt a throwback to Eleanor's days interrogating suspects back at her former post.

'At about six o'clock. I remember that because I had to get the footage we'd shot sent off in time to make the deadline. I was cutting it a bit fine.'

'At about the time of the guards' handover,' Eleanor said, more to herself than to her guests. She pursed her lips and sighed. 'Sloppy. Would never have happened in my time. The areas around the masts are closely monitored. Your little friend must have picked just the right moment to slip past them. You won't be that lucky twice.'

Cowper turned to his daughter. 'You see? It's not possible. If the monkey can't get back inside without being detected, your whole plan is doomed.'

The former head of security gave her friend a sly smile. 'I didn't say it was impossible. I said you were *lucky* last time. If you were to try it again, you'd need to replace that luck with . . . something else.'

The look Cowper gave her was anything but warm.

'What do you mean?' Tia asked, feeling her hopes rise again.

'As former head of security, I'm still employed on a consultancy basis by the Principia. That means I still have access to certain areas that are closed to others. It would be simple for somebody like me to create a momentary diversion at the handover.'

'I don't want to implicate you in all of this, Eleanor,' Cowper protested.

Tia watched as the woman stretched her neck. She had a cat-like grace about her. 'You already have. Merely by revealing these plans, you've involved me.' She held out a hand to halt his interruption. 'I'm not blaming you and I'm not angry. Who else could you ask about all this stuff? But don't think you can turn around now and use me as an excuse for Tia not to give this a go. You know how I feel about the ARM and its treatment of those poor unfortunates out there. Their agents are vicious thugs, just like the man who set the agency up in the first place.'

'How is our beloved president?'

'Sick. He seems to be worse than ever. Thanks to blood replacements and a cocktail of drugs he's able to hide it from most people. I find it hard to have any sympathy for the man.'

Cowper nodded. 'I just don't want you to take any unnecessary risks.'

Eleanor shook her head and took a sip from the drink she was holding. That mischievous smile was back on her face. 'It doesn't have to be anything big. Merely turning up at the observation point should be enough to do it. I can still cause a stir, you know.'

Looking at her, Tia had little doubt about that. Not yet reassured, her father continued.

'There's still the matter of the security log at the entry gate.'

Eleanor wafted a hand in his direction. 'Easily put straight. To be honest, and despite what our leaders would have the Citizens believe, glitches in the system do occur from time to time. Upon the monkey entering your apartment, the chip will be flagged as being there. The anomaly with the lack of an entry log will be followed up, but it'll almost certainly be little more than a comms call from a city security officer, asking you to confirm Tia is indeed home. Your confirmation will be enough for them to write it off as a software error.'

'Then what?'

'It's important that the monkey – or, as far as the CSP are concerned, Tia – moves about. You can't just keep the animal confined to your residence. That would bring unwanted attention.' She looked over at Cowper. 'You'll have to take the animal around with you while Tia's gone.'

This was greeted by a snort of derision. 'It's a monkey! What am I going to do? Turn up to business meetings with a monkey on my back?'

'I think you could do with a well-earned holiday, Cowper. Take some time off. Maybe visit some of our city's tourist spots.' She looked from father to daughter. 'Nobody will bat an eye at a man with a pet in those places, and the crowds mean the security services won't be able to spot who's where and with what. As far as they're aware, Tia is with you on a little vacation.'

Tia narrowed her eyes at the older woman. 'Have you done this sort of thing before?'

'No, but I've arrested people who have tried.'

'That doesn't sound too encouraging.'

'That's why I'm telling you where they went wrong – so none of us suffers the same fate.' She smiled back at the girl. 'You're the one taking the biggest risk here though, sweetie. Your father might be able to protect you from the powers that be while you're in City Four. But once you're out there you'll be cut off from everything and everybody inside the wall. Not just that, but you'll be unchipped and therefore viewed as a mutant by the ARM and anyone else. Not all mutants have physical deformities or unusual appearances to identify them as such, you know.' She peered intently into the girl's eyes. 'Are you *sure* you want to do this?'

There was a moment as the girl took in everything she'd just been told. 'I'm sure.'

'Then I'll hook you up with a man on the other side. He's a good person – runs a school for orphans and abandoned kids. If I were about to do what you are, I couldn't think of anyone I'd rather have on my side.'

'What's his name?' Cowper asked.

'Silas. His name is Silas.'

Silas

'Is that her?' Silas asked. 'Is that Flea?' He was standing next to the tall, skeletal Jax, the two of them watching the girl as she moved among the people in the marketplace. It was getting late in the day, and the traders were eager to shift their stock before the darkness closed the market and the night people came out to sell their own particular brand of goods and services. Silas narrowed his eyes. Something was wrong with the way the girl moved, but despite all his senses telling him this was the case, he couldn't quite put his finger on what it was.

Jax gave a nod. 'Watch.'

Silas studied the scene. The girl, elfin-featured and extremely small for her age, moved between two people waiting to be served at a stall selling dubious-looking meats of unknowable origin. The trader was calling out the late bargains he was willing to make when the girl did that odd, jerky thing again, as if her arms and legs were in one position one moment and then seamlessly in another. It wasn't a big change, and you could only spot it if you were watching very carefully, but it was definitely there.

'She did it, didn't she?' Silas asked the albino. 'Wow, she's fast.'

Never one for many words, Jax just tilted his chin in the direction of the girl who was moving back across the other side of the street towards the entrance to an alley, where she handed a couple of items to a man. Words were exchanged, and the man gestured back in the direction of the crowd. When the girl shook her head, Silas didn't like the look the man gave her. The creep leaned forward, pushing his face into hers, and said something, jabbing his finger over her shoulder to emphasise each word. Her shoulders sagged and she moved off into the thronging mass again. The man stood and watched her for a few moments, as if to be sure she would follow orders.

'Come on,' Silas said, moving out from their hiding position. 'You get Flea. I'll deal with our friend over there.'

The creep was opening the second wallet, the first one already emptied and discarded at his feet, when Silas stepped up and took it out of his grasp.

'Hey!' the man said. 'What the hell –'

'Didn't your mother teach you not to take things that aren't yours?'

The man reached into his coat pocket, whipping out a small but vicious-looking knife. It was only in his hand for a moment. Silas moved in, grabbing and twisting the man's wrist so the knife skittered to the ground at the same time that Silas's right knee connected solidly with his opponent's groin. There was a loud *'Oof!'*, and Creep sagged to his knees, eyes bulging in a plum-coloured face.

Silas kicked the blade away up the alley as Jax and the girl turned up.

'Do you know who I am? Who I work for?' Creep said through gritted teeth.

'A lowlife piece of trash that forces little girls to steal for him?'

Creep glanced over at the girl and the albino. 'Hey, I'm just the middleman. She don't belong to me. But the man who owns her –' he gave Silas a look of warning – '*he* would not be very happy to find out you'd interfered with us in any way. You wanna muscle in on someone's patch, take my advice and do it somewhere else.'

'*Owns* her?' Silas took a step towards the man, who put his hands up in front of him as if to ward off any further attack.

'OK, OK. *Employs* her.'

Fighting back the urge to inflict more physical damage on the man, Silas turned his back on him and faced the youngster.

'Are you OK?' he asked.

He was about to say something else when the man on the ground spoke up. 'She don't speak. She can't.'

'You're safe now,' Silas went on, ignoring him. He looked at Jax and raised an eyebrow.

The albino took a deep breath, his expression becoming one of concentration as he stared at the teenage girl. 'She doesn't know what his name is, but the man who sent her out to steal still has Lana,' he said, referring to the female guardian who'd looked after the youngster all these years. 'It seems our odious friend here is telling the truth when he says he's a middleman. Flea has been told that the only way she'll be reunited with Lana is if she uses her gift to steal enough money to buy her freedom. This is her first day on the job.'

'How the hell does he know all that?' Creep spluttered.

'Who's the man that's holding my friend prisoner? The woman – Lana,' Silas asked the man.

'Go to hell,' Creep spat.

Silas dropped down beside him and put his hand around the man's throat, forcing him to shuffle backwards until his back was up against the alley wall. There was a strangled cry.

He leaned forward and whispered into the man's ear, 'You have three seconds to tell me what I want to know. Believe me, right now nothing would give me greater pleasure than to wipe you off the face of this earth. I'd rather not do that in front of the little one, but you give me no choice. One . . . two . . .'

'A' righ', a' righ',' the man managed. He massaged his throat and glared up at his assailant. 'Mange. Steeleye Mange.'

'The Mute who runs Dump Two?'

Creep nodded. There was a triumphant look in his eye. No doubt, in the past, the mere mention of his boss's name had been enough to get him out of any scrape he found himself in.

The two remote refuse dumps fed by the inhabitants of the city were hot property in Muteville. They were fought over by vicious gangs because the pickings from them were so profitable: food, clothing, building materials, even electronic equipment could be scavenged from the huge industrial sites. Dump Two was currently controlled by Mange, while another gang boss, a mutant called Hogg Venschen, was king of Dump One. Silas knew of Creep's boss, but their paths hadn't ever crossed. The fact that Mange was in charge of one of the dumps showed he'd risen considerably up the Muteville scumbag rankings, no doubt proving his ruthlessness to anybody who chose to cross him on the way.

'Get up,' Silas said to Creep, half dragging the man to his feet. He held a hand out, palm up. 'Return the things you made her steal.'

Mumbling under his breath, Creep dug the money out of his pocket and handed it to Silas, who replaced it back in the discarded wallet.

'That didn't all come out of there.'

'Shut up and get out of here,' Silas said to the man.

'You're letting me go?' Creep stared at him incredulously. 'Just like that?'

'Go to Steeleye and tell him he has exactly two hours to release our friend. He can take her to the Dog and leave her there. Tell him that failure to do so would not be in his best interests.'

'Are you insane?'

'Tell him what I said. Word for word. Now go.'

The man needed no further invitation. He turned on his heels and hurried away. When he felt he was at a safe distance, he paused and called back to Silas, 'You are a dead man! You hear me? A dead man!' With that he scurried off.

Turning to the girl again, Silas knelt down so he could be closer to her level. She was beautiful. Reddish blonde hair hung halfway down her back, and her blue eyes looked out from a delicate face whose cheeks were bedecked with tiny freckles. 'You won't remember me, Flea, but we've met before.' He smiled at her and handed the wallets over. 'Do you think you could use your gift to give these back to the people they belong to? Without getting caught?'

The girl shrugged and nodded as if it would be the easiest thing in the world.

'Good. You go and do that. I'm going to wait here for you. When you come back I'd like to take you to a place where you'll be safe. Then Jax and I are going to find Lana and bring her back there too. Would you like that?'

The girl smiled for the first time. She nodded and beamed up at Jax.

'OK.' He smiled as the girl disappeared, a blur that moved too swiftly for his eyes and brain to register properly.

Alone again, the two men faced each other.

'Do you think Steeleye Mange will just give Lana up?' Jax asked.

'I doubt it. Men like him are used to getting their own way, and they tend to get pretty ticked off when people spoil their plans.'

'So what are we going to do?' Jax asked, but the smile on his face suggested he already knew the answer.

'I think we'll have to pay our friend a visit.'

Rush

Much to his dismay, there was no sign of the mountain men or of Dotty when Rush came across the camp they'd clearly used the night before. The group had already packed up and moved on. Alone, Rush would easily have caught up with them, but despite the big guy healing faster than the younger mutant believed possible, Brick's leg was still causing him considerable pain. So Rush scouted ahead, using the hunting skills Josuf had taught him as a young boy, and when he returned he was satisfied he knew in which direction the men had gone.

'There are at least two of them. There might be more but it's hard to tell,' he told Brick. 'They're not travelling particularly quickly, probably due to Dotty slowing them down.' He nodded encouragingly at his friend. 'We'll catch them. And we'll get Dotty back.'

They set off together. Rush had become so used to having the rogwan at his side, it felt wrong to be travelling without her. In her absence he realised how very fond of the ugly little creature he had become. After three hours of monotonous walking, they spotted a clearing where the trail stopped and the men had made a new camp. Putting a finger to his lips and pointing, Rush signalled for Brick to halt. They'd agreed on a simple plan: find the men, wait until dark, creep into their camp and free the rogwan. Watching the encampment from behind a bush, Rush thought he might not even have to wait for nightfall; the men were off somewhere, probably hunting or collecting wood for a fire. There was a big pile of animal skins on a wooden sledge device. The men must be trappers, the skins merchandise to be sold.

Behind the pile of animal pelts he spotted Dotty. She was attached to an ingenious device: a long pole with a hole running through the length of it, through which a rope had been passed. One end of the rope was a loop that could be passed over a creature's head and pulled tight from the other end. In this way the creature could be led anywhere with no possibility of attacking the pole-bearer. The noose-pole was firmly staked into the ground now that the men were away, but it would be an easy matter for Rush to loosen that loop around Dotty's neck and free her. If he did it now, they could use what daylight remained to put some distance between themselves and the mountain men. His heart beating faster in his chest, he made his mind up and started to creep towards the clearing. A voice from behind him barked, 'Stop where you are and do not take another step.' He froze.

'Put your hands up, youngster. When you've done that, turn round real slow. Don't get smart. That is, unless you want my brother here to put a bolt in your big friend's head.'

Rush slowly lifted his hands, palms out. Turning, he was confronted by two of the hairiest men he'd ever seen, one of whom was aiming a crossbow straight at Brick. He hadn't heard a sound as the pair had crept up on them. They moved like ghosts. As well as every visible inch of skin being covered in hair, they were draped in the skins and furs of assorted animals. Their hair and beards were plaited into long, dirty braids, at the end of which were small, bleached-white animal skulls. The one pointing the crossbow at Brick gave a little whistle, and two more hirsute men appeared from behind trees, both similarly armed. One had a splint on his leg and wore a necklace of animal paws. The similarity in the men's faces left Rush in no doubt they were all from the same family.

The one who'd addressed Rush was missing a hand. In its place a vicious looking three-pronged fork, like a trident, had been bound to the scarred stump. He jabbed towards Rush with this crude implement. 'Well, look at this pretty one, boys! Hell, he could almost pass for a city dweller.' He took a sniff. 'But you're Mute all right. You smell of mutant.' He paused as if waiting for Rush to disagree. 'Care to tell me what the hell you two were doing creeping up on our camp?'

'You've got something that belongs to us,' Rush said, doing his best to sound brave as his eyes moved from the crossbow to the fork-hand and back again.

'That so? And what would this "something" be?'

'My rogwan.'

The man paused. 'What the hell is a rogwan when it's at home?'

'The animal you have in the noose over there.'

'That thing?' Forkhand raised his eyebrows, then nodded at the nearest of his brothers. 'There, now we know. It's a rogwan.'

'She's mine. I don't know what you're doing with her, but if you'd give her back we'll be on our way and –'

The man cut him off with a cruel laugh, looking round at the other three, all of whom joined in. 'You hear that? Just give the thing back and they'll be on their way!'

'Why is that funny?' Rush asked, not sure he wanted to know the answer.

'Well, first of all, that critter was caught by us out here on our mountain. Me and my brothers trap all manner of creatures up here, and we are not in the habit of just giving them away. No, siree.' He shot the boy a menacing look.

'But –'

'Secondly, you and your friend are in no position to "be on your way".' Forkhand leaned forward, giving the boy a ghastly, black-toothed grin. He smelled terrible. 'You see, the pair of you are also on our mountain, and that makes *you* fair game too.' He paused to let that sink in. 'Now it just so happens we were on our way to Logtown to do a little business, and it appears as if our stock has increased by two.' He nodded to himself as if deciding on a course of action. 'Bo,' he called out to the man with the damaged leg, 'get two more noose-poles – the longest ones we got.'

The man hop-walked into the camp and came back with the devices.

'Now stand still while my brother puts this loop over your head, and tell your friend to do the same,' he instructed Rush. 'We wouldn't want any crossbows accidentally going off, now would we?'

Knowing he couldn't make a run for it, Rush did as he was told, gasping as the rope at the other end of the pole was pulled tight and knotted, the knot jamming up against the far end of the pole to secure the noose. Brick was

147

instructed to stand and was likewise leashed. Finally the trappers tied their prisoners' hands behind their backs.

'I'm sorry,' Rush said to Brick as the two were led to the camp and pushed to the ground.

Dotty went crazy at the sight of them both, *hurghing* like mad and pulling violently against her restraints. Eventually one of the men went over and gave her a vicious kick, ordering her to 'calm the hell down'.

Rush saw Brick shake his head angrily and a low rumbling sound came from his chest as he glared at Dotty's assailant.

'All right, Brick. Calm down,' the youngster said in a low voice. 'I'll figure out a way to get us out of this, I promise.'

The next day they were awoken with kicks and shoves, told to get to their feet and prepare to move out.

'We wanna get to Logtown before sundown,' Forkhand said, nodding in the direction they were to take. 'They have a tournament every Friday night, and your rognam, or whatever the hell you call it, is going to be putting in an appearance. If he's half as mean as he seems, he might make me 'n' my brothers some serious tokens.'

Rush glared at the trapper. '*He* is a she. And she's a rogwan.'

'Like I care,' the man said, with a dismissive wave. 'Let's get goin'. Any funny business and I might just let my brother Bo, who's feeling pretty angry after having his leg all mauled up, take out his frustration on your stupid friend here.' He said this in a matter-of-fact way that left Rush in no doubt that he meant it.

'Why are you doing this?'

'You shouldn't have come on to our mountain,' said Forkhand, as if this was an answer.

With their hands tied behind them, it was difficult to walk up the mountain slopes, some of which were scattered with loose rock fragments that were treacherous underfoot. Brick, his leg still not right, slipped and fell on a number of occasions, eliciting curses and blows from their captors. He took the beatings without a sound, shaking his head in Rush's direction whenever the young mutant began to protest.

The entire party, trappers and their captives, were exhausted by the time they reached the summit. There was a huge sunken crater at the top of the mountain, its caldera full of garishly coloured water. It was wonderful and eerie at the same time. Sunlight played on the surface of the vivid green lake, but there was no sign of life, and the rotten egg smell the pair had encountered in the mountain's interior wafted up at them from the vast hollow.

'We need to rest.' Rush said to Forkhand.

'No rest. We keep going. I told you that.'

'Brick has an injured leg.'

'So has my brother, thanks to that beast of yours. We don't stop until we reach the other side of this crater.' He turned to the two men bringing up the rear. One of them held the noose-poles, the other a crossbow. 'Keep these two moving. If they stop again, hit the big guy. Hard. Got that?' He marched off again, kicking and shouting at Dotty to get up, after she too had flopped on the ground.

The going around the crater ridge was tough, and at times it felt as if the noose-poles were the only thing stopping Rush falling to his death. The trappers had clearly made this journey before. Eventually Forkhand came to a halt, peering down the slope ahead of him until the others caught him up.

Rush and Brick took in the view ahead. If the lake had been a sight to behold, the landscape they now surveyed was a wonder. This side of the sierra, the one facing the wind, was verdant, with no similarity to the arid scrubland they'd left behind. Rush thought the mountains must act as a barrier to the moisture in the air, straining off all the goodness before it hit the parched wasteland beyond. Trees had taken root on these slopes. Indeed, a small forest had established itself in the nutrient-rich soil of the volcano's flanks.

It was the first sight of so much foliage either of the young mutants had ever seen, and the pair simply gawped in awe as the harsh sunlight painted the top of the bright green canopy, transforming it into something magical-looking.

'I like the trees,' said Brick in an almost reverential voice.

'Me too.'

A number of large, black-feathered birds with saw bills flew out of a tree below them, protesting loudly as they took to the skies.

'Look, Brick,' Rush said. 'That's it.' The birds and the trees were forgotten as they focused on a vast shape visible on the horizon, the sunlight reflecting back off metal and glass walls and the many structures that made up City Four. It was still too far off to properly make out any details, but that it was their final destination neither of them had any doubt. Nor could there be any doubt about the immensity of the place: a vast metropolis with impossible towers that thrust upward into the sky. Rush tried to imagine how many people must live in a place like that. Tens of thousands? Hundreds of thousands? However many, it was more than the young mutant could envisage. He wondered what it was like inside its walls, and what incredible sights there might be to see there. He knew that Mutes weren't allowed inside, of course, but even so, he was excited even to be this near to it.

When Rush looked at Brick again, he saw his friend's attention was no longer on the vast, glinting metropolis. Instead he was staring at a settlement at the foot of the mountain. It was surrounded by water on all sides, a lemon-shaped islet linked to the mainland at its south and north by what appeared to be large rafts.

'Logtown,' Forkhand announced, flashing those black-ened teeth again. 'A man called Kohl runs the place. You'll be meeting him soon enough.'

Brick nudged the boy at his side, gesturing with his chin.

Not far from the largest building on the small island, trees were being hauled out of the water. Long chains were wrapped around their trunks, and animals, four or five of them linked together in a leather and rope harness, were dragging them towards a large building with a spinning waterwheel on the side.

'What are they?' Rush asked their captor.

'The critters? They're boarnogs. Some half-pig, half-dog things the loggers breed. Strong they are. Mean too.'

'They're what you want to fight Dotty against, aren't they?'

The mountain man gave the boy a ghastly grin. 'Let's go,' he said.

Tia

Tia watched in frustration. The marmoset had stopped for a third time – sitting on top of the steel cable, gripping it with her feet, her prehensile tail wrapped around beneath it just in case. The animal was still only about two-thirds of the way up the twisted metal rope that stretched from the ground to the mast above the massive wall that, even at this distance, loomed over the ramshackle shanty town.

'Don't stop again, Buffy,' Tia said under her breath. She knew from her cameraman – who'd seen and filmed the monkey climb the cable on that first occasion – that it had taken the marmoset about seven minutes to reach the mast. Buffy had already taken at least four times that long. The animal seemed nervous about something, but Tia had no idea what.

Tia looked about her, hoping again that Buffy's presence had not been noticed. Despite being on the edge of the sprawling slum, there were still people about, and any commotion about a monkey on the wire would almost certainly bring the situation to the tower guards' attention. At the same time, Tia also had to take care not to behave suspiciously in case the cameras mounted on the ramparts should decide to swing round to find out what she was up to. Anybody seen loitering for any length of time this close to the no-man's-land that separated the edge of the slums and the wall would inevitably call attention to themselves, and since the mutant rallies had started, the guards seemed more trigger-happy than ever.

She glanced at her watch.

Eleanor would already be at the guard station. She'd planned a surprise visit, hoping that her presence would fluster the watch commander and his troops enough for the monkey to slip inside the city unnoticed, but with Buffy taking so much time to make her way back on this occasion, Tia hoped Eleanor could keep up the charade without the guards beginning to suspect the reason for her presence.

The camera nearest to her began to swing round in her direction, and she ducked into the shadows of the nearest ramshackle hovel, telling herself it was nothing more than a routine sweep. Through the thin walls she could hear a woman inside shouting at her children, telling them not to fight with each other while she was getting their dinner ready. The dwelling – it could hardly be called a building – was typical of the vast majority of places the people here lived in. Inside there would only be the one room, and it would be used for eating, sleeping, playing and everything else. In parts of the shanty town these homes were packed so closely together, jammed up against each other with no space between them, that it was impossible to see where one hovel ended and another began. There would almost certainly be no toilet inside, and if there was it would not be plumbed in any way. A bucket often had to be used by all, emptied regularly to keep the flies at bay. If they were fortunate, there might be a communal latrine somewhere nearby that could be shared by as many as twenty or thirty families. If that was fully occupied when the shack's inhabitants needed to go, they would have to use the stench-filled gutters that ran through the streets. No wonder disease and infection were rife in the slums.

Tia's head whipped around when she heard the unmistakable high-pitched trills of a marmoset's distress calls. Looking up at the wire, she could see Buffy was still on top of it, her little head oscillating wildly back and forth as she appeared to scan the skies above.

'What's the matter now, Buffy?' Tia whispered. Then she saw it. The hawk turned lazily in the air, banking on the thermals as it took in the tiny figure below it.

'Run for it, Buffy, run!'

Tia watched the little monkey start to scamper further up the cable, its tiny hands and feet a blur as it tried to get to the top as fast as possible. The hawk had disappeared, and Tia craned her neck, frantically searching the heavens for sight of it. Then, in a flash, she saw it. It came in low from the right at great speed, wings folding at the last minute, hooked talons outstretched. There was no way the marmoset could avoid the raptor, and Tia held her breath as she waited for her little pet to fall into the clutch of those deadly spurs. Just as the hawk was about to grab the monkey in a last fatal embrace, Buffy jumped high into the air, twisting acrobatically and lashing out at the aerial killer's wings with small hands and feet as the predator passed beneath. The marmoset's efforts might all have been in vain because Tia was certain her pet would plunge to its death, but at the last second Buffy managed to grab hold of the cable again with her tail, swinging about underneath like a circus performer, before pulling herself up. With a quick look left and right, the monkey scurried up the remainder of the wire and into the metal skeleton of the mast, where she was at least safe from further aerial attacks. Tia heard the cry of frustration from the unseen hawk before it flew off in search of easier prey.

Tia breathed a huge sigh of relief, only to realise that everything could still go horribly wrong. While the marmoset was on the mast, she was in most danger of being spotted by the guards in the observation post right next to it. Tia prayed that Eleanor was still inside, doing her best to keep them distracted, but Buffy needed to get moving again. Instead, the little animal was cowering among the struts and supports that made up the tall aerial, no doubt shaken to the core by her near-death experience at the claws of the raptor.

'Go, Buffy. Get a move on!' Tia urged under her breath.

Almost as if the monkey had heard and understood, the creature shook itself down, jumped on to the top of the roof and disappeared from sight.

Tia gave a little clap of delight and turned round, startled to find she was being observed, not by a CCTV camera, but by one of the children from the shack behind her.

The youngster smeared his running nose on his cuff and stared up at her from eyes of the deepest blue Tia had ever seen (without surgical or genetic enhancement, anyway). Those eyes were beautiful; the rest of the face, covered as it was with coppery-red growths, was not. The child was a victim of Rot, a terrible disease that in the last few years had swept through the Mute communities based around each of the Six Cities, killing many thousands. Tia's father suspected the disease might have been engineered by Melk's people, but had, as yet, been unable to prove it.

'What you up to?' the boy asked.

'Nothing.'

'Yes, you were. You was watching that fing climb over the wall.'

'What thing?'

'The one what the bird nearly got.'

Tia didn't say anything.

The child sniffed, his eyes tracing the cable up to the mast and the guard tower beside it.

'How many of you live here?' she asked, gesturing towards the shack.

'Six.'

'That's a lot of mouths to feed.'

'We was seven, but Uncle Gorp died last month.'

'How would you like some food coupons?'

The child's eyes regarded her suspiciously. He scratched at his face, then quickly took his hand away, as if it was something he'd been told not to do. 'How many?'

'Two?' She saw the child's interest dwindle a little. 'They're gold star tickets,' she added.

Coupons that could be exchanged for food were hard to come by in the slums. A gold star ticket would be enough to feed a family for three or four days.

'What'd I 'ave to do for 'em?'

'Forget.'

The boy glanced up at the cable and back at Tia again. A mischievous look spread across his face. The kid was street-smart. 'Forget what? I ain't seen nuffink.'

'The Agency for the Regulation of Mutants can be very persuasive. They might try to "help you to remember" after I've gone.'

The boy spat on the ground. 'I hates the ARM! It's cos of them Uncle Gorp's dead. Mum says they beat him senseless when they found him selling stuff he shouldn't 'ave been. Conkerband or sumfing.'

Tia dug in her pocket and pulled out the tokens.

The boy quickly snatched them from her fingers, as if he thought she might change her mind. He stared down at them.

'They're real,' she said.

'Was it yours?' he asked without looking up.

'What?'

'The fing I never saw.'

'The monkey? Yes.'

'Was it important for it to get back inside?'

'Yes, it was.'

'Ain't you scared?'

'Of what?'

'Me touching you. I've got Rot.'

'No, I'm not scared.' Every Citizen had been given a jab to inoculate them against the disease. It cost next to nothing, but had not been offered to those outside the walls.

The boy sniffed again. 'I'm glad it got away from the bird.' With that, he disappeared back inside the shack.

Tia watched him go. 'Me too, kid,' she said. 'Me too.'

Rush

The route down the mountain was much easier than the ascent. A path of sorts wound its way through the forest, and the group made good time as they followed it. Animals lived in the overhead canopy, their calls ringing out in warning as the intruders entered their leafy world, but try as he might, Rush only caught a fleeting glimpse of one of the tree-dwelling creatures. It was a huge hairy thing with a rodent face, and it was gone almost as soon as it appeared.

They exited the tree line close to the river, their captors pushing them forward at the end of the poles until they were standing at a small dock.

Making its way towards them from the islet was a ferry, a dilapidated old thing that looked as if it might sink at any moment. In the centre of the deck the figure of an old man was cranking on a large winch, turning the handle at the top of it round and round so the device gobbled up the wet links of a half-submerged chain stretched from one shore to the next. The winch filled the air with a loud *cling!-cling!-cling!* noise that was almost painful on the ears. As Rush watched, something broke the surface next to the ferry; a long scaly head with black eyes appeared, rolling over for a moment and revealing a mouth filled with teeth. The head disappeared beneath the murky surface again, followed by a snake-like body that must have been as long as Brick was tall. The boat bumped up against the edge of the dock, the vessel's operator straightening up and turning to face them.

The man was older than Rush expected. Like the mountain men, he was wiry and thin, his face all angles and sharp points. He wore a long coat, leather of some kind, that hung down past his knees, with muddy boots of the same colour and material. His long grey hair was shoulder length. There was something in his mouth that he chewed on one moment, shoved into the hollow of his cheek the next. He reminded Rush of a scarecrow figure he and Josuf had made to ward birds away from a plot of land where they tried to grow vegetables.

Even in dock the ferry listed alarmingly in the water, and the scarecrow caught Rush looking at it sceptically. The old man sucked his brown teeth, nodding his head, and continued his chewing.

'She in't too pretty, is she? But she gets herself back and forth over this river when I ask her to, and that's all 'at counts. Yup.' He nodded to himself as he said this last word, then he spat a long thick stream of something brown and vile into the water, wiping the rest of the juice off his chin with his sleeve.

'Usual fee?' Forkhand asked.

'You got business –' it sounded like 'bezznezz', the way the ferryman said it – 'in Logtown?'

'Yep. We got trade to do with Kohl.'

'Then it's the usual fee – payable upon leaving.'

As the mountain men and the captives climbed on board, the scarecrow ferryman pushed a lever on top of the winch and started turning it again so the vessel began to pull away from the dock.

Forkhand turned to Rush and Brick. 'When we get to Logtown, I intend to sell you both to a man called Kohl. He's like the mayor of the place and he owns the mill. He'll put you to work. Now I guess you might get it into your heads to try and run away, but I'm telling you right now, that would be foolish.' He raised his voice so the old man on the winch could hear him. 'The only way on and off the islet is via the two ferries, isn't that right, old man?'

'You could try to swim it,' the ferryman answered without looking up, 'but I wouldn't recommend it. If the tide didn't carry you away and drown you, the eelsnakes in the water would get you. I seen 'em strip a harg to the bones in less time 'an it takes me to say my own name.'

'Besides,' Forkhand said, 'Kohl don't take too kindly to runaways. I hear he's taken to cutting a foot off anyone who tries it these days.'

The 'town' consisted of little more than a hard dirt road lined on either side by poorly constructed wooden buildings, many of which were in need of repair. The huge mill, in contrast, appeared to be sturdy and well maintained.

Just as Rush was beginning to wonder where the people who worked the place were, a drawn and haggard-looking woman emerged from a narrow alley dragging a heavy-looking sack of sawdust. She glanced out at them, quickly averting her eyes when she saw the trappers. Rush's heart sank when he saw the woman was missing one foot; a crude wooden stump was strapped to her leg where it had been.

'Take a good look,' Forkhand said when he caught the boy staring, 'and remember what I said about runaways.'

They approached the building nearest to the mill. Before they reached the wooden veranda outside, a man came out wiping his hands on a cloth. Another man, this one almost as big as Brick, was with him. 'Well, well,' the man with the cloth said, 'if it ain't the four Tapp brothers.' There was no sign of welcome in his voice or in the look he gave the trappers. 'What brings you here this time? Caught me another wild boarnog?'

'No, sir, but we got some merchandise for you, Mr Kohl.'

Kohl looked at Rush and Brick.

'Got you some more workers for your mill. Also brought along some furs and pelts. Winter is coming and –'

Kohl cut Forkhand off with a wave of his hand. 'These two mutants – where'd you find them?'

'Up on the mountain.'

There was something about the way Kohl kept looking at them both that made Rush even more uneasy than he already was. Nevertheless, the young mutant spoke up.

'These men captured us! They have taken us and – urgh!' Rush's words were cut off by the brother behind him yanking down on the pole, momentarily strangling him with the noose.

'Brick!' the giant bellowed, starting to move to his friend's aid.

'You shut your food-hole, young 'un,' Forkhand said, 'and tell the big dummy to do likewise. When I want you to speak, I'll let you know.' He turned to Kohl again. 'I can tell you're interested in these two. How much . . . ?'

'I'm not buying these mutants from you.'

'But –'

'I am taking them from you though.'

There was a beat as Forkhand took this in. 'Now you wait just a minute, Kohl.'

'No, *you* wait just a minute. I had a visit from an ARM unit yesterday. I don't like visits from the ARM. They came on to my island and demanded to know if I'd come across any young Mutes on the run. I said no, but clearly my word wasn't worth a damn to them, so they went through the town, house by house, broke some stuff and beat up some of my men. They didn't find anything, but they told me I was to look out for a boy of around fifteen, a couple of girls of the same age, and a giant man-child who is thought to be none too bright.' He looked from Brick to Rush and back again. 'It appears as if two of them have just landed on my doorstep. When the ARM left they said they would be back in two or three days. They also said that if I was to come across any stray young Mutes travelling this way, I was to keep them under lock and key until their return. They'll be back tomorrow or the day after, so I'll be taking these Mutes off your hands to give over to the ARM in the hope that they will leave me the hell alone. You don't want that to happen, you tell me where you're going on to, and I'll be sure to send the ARM after you so you can explain your reasons in person.'

Forkhand shook his head and swore. When he looked at Kohl again, he narrowed his eyes at the man. 'They say anything about a reward?'

'If you're around tomorrow, you can ask them that yourself.'

'Shoot, I ain't going near no ARM.'

Kohl was about to say something else when he stopped, noticing the rogwan for the first time. 'What the hell is that?' he said.

'That? *That* is the other reason we are here.' Forkhand straightened up and puffed his chest out. 'Got ourselves a fighting critter we intend to enter into your contest this evening. Reckon this thing could be a match for any of your beasts.'

'Dotty isn't theirs! She's –' The air was expelled from Rush in one go as Forkhand hit him, thankfully with the hand made of flesh, in the stomach. Brick gave another roar and would have charged in if a crossbow had not been levelled at his friend. 'Uh-uh, big fella,' Forkhand said. 'You've been a good boy up until now. You keep it that way. Don't know what you've done to get the ARM on your tail, but you two ain't worth a damn to me now, so there's really no reason for me to be as nice to you as I have been.'

'Nice?' Rush glared up at the man. 'You've treated us like animals!'

Forkhand sighed and turned to Kohl, shaking his head. 'Some people, eh?'

Kohl turned to the hulking figure standing beside him and gestured at the pair. 'Lock these two in the jail, Henk. Give them some food and get those damn pole things off them. The boy's right. After all, we're not all barbarians, are we?'

Rush tentatively touched at the red line around his neck where the rope noose had rubbed it raw. Brick's seemed to have healed already. Despite not being tied up any longer, their situation, at first glance at least, had not particularly improved. Their cell was a small room with a hole in the floor at one corner that served as a toilet; the smell emanating from it was truly vile, and neither of them had any wish to use it. A heavy wooden door dominated one wall, and set into this, at eye level, was a square opening. Standing on tiptoe, his face pressed against the door, Rush could just make out the short passageway linking the three cells. At the far end, standing in the doorway leading to the street, was Henk, the giant who'd been charged with guarding the two prisoners for the night. Rush watched him. The man was muttering under his breath, clearly unhappy at being given the task while the rest of the town gathered for the evening's festivities. Earlier, a group of loggers had passed by outside, shouting out to the jailer and mocking him.

They'd told him how they'd get extra drunk on his behalf and left, their laughter slowly fading away. The language the man had used to tell the group what he thought of their offer was colourful, to say the least.

Go on, Rush thought. *Move out a little further. Just for a few moments . . .*

Raucous laughter, followed by a loud cheer, drifted down to the jail from the hill, and it was this that finally drew the man out to stand on the steps and look off in the direction of the noise.

Rush wouldn't have long. His heart was beating fast, but he tried his best to ignore it. He needed to focus on the task in hand.

Hanging on a small hook beside the front door were keys to the three cells. Rush knew the top one opened the door he was pressed up against, and he concentrated on it with all his might.

Brick looked up from the corner he was sitting in. 'Rush?'

'Shhh.'

Metals, particularly alloys, were sometimes hard for Rush to control. He reached out with his mind, focusing on the metallic object and trying to merge with it until he felt that familiar *connect*. Silently, the key swivelled upward, as if an invisible finger was tilting it to the horizontal, then rose off the hook. It wavered in the air a little, before slowly moving along the corridor towards him. At the door it paused, turned on its axis, and headed for the lock, slipping silently inside.

Unaware he'd been holding his breath, Rush suddenly let it all out, gasping and collapsing against the door while his head buzzed with the exertion of what he'd just done. Moving the key had drained him, but he had to get himself back together again before going through with the rest of his plan.

'Brick,' he whispered after a few minutes, beckoning the big guy over. 'In a second, this door is going to open. The man guarding us won't know anything about it until it happens, but you heard the noise the hinges on this thing made when they put us in here. As soon as it opens, he'll know.'

'Who's going to open the door?'

'I am.'

The hulking mutant thought about this for a second or two before nodding his head and saying, 'OK.'

'I need you to stop that man from raising the alarm.'

'How?'

'Hit him.'

It was clear from the look on Brick's face he was unhappy at the idea of having to injure anyone.

'If you don't, we won't stand a chance of rescuing Dotty, and the people here will hurt her. They'll also turn us over to more bad people, people who will hurt *us*.'

'Hit him?'

'Just hard enough to make him go to sleep, that's all.'

Brick considered this. 'OK.' He nodded.

The guard lay in a crumpled heap on the floor of the cell. Rush tore the sleeves off the man's shirt, stuffed one into his mouth and tied it in place with the other. They shut the door and locked it again, returning the key to its home.

'Let's go,' he said to Brick.

'Your bag.' Brick gestured towards something hanging from a large hook, on the far wall.

Rush was surprised to see his rucksack, and even more amazed to discover inside it all the things Tink had given him for the journey. Thanking his lucky stars, he threw it over his shoulder, checked the street outside was clear and headed off up the hill with Brick loping along at his side. His mind was working overtime as he tried to figure out what to do next. They were out of jail, but he still had no idea how the hell the two of them were going to rescue Dotty and get off an islet surrounded by deadly unswimmable waters.

Tia

Tia warily approached the establishment known as the Three-Eyed Dog, pausing to check if she was being observed. There were a few people milling around the narrow passage-ways surrounding the place, but nobody seemed particularly interested in her. Even if she had not already known about the Dog – she'd once filmed a report outside here, using the premises as a backdrop – there was no way you could miss it. Built on the ruins of old, decaying concrete that had some-how survived the war, it was one of the biggest buildings in Muteville, both in size and reputation. The noise that poured out of the front doors was loud and raucous, an alcohol-fuelled buzz over which music could just be made out. As she got nearer, Tia could hear the unmistakable sounds of laughter, both female and male, chairs scraping against the wooden floor and glasses being chinked together.

She cursed beneath her breath, wondering why her contact had insisted they meet here, of all places: a dive where the seedier elements of life – from both sides of the city's wall – came to hang out.

She hesitated at the door, steeling herself before pushing it open and taking in the interior.

Men and women in various states of inebriation filled the large barroom, most of them appearing well on the road to drunken oblivion thanks to the cheap hooch that was brewed and sold on the premises. Such establishments were not found inside the city; they were considered *vulgar*. The air was a thick blue smoke-filled fug, and Tia shuddered at the idea of having to breathe in the second-hand exhalations of whatever it was the patrons were puffing on. Just as alcohol was frowned upon inside the city, hardly anyone smoked there, and *never* in a public place.

Many of the Dog's customers sat at large round tables, betting food tokens and other items on cards held in their hands. By the look of their clothing, quite a few of the patrons were Citizens – on a day trip to Muteville to 'take in the freaks', or 'slumming it' as it was known. Her own dress also marked her out as a visitor. She wondered if any of the day-trippers was Eleanor's go-between, the man or woman she'd used to make contact with this Silas person.

A number of women meandered around the place,

talking and laughing raucously with the male clientele. That these women were popular with the city day-trippers came as no surprise to the young journalist. She'd done a report on this once, keen to show how, despite the Principia's edict that Citizens and Mutes did not 'cross-breed', many of the visitors seemed only too happy to fraternise with pretty mutant girls. Her piece, broadcast on her father's media channel, had been dismissed as 'subversive nonsense' by President Melk.

Tia took a deep breath and stepped inside, half expecting to be turned round and marched straight back out again because of her age.

She needn't have worried; nobody so much as batted an eyelid. As she approached the high wooden bar, the green-haired man behind it turned to her and asked her what she was having. Age restrictions clearly weren't a big thing in Muteville drinking establishments.

'I was wondering if Bella was here.'

'Who wants to know?' the man asked, continuing to polish the glass in his hand.

'Tell her Eleanor is looking for a job.' She repeated the phrase her father's friend had made her remember.

The man pursed his lips, called one of the girls over to mind the bar and disappeared through a door at the rear.

She sensed somebody behind her.

'How you doing, sweetcheeks?' The voice close to her ear was accompanied by the sour breath of somebody who'd had their fair share of the cheap drink sold in this place. 'What's a pretty little thing like you doing in here, huh?'

Tia decided it was best to ignore the man. Unfortunately the drunkard was too far gone to take the hint.

'Ooh, the strong, silent type. I like that. Why don't you and I –'

His mistake was reaching out and putting his hand on her waist.

Tia's father insisted she learn self-defence from a young age, signing her up for classes with an ancient-looking Russian who, on the face of it, didn't look capable of hurting a fly. What old Bogatyr lacked in vigour, he made up for in technique, skill and knowledge.

Tia shifted her hips, creating space between herself and the man. At the same time she drove the outer edge of her hand backwards, connecting with his most sensitive area. The air left his lungs in one big *Ooof!* and the man bent forward. As he did so, Tia brought her elbow up sharply and drove it forcefully into his face. There was a satisfying crunch of cartilage and the man staggered backwards. Tia was still in motion. Spinning on one foot, she brought her other leg up and round behind her, catching the man solidly on the side of the head. Her assailant sank to the floor, where he stayed, eyes screwed tightly shut in a purple-red face as he clutched his head with one hand, his groin with the other.

A few people turned to look, but they quickly went back to whatever they'd been doing. Most of the customers weren't even aware anything had happened. Clearly fights, like underage drinking, were an everyday occurrence at the Dog.

The barman returned. 'Bella will see you.' He nodded to a staircase at the far end of the bar. Noticing the flushed look on the young girl's face, he stepped forward, leaning out over the counter to take in the man as he groaned and spat blood on to the floor. 'Your work?' he asked Tia.

'He grabbed me.' She gave the barkeep a hard look, as if defying him to take her to task.

'Hey, no problem,' he said. 'The guy's a pest. Some big shot from the city. Claims he's high up in the council, and thinks that because he comes in here flashing a few tokens about, he can do what he pleases. Looks like he got his comeuppance. And from one of his own. Nice.' He signalled to a pair of women, who came over. 'Get this slimeball out of here. Tell him he's no longer welcome.'

'He's barred?' one of them asked, raising an eyebrow over her purple-coloured eye. She had a slight lisp and Tia guessed she could only be a few years older than her.

'Yep. Don't say it never happens, Bonny.'

Despite his groans and protestations, the two girls dragged the man out by his heels. From the side of the bar a small hunchbacked figure emerged carrying a bucket, from which he flung handfuls of sawdust at the floor to soak up the blood.

'Thank you, Gram,' the barman said when the hunchback had finished. 'As efficient as ever.' He poured a small glass of some cloudy green liquid, which was snatched up and drunk in one swallow by the bucket wielder who then slunk back into the shadows. The barman turned to Tia again. 'Just take those stairs and knock at the door of Room 3.'

He picked up the glass and started polishing it again.

Tia rapped her knuckles on the door. She wasn't surprised when it was a man's voice that told her to enter. She did so, noting how the curtains were drawn over the window so the room she stepped into was dim and murky.

'Close the door behind you, please.'

She reluctantly did so.

There were in fact two men in the room: one in a chair facing her, while a tall pale figure sat in the deepest shadows of the furthest corner.

'Bella?' Tia said, noting the slight catch in her voice.

'I think we can dispense with the cloak-and-dagger routine now, don't you, Ms Cowper?'

'Tia, please.'

The man facing her paused. 'I am Silas, and my friend over there is Jax. We have a mutual friend in Eleanor, I understand.'

'She said I could come to you, that you would be a good person to know during my time outside the city wall.'

'That depends on what you intend to do here.'

'I'm a reporter.'

'I know.'

'I want to highlight the mutant plight. Show people inside the Six Cities what's really going on out here. Make them understand that the Mutes are not the threat they are made out to be by the Principia and –'

'Why?'

'I'm sorry?'

'Why do you want to do this?'

She frowned. She hadn't expected to have to explain her reasons. 'Because it's wrong. Because it's unjust. We *all* survived the Last War. Those topside had the worst of it then, and have continued to have the worst of things ever since. Regardless of what President Melk –' she spat this last word as if forming it had left a bad taste in her mouth – 'and his kind say.'

'And you think your reports will make a difference?'

'The best thing you can do is the right thing, the next best thing is the wrong thing, and the worst thing you can do is nothing.'

'Roosevelt,' Silas said with a nod. 'Clever as well as pretty.' He put his head to one side and frowned, as if contemplating the exchange that had just taken place between them. After a moment, he turned and looked towards the figure in the corner.

Tia was about to say something else when she felt a sudden and unusual sensation of nausea. Her stomach rolled and she involuntarily put a hand out to steady herself. The inside of her head felt strange: light and woozy in a way that made her vision swim. The experience was over almost as soon as it had begun.

'Are you all right?'

She swallowed. 'I'm fine. Just a little dizzy. Maybe I need to eat.'

'A common problem out here in the slums – what with the food shortages.'

He looked across at the room's other occupant again, and the boy nodded back at him. With that, Silas stood and walked over to her, holding his hand out. 'Welcome on board, Tia Cowper. It's good to have you with us.'

Rush

Half expecting to be spotted at any moment, Rush and Brick, having successfully escaped their prison, moved stealthily uphill, following the noise of the crowd. When they reached a copse on a ridge, they took cover behind the trees. Below them, in a clearing, they stared down at the event that had so galvanised the people of Logtown. What they witnessed was a scene of horror.

Men were standing around the edges of a pit dug into the earth, its sides shored up with wooden planks, shouting excitedly at a barbaric and cruel spectacle. A strong smell hung in the air: a pungent mixture of blood and fear and excitement.

Three of the pig-dog creatures – boarnogs, Forkhand had called them – were in the pit. They were thickset beasts, covered in short, wiry bristles, with small black eyes set deep into heads that looked too big for their bodies. Large curved tusks protruded from their bottom jaw, so the overall effect was of an animal more porcine than canine, except they growled like the wild-dog creatures Rush had occasionally seen near the farmhouse where he'd grown up. Two of the trio had taken up positions on either side of a massive creature, some bear-like mutation that was chained to a pole in the centre of the arena. The third was lying on its side, blood pooling around it, its flanks heaving and jerking as it struggled for breath. The bear-thing was far larger than the boarnogs and easily outweighed them, but even with one of them seriously injured, their numerical advantage allowed them to dart in and attack the animal's blindside, tearing and worrying at it until it swung about with a claw or brought its huge head round to defend itself. When that happened, the other would dash in from the rear. All of the animals were already bloodied from their injuries, their coats matted to their skin.

Men, most of whom appeared to be extremely drunk, were betting on the outcome of the fight, shouting out the name of the side they thought would win and handing over food tokens or credits to a group of men wearing red scarves who moved among them, acting as bookmakers. Even from where they hid, Rush and Brick could sense the excitement in the spectators. There was a cheer as one of the boarnogs leaped up to sink its teeth into the shoulder of the bear-thing, the victim roaring in pain and bucking around to try to shake its attacker off. Blood ran freely from the wound, the sight of which seemed to ignite a new wave of betting.

Rush could see Kohl standing on a small stage at the edge of the pit. The mayor was holding a cone-shaped instrument up to his mouth and bellowing out to the crowd, commentating enthusiastically on the horrors and whipping them into a frenzy.

Rush fought the need to throw up.

'Where's Dotty?' Brick asked him in a voice that expressed his own outrage at the scene.

The younger mutant scanned the ridge until he spotted what appeared to be a number of wooden cages a stone's throw away from where they stood. 'Over there, I think. Let's go. Maybe we can get her out while everyone is distracted.'

The smell was the first thing to hit them: the harsh stench of animal faeces liberally mixed with a wet, mildewy odour. There must have been about thirty or forty cages, some stacked two or three high. Not all were occupied, but those that were housed the saddest, most miserable creatures Rush had ever laid eyes on.

Most of the cages contained boarnogs, who had with few exceptions been scarred or mangled in some way. Many had teeth or parts of their ears missing, and one or two appeared to only have one working eye.

'Wait,' Rush said to Brick, halting him just in time for them to avoid being seen by a man who was also lurching towards the holding area. Ducking down behind a couple of empty cages, they watched as the drunkard turned his back on them and began to relieve himself up against one of the enclosures. At the sight of him the caged pig-dogs began attacking the walls of their cage, smashing against the bars in an effort to get at him.

These creatures hate the men here, Rush thought to himself.

There was a terrible roar from the direction of the pit, which was echoed by an eruption of noise from the crowd. The man cursed, quickly finished what he was doing and hurried away to find out what he'd missed.

'We have a result!' Kohl shouted out, the megaphone amplifying his voice so it could be heard over the cheers. 'The boarnogs are victorious!' There was another cheer. 'Gentlemen, if you please, a little hush. We have a night of murderous mayhem for your entertainment this evening. The bar is still open and serving drinks, so fill your glasses, folks, because up next we have a new challenger! A specimen brought here from beyond the mountains. A creature we have not encountered before! It's our next fight, so get a drink and hurry back.'

Rush knew he had mere moments if he was to get Dotty free. He hurried from his hiding place, hissing her name and frantically looking around him into the cages' dark interiors. Spinning about when he heard the rogwan's familiar *hurgh*, he almost cried aloud as her face appeared at the bars of a cage a short distance away. The doors to the crates were secured by thick wooden rivets pushed through a clasp. Rush pulled out the one holding Dotty's cage door, almost falling over backwards when the rogwan leaped out at him and licked his face with her rough black tongue.

'Quick, Brick!' he said, beckoning the big guy over. 'Get Dotty out of here. Take her down to the ferry. Not the one we came on, the one on the other side.' They had to get out of there before it was too late.

'What about Rush?'

'I'll be along right behind you. Now go!'

'These animals,' Brick said, patting his leg so Dotty would come to him, 'they don't belong here with these bad people.'

'You're right. But if we're going to do anything about that, I need you to take Dotty now, OK?' He shrugged the backpack off his shoulder and handed it to his friend.

'Rush got a plan?'

'Don't I always?'

Brick gave him a nod, and without another word set off down the road leading out of Logtown with Dotty at his heels.

Rush watched them go for a moment before turning to face the cages again. 'OK, boarnogs,' he said to them. 'Let's see how much you really hate these loggers, shall we?' He focused on those wooden rivets, concentrating his mind and connecting with as many of them as he could . . .

Rush was shouting as he ran full-tilt down the hill, his arms windmilling to keep him upright. Blood flowed from a cut on his right thigh, but he appeared not to notice. There was a shout from the top of the hill as somebody spotted him, and five or six men set off in pursuit.

Brick and Dotty were waiting on the quay, watching, their attention half on Rush, half on the mayhem unravelling behind him. They had the boat to themselves. A ferryman had been on duty, but he'd taken one look at the rogwan and Brick as they pounded up the jetty towards him and wisely decided to abandon ship.

On the hill, boarnogs were running everywhere, attacking anyone foolish enough to get in their way. Men were crying out in panic. A huge specimen could be seen under a tree, angrily eyeing the men who'd scrambled up into its boughs to escape. When one man lost his grip and fell, the boarnog set about him, goring at his body with its tusks until his screams abruptly stopped.

'Get it going!' Rush shouted out to Brick. 'Start turning the winch! Don't wait for me – I'll make it!'

The clanging sound of the winch as it drew in the chain began to fill the air. Dotty darted to the back of the ferry, shifting from paw to paw, her eyes fixed on Rush. When the noise of the winch was accompanied by his feet on the wooden jetty, she shook her head and *hurghed* as if urging him on. The boat was perhaps a body length away from the dock when he leaped. He landed in a heap on the deck next to the rogwan, who set about him with delight.

'You set them free!' Brick shouted. He was grinning from ear to ear, all the while whipping the handle of the winch round and round, dragging the craft through the water.

Rush watched as the men pursuing them came to the bottom of the hill, hurrying towards the quay. He wasn't particularly surprised to see Forkhand among them. A bloody and limping Kohl was bringing up the rear. The men began shouting threats in their direction. Rush was going to give them a hand gesture he thought would leave them in no doubt about what he thought of them, when he saw Forkhand grab for the crossbow hanging around his shoulders.

'Brick, can you make this thing go any faster?' Rush asked. They were halfway across the river, but suddenly that didn't seem nearly far enough.

Forkhand raised the loaded weapon, resting the front end between the upturned prongs of his trident, and took aim.

Rush hurled himself at his friend. 'Get down, Brick! Get down!'

They hit the deck as the crossbow bolt thudded into the housing for the winch where Brick had been standing seconds before.

'You OK?' Rush asked.

'Uh-huh.'

The ferry gave a little jerk. Rush looked up to see three things: Forkhand reloading the weapon, two men pulling on a rope attached to the back of the vessel, and another man pulling the cover off a wooden canoe. The craft lurched again and began, very slowly, to move back towards the islet.

Rush called out to Brick, 'Winch again. It's you against them. If I tell you to stop, you drop for cover. Got it?' He scurried over to the backpack and began pulling the contents out.

Two men got into the canoe, the one in the front paddling out into the current while the other sat armed with a bow. He notched an arrow to the string, but sat with the weapon in his lap, clearly waiting until he felt he was within range. Rush could see what would happen: either they would be dragged back to shore by the men on the rope, where they would be killed by Forkhand, or the men in the canoe would get close enough to do the job.

Finding what he had been looking for in the bag, Rush peered up just as Forkhand lifted his weapon and took aim again. 'Down!' he shouted, and the ferry rocked alarmingly as Brick did as he was told. There was a pause, and Rush thought the shot might have flown harmlessly over their heads. When he dared to peer out over the top of the large pile of cut timber he was sheltering behind, there was a *thunk!* as the bolt lodged into the wood inches away, sending sharp splinters into his face.

'We're dead,' Brick moaned, climbing back up to continue to operate the winch.

'Not yet, we're not,' Rush said as he got to his feet, allowing the sling to hang down from one hand. The stone he dropped, almost casually, out of the same hand landed perfectly in the small square of leather between the long thongs, and he twirled the entire thing about his head, the weapon making a low *whoosh* that grew louder with each revolution. On the third turn he leaned into the throw and released one of the thongs so the stone flew out at terrific speed, streaking through the air like a bullet. There was an audible *crack!* as the projectile connected with its target, followed by the sound of the crossbow clattering to the ground. For a moment Forkhand seemed unaware he'd been hit. He stood as a rivulet of blood flowed down his face from the centre of his forehead. Then his eyes rolled up towards the heavens and he collapsed.

Brick looked over at his friend. The whooshing noise had already started again, and this time it was the man paddling the canoe who took the hit, this one to the side of the head. The blow had exactly the same net effect as the previous one had on Forkhand: the man gave a cry and collapsed over to one side, unsettling the craft so both men were tipped out. There was a scream and the water appeared to boil as the eelsnakes set about their unexpected meal.

'Let go of that,' Rush shouted out to the men hauling on the wet rope, 'or you're next.'

'Don't you listen to him!' It was Kohl. 'Those shots were lucky! You keep pulling that damn ferry back in or I'll – GARGH!' The third stone caught him in the throat, collapsing his windpipe and shutting off both his threats and any doubts about 'lucky shots'. The pair took one look at each other, dropped the rope and ran off.

There were no more attempts to stop the ferry leaving.

Brick winched them to the far quay, where, once ashore, the big mutant used his colossal strength to heave a thick wooden jetty post out of the ground and throw it through the deck of the ferry. The two friends watched it slowly sink beneath the surface for a few moments before turning their backs on Logtown and the mountains beyond.

They stared across the landscape before them in the direction of the vast metropolis that was City Four.

A splash made them whirl about, only to see Dotty in the shallows, her teeth clamped on to the head of one of the eelsnakes. The creature curled and twisted its body in a vain attempt to escape the rogwan's deadly jaws, but Dotty held on, bracing her short legs in the thick mud as she made her way backwards towards the shore. Once there, she dragged the thing to Brick and Rush and deposited it at their feet, letting out a deep *hurgh*. She nudged the catch with her nose, looking up at the two of them for a moment before shaking herself off and covering the pair with muddy water droplets.

'You're welcome, Dotty,' Rush said with a smile, recognising the gesture for what it was.

They were all exhausted. Brick insisted on looking at the

wound on Rush's leg where he'd been caught by a boarnog's tusk, so they agreed to make camp where they were. Nobody was coming over the river after them – they were sure of that. Rush was worried about the ARM's imminent return to Logtown, but if they were to stand any chance of making it to C4 ahead of them, they would have to rest tonight.

They built a fire to cook the eelsnake, the meat of which was dense, with a slight earthy flavour. Despite this, the three of them ate the entire thing.

Bellies full, they eventually lay back on the ground and stared up at the stars.

Brick started humming, and Rush smiled. The sound no longer bothered him. In fact, he rather liked it.

'Rush?' Brick asked after a few minutes.

'What?'

'How'd you hit those men? With the stones?'

The teenager sighed and looked over at his friend. 'Want to see a trick?'

Brick nodded. He sat up and Rush did likewise.

'Hold up your index finger.' His grin widened when he saw Brick frown, trying to work out which of his digits was required. 'The one you point with. Or in your case, the one you pick your nose with!'

Brick pulled a face at him, but obliged by sticking the digit straight up towards the night sky. Rush dug a round pumice-coloured stone from the earth, wiping the mud from it on his trousers. 'Keep still,' he said, and placed the stone on the very tip of Brick's upraised finger. It wavered for a couple of seconds and then became completely still, as if steadied by some invisible hand.

'Wait just a moment.' This time Rush picked up an old dry stick, which he placed on top of the stone, holding it there. He couldn't help but smile at the look of bewilderment on the big man's face. 'It gets better,' he said. With all the flourish of a stage magician, he took his hand away and sat back, his hands on the ground behind him. The stick remained, perfectly balanced on the uppermost tip of the stone, and then began to very slowly rotate about its centre point, gradually picking up speed. If Brick had looked up at that moment he'd have seen the intense look of concentration on his friend's face and the tiny beads of sweat that were beginning to form on his lip and forehead, but the big guy's eyes were glued to the little propeller set-up on the tip of his finger.

'Ha!' Brick said. 'It's magic!'

Rush clapped his hands and both the stone and the twig fell to the ground.

Brick looked at his friend in amazement. 'How'd Rush do that?' he asked. He picked the items up, staring at them as if they might come to life again.

'That's rich, coming from the man who healed me with nothing but his hands!' Rush shrugged and lay on his back again. 'Like you say, it's magic or something. I don't really *know* how I do it. It's like when I launched the stones at those men; they weren't going to miss, because I *made* them hit their targets.'

'You made a stone do something?'

'Yeah. It sounds weird, I know, but . . . it's like I'm able to *connect* with an object. I can feel the tiniest particles that make something what it is – the atoms or maybe something even more fundamental than that – and affect the way it interacts with other things around it. It's difficult to explain.'

The big man slowly nodded his head. 'Like the hurt. I can see it and take it out. Sometimes.' He started to hum again.

'Have you always been able to do that, Brick?'

'Uh-huh.'

'Me too. Although Josuf, the man who looked after me, said I shouldn't.' He paused, remembering his guardian. 'I wonder how many more of us there are? How many other mutants have special gifts like you and me? When I was growing up, I imagined it had to have something to do with all the radiation and chemicals left over after the Last War – that they screwed up my DNA and gave me weird powers. If that's true, there could be thousands of us out there.'

'Five,' Brick said, pausing mid-hum.

'What?'

'Five. There are five of us. The bad man, the *really* bad man, made us. He made others, but they died. You were all babies. 'Cept Jax. "Waaah, waaah, waaah" – that's how you went. "Waaah, waaah, waaah."'

'Wh . . . ? What do you mean?'

But Brick was no longer listening; he was too engrossed in trying to balance the stick on the pebble, humming tunelessly to himself.

Anya

At the girl's signal, Tink pulled on the reins, bringing the harg and the wagon it pulled to a halt. He looked across at the teenager sitting beside him.

'They're just around this next bend,' Anya said. 'I saw three of them, but I can't be sure there weren't any more hiding out of sight.'

'And they'd already captured some travellers?'

'Uh-huh. One of the captives looked younger than me.'

Tink frowned, still not sure what their best option was now they'd arrived at this point. To his mind they were extremely limited.

'We have two choices,' he eventually said. 'Either we trust in this old harg of mine to somehow find it in him to go round this bend at top speed, hoping it's fast enough to get us past these men before they have a chance to attack us, or we get sneaky and play the ambushers at their own game.'

Anya considered this. 'If we try to rush through, what happens to the people they've already captured?'

'We'd be leaving them to their own fate.'

The teenager shook her head. 'I'm not sure I'm happy doing that.'

'Neither am I, but I thought it best to let you know what the alternatives are.'

'So we get sneaky?'

'It looks that way.'

The sound of the harg's hoofs echoed back off the trees that lined the track on either side. It was a good place for an ambush, Tink thought to himself, looking out from beneath the brim of his hat. In fact, it was almost too good. He was wearing a long woollen poncho so only his head could be seen. Even the reins disappeared beneath the thick folds of cloth. He did his best to look weary, slumping forward on the jockey-box as if he might topple off at any moment.

Tink pulled the animal to a halt when he saw a man armed with a crossbow step out into the middle of the track. He didn't need to look to his left or right to know the other members of the gang were taking up positions, so the wagon would be boxed in from all sides. The group had clearly done this many times before.

'Whoa there!' the man shouted, pointing the weapon at the wagon driver. One side of the ambusher's face was withered, like melted candle wax.

Tink stared at the man, but sat unmoving.

'Where you going, old-timer?' the man asked.

'Muteville. I'm a trader, and I have some business there.'

'That so?' He nodded to himself, taking this in. 'What you trading?'

'Oh, you know, this and that.'

'What you got?'

'Nothing you'd be interested in,' Tink answered.

'Maybe I should be the judge of that,' the man said. Without taking his eyes off Tink, the man with the melted face called out to one of the other men, 'Bern! Have a look and see what our mysterious friend here has in the back of his wagon.'

'You planning on robbing me?' Tink asked, aware of a man slightly behind him and to his left, emerging from cover and approaching the rear of his cart.

'Robbing you? No. I like to think of it as a toll. This here is a toll road, and if you haven't got the right fee, I'm afraid you'll have to pay in some other way. Like with your freedom.'

Tink sat unmoving, waiting.

As the man pulled up the tarpaulin at the back of the wagon, there was a terrible scream. The creature waiting beneath the cover was hideous to behold, a great coiled dragon-like beast with bulging eyes and a huge mouth full of deadly teeth. It lunged out at the man, and the scream was abruptly cut off.

Tink threw back the poncho and rose to his feet, pulling out a weapon. It was an ancient device, a leftover from before the Last War, and unlike the guns used inside the cities that fired pulsed energy, this one still fired projectiles. Two barrels, side by side, swung up as he pulled the first trigger, doing his best not to be blown off his feet and end up in the back of the wagon by the recoil. The shotgun boomed, causing birds and other winged creatures of every description to take to the skies from the trees. The two remaining ambushers also managed to get off their own shots. One of the crossbow bolts flew through the air no more than a hand's width in front of Tink's nose; the other hit him above the eye. If Tink hadn't turned his head in response to the first, the second shot would have killed him. Fortunately it was more of a glancing blow; the bolt cut through the flesh and had enough momentum to snap the old man's head back so he spun around. He fell from the wagon, already unconscious before he hit the hard ground.

Out cold and bleeding, Tink couldn't know that his shot had killed the man standing before him; neither did he see that the monster in the wagon behind him had already slid from the vehicle, snaking across the ground at great speed towards the third ambusher as he desperately scrabbled to reload. The man never got to fire another shot.

Later, Tink would have no recollection of being put in the back of the cart and covered over with the tarpaulin. Anya, despite the agony, had struggled back into her human form and, after freeing the other captives, who were tied up and face down in the men's own wagon, had jumped in behind Tink's harg, urged the animal into a gallop and set off for City Four, determined to get her friend and saviour the medical attention he needed.

Rush

Two days after they'd crossed the river and left Logtown behind them, Rush, Brick and Dotty finally reached the outskirts of Muteville. Despite spending most of the journey from there glancing over their own shoulders, there had been no sign of the ARM, and Rush was glad they'd destroyed the ferry so completely. Tired and hungry, they shuffled along, too exhausted even to speak. It wasn't just fatigue from the journey that had rendered them voiceless; the nearer they'd got to the sprawling slums, the clearer it became how different were the two worlds separated by the colossal city wall. From a distance, the dark sprawling ghetto that had grown up in the shadow of the city had not seemed so bad, but now that they were within touching distance, their souls had become infected by the misery of the place.

As if unwilling to enter the slum straight away, they skirted around the fringes, moving inexorably closer to the vast wall that, even from a distance, loomed over everything.

Most of what Rush knew about the cities he'd gleaned from advertisements and reports he'd seen on a battered old comms screen at a neighbouring ranch. The screen was cracked and it was difficult to make anything out on the ancient device, but even so, it had been clear to him that life in the cities was something worth dreaming about. Whenever the InterCity Games were on, he and Josuf would make the long journey out to the nearest trading post and watch some of the events on a screen set up in a tent, paying two credits each for the privilege. This place was nothing like the images he had seen. The Mute settlement was dismal. If Rush needed any further proof of how disparate the two societies were, their experience when they approached the no-man's-land immediately at the base of the wall provided it.

From the mutant side, the start of this no-go zone was a fence topped with razor wire with guard towers placed at regular intervals along it. Uniformed armed men occasionally paused on the parapets, and it was as Rush and Brick came close to the wire barrier that they drew the attention of one of these sentries. A device like a metallic insect the size of a man's head immediately took off into the air from the tower, the high-pitched whining of its propellers adding to the impression of its being a living thing. It headed towards them, hovering in the air out of reach above them. Rush looked up, straight into the domed lens suspended beneath the thing's 'torso'.

'You there!' An electronic voice addressed them. 'Step away from the fence.'

Brick looked from the remote-controlled surveillance drone to the source of the noise: a small speaker mounted to a post nearby. He approached the stanchion, straining his neck to get a better look at the box and grille.

'STEP AWAY, MUTE,' the voice barked at him.

Rush cast his eyes in the direction of the tower nearest to them just as a guard swung something up to his shoulder. The youngster screwed his eyes shut as a bright red beam of light flashed across his vision for an instant. When he opened them again there was a red spot dancing on his chest.

'Er, Brick . . .'

Brick grinned at him, oblivious to the danger. 'That voice. The man's up *there* –' he pointed at the tower – 'but we can hear him through the box thing *here*.'

'We need to move, Brick. The man up there is getting angry.'

'Say something else, soldier man!' Brick called in the guard's direction before turning to look eagerly at the speaker, hoping to hear the disembodied voice again.

'Come on, big guy.' Rush put his hand in the crook of

Brick's arm and gently pulled him away, aware that a second red dot had joined the first, this one firmly fixed on Brick's head. The dots stayed with them as they moved off, only disappearing when they were well away from the fence and heading back in the direction they'd come from, towards the hovels of Muteville.

The buildings at the outermost edges of the vast, sprawling slum were little more than hastily thrown up lean-tos, many of which were still under construction as new arrivals added to the existing mass of mutants. The people who sat outside these poor excuses for a home looked wretched, and Rush found it difficult to meet their eyes. Moving deeper into the shantytown the pair discovered that the shacks lying beyond these were slightly better made; the walls firmed up and fixed with nails or ropes, the roofs more solid and gap-free. Those beyond *these* were better yet. Rush imagined that if he was able to fly over the squalid settlement he would see that the slums grew outwards from some central point; each new ring poorer and humbler than the one preceding it, until its residents could improve their dwellings.

The smell was terrible, although it didn't seem to bother the children who laughed and chased each other among the filth and sewage running down open ditches at their feet. A mangy-looking dog raised the hackles on its neck as Rush and Brick approached, but the animal quickly put its tail between its legs and scampered away when it got a look at the rogwan trailing along behind them. The three of them moved deeper inside the slums, and it became clear what a daunting task lay ahead of them: the place was a maze filled to the rafters with people of every description. Every inch of space was taken up, the gaps between the buildings so narrow in places that they were only navigable side-on. Mutes sprawled out of the buildings, and everyone eyed the newcomers with distrust. Nobody seemed to know anything about a man called Silas, and most of the people Rush asked were openly hostile as he approached their living space, as if suspecting he might try to take it from them.

'Go to City Four and find a man called Silas,' Rush had been told. *How? How were he and Brick ever going to find one man among this chaos?* After everything they'd already been through, this was the last thing he'd expected, and he was soon filled with desperation and hopelessness.

After about an hour of walking along aimlessly, the way ahead opened up and they stepped out into a small square with houses facing inwards towards a small water pump in the centre. Although the space was small, it came as a relief to Rush, who'd begun to feel claustrophobic among the rat runs they'd been negotiating until now.

The three approached the pump. As Rush reached for the handle, a voice called out to him.

'I wouldn't touch that if I were you.'

He stopped and looked across at an old woman standing in a doorway.

'Excuse me?' he said, giving her a friendly smile.

'That pump belongs to Green Ward. You're not from this ward, so you've got no right to our water.'

'We're thirsty. We've been travelling for a long time, and –'

'I don't care who you are or where you're from. That water is for the people of Green Ward, and you are not welcome to it. Move on. You can buy water at the market.'

Rush eyed the pump longingly. With a shake of his head he approached the woman.

'If we're not welcome to your water, maybe you can help us with something else. I'm looking for somebody.'

The woman said nothing, just gave him a look that suggested she was not impressed by having strangers wandering up and talking to her.

'He's my uncle.' He had no idea why he told this lie, but it was out of his lips before he knew it. 'I was sent here to find him. His name is Silas.'

He thought he detected the hint of something in her eye, but she shook her head and addressed him in the same stark tone she'd used to warn him away from the water. 'Never heard of him.'

'Do you know where I could ask? It's very important that I –'

Brick, who'd been silent up until now, tapped Rush on the shoulder. 'Rush,' he said.

'Not now, Brick. I'm trying to –'

'There's someone in there.' He nodded towards the dark interior. 'Someone who needs me.'

The woman looked at the giant with open distrust. She was about to speak when Brick walked up to the door, pushed past her and entered the shack.

'Hey!' the old woman said, following the hulking intruder inside. 'What the hell do you think you're doing? You can't just barge your way in here. Get out!'

But if Brick heard her, he didn't show it. He stood, perfectly still, staring at a small, unmoving figure on top of a thin and grimy mattress at the back of the room.

'She's sick.' His voice was so low Rush had to strain to hear him. Brick took a step towards the bed.

'Don't you touch her!' the old woman said. 'Don't hurt her!'

'Already hurting,' Brick said. 'I can see it. She doesn't have very long.'

'Horace! Janek!' the woman cried out of her front door to her neighbours across the square. 'Anyone! Come quick! Help!'

'Brick . . .' Rush put a hand on the big guy's arm and tried to pull him back. He might as well have been tugging at the giant wall that loomed over this place. Brick knelt down beside the pallet and reached out, gently brushing the sick young woman's thin hair away from her forehead with his fingertips. Then he put his enormous hand on the top of her head and gently curled his fingers around it as if her skull was a ball.

The woman went to grab Brick, but Rush held her back. 'Wait,' he said. 'You have to trust him! He can help!'

'Let go of me! Get him away from her!' the woman shrieked. 'Janek!'

Brick's entire body went stiff. His face contorted into a ghastly rictus – mouth drawn down, jaw clenched shut so the muscles at the side of his face and the cords on his neck stood out. It looked as if a powerful invisible force was flowing through him from head to toe. The figure on the bed gave a little moan and then she too went ramrod stiff. Rush tore his eyes away to look at the woman. Dumbstruck now, she gawped at the scene unravelling before her. The little shack was filled with a harsh ozone smell.

Brick still had the sick girl's head in his hand, both of them vigorously jerking and twitching for what could only have been seconds but seemed much longer to those watching. The look on Brick's face was terrible. Thinking something had gone horribly wrong and that his friend was in danger, Rush was about to try to physically pry them apart when Brick flew violently backwards, his meaty shoulders slamming into the hard ground. There was a low, terrible groan, and the giant rolled on to his side, drawing his knees to his chest. He closed his eyes and lay there unmoving.

Rush dashed over to his friend's side, taking Brick's huge head in his hands and asking him over and over again if he was all right. He could hear the desperation in his own voice when Brick didn't respond.

'What just happened?' the old woman asked in a shrill voice. 'What has that thing done to my –'

'Mama?'

The woman stopped. She stared in disbelief at the girl on the bed, who'd turned to look at her for the first time in three weeks. 'Yala!' she cried, throwing herself down beside the makeshift bed and gathering her daughter into her arms. As the tears ran down her face, she failed to notice the arrival of some men at her door.

'What's going on in there?' a gruff voice asked.

Rush looked over his shoulder. Dotty had taken up a menacing posture in the doorway, blocking the men's entry. 'It's OK, Dotty,' he called out. 'Easy, girl.'

'We heard you calling out for help, Elder Yesmin,' the man said, looking from Dotty to the old woman and back again. 'Who are these strangers? Have they tried to hurt you?'

The woman stayed on her knees, her daughter's head resting in the crook of her arm. An odd laugh-sob escaped her lips. Without taking her eyes off the girl, she waved her free hand in the direction of her neighbours. 'No. No, they have not tried to hurt me. They have helped Yala. They have saved her.'

The men hesitated, uncertain what to do. 'You're sure?'

The old woman nodded. Tears of happiness ran down her cheeks. 'I'm sure. They are my guests. They are guests of Green Ward.' This time she turned to look at the men, nodding and smiling through her tears. 'Go now. I'm fine.' She looked lovingly down at her daughter before adding, 'We're all fine.'

Yesmin – that was the mother's name – prepared a meal while her guests sat around her single-room house. Despite protests that she felt perfectly well, Yala was ordered by her mother to rest. Rush hardly recognised the girl as the same person who'd been lying on her deathbed when they'd arrived, and he doubted there would be any kind of relapse; whatever Brick had 'taken away', he had made the girl completely fit and healthy again. She answered Rush's questions about the slums, explaining the layout and the politics of the place.

Word of Brick's healing quickly got out. It turned out that there were currently three more victims of Rot in Green Ward, and Brick, having recovered slightly from healing Yala, was asked by their families if he would visit them too. Rush, seeing how progressively ill his friend was becoming after the first two treatments had begged him to stop, but to no avail.

Now the big guy sat hunched over on the edge of the mattress. He looked terrible: pale with deep purple shadows under eyes that had lost all their shine. It was clear to everyone he was suffering, despite his insistence that he was 'fine'. When he'd healed Rush back in the cave, his eyes had gone completely black. Now the same blackness was in his veins, all of which seemed to stand out luridly in stark contrast to his sallow skin, on which dark, nasty-looking sores had erupted. His breathing was laboured, and when he coughed it was a nasty wet noise.

'It's not much,' Yesmin said as she placed the food on the low table in the centre of the room, 'but you are welcome to everything we have and much more.' She gave Brick a worried look. 'Will your friend be all right?' she asked Rush.

He shrugged. 'I don't know. I haven't known him long. He did something similar to me when I was blinded.'

'You were blind?' Yala asked, looking between the pair.

'Temporarily. But Brick healed me.' He glanced across at his friend, shaking his head at what he saw. 'He recovered quickly that time, but he didn't look anywhere near as bad as he does now. I don't know how or why, but I think he takes into himself whatever it is that has made the person sick. In doing so, he gets ill until he can make it go away.'

'You must both stay here until he recovers. The slums are not an easy place for those new to them.' She spooned a thin stew into a bowl and handed it to him, setting another, bigger bowl aside for Brick, who did not even look up.

'That's kind of you, but I think we should press on and try to locate the man I've come to find.'

'Silas?'

'You know him, don't you?' Rush remembered the strange look on the woman's face when he'd first mentioned the man's name.

'I know of him. He's a troublemaker. His name has been mentioned in connection with the mutant rallies, talking in front of the crowds about our rights and how we should strive to make our voices heard. From what I gather, he also runs a small school for children who have been orphaned by the very disease your friend took away from

211

Yala. Again, I'm not sure, but it's rumoured to be some-where in White Ward. Some say he is not even a Mute, but I find that impossible to believe.' She paused for a moment. 'You are not from here, so you don't know what we have to live with – the ARM crews and their thuggish tactics: coming into our houses and demanding to see our ID papers, hauling us off in the middle of the night to experi-ment on us or take blood samples. People like this man, Silas, have sown the seed of hope in many a mutant's head, but he's setting himself up for a fall. Melk and his ARM brutes will not stand for opposition.' Another pause, this one accompanied by a long, searching look. 'Thankfully, the ARM has been quieter of late. Apparently, half its units have been sent out from the cities in search of mutant children with strange abilities.'

She smiled when she saw the look on Rush's face. 'Don't worry. Even if you are the ones they're looking for, you're safe here. There is no love for the ARM in this, or any other, ward, and the two of you have more than earned all the protection Green Ward can offer. You can be sure of that.'

'Our being here might put you in danger.'

'Nonsense. The ARM are not expecting you to turn up here. They think you are hidden out there somewhere.' She waved her hand.

Rush glanced over at Brick again. He hadn't touched his

food. Despite his reservations, it looked as if staying in Green Ward was their only option until his friend was back on his feet. Something else Yesmin had said struck him. She'd said the ARM was looking for *children*, not just one child. It was what Kohl had said in Logtown, and Tink had spoken about there being at least one other 'like him'. He felt his heart thudding as he remembered what Brick had said a few days ago in the mountains: 'Five.' There were five of them. Although strictly speaking Brick wasn't a child, he was more like one than Rush in many ways. Were Silas and Jax bringing them together, here in the slums of City Four? If so, why? His head was spinning with it all.

'There is a safe house a little way from here,' Yesmin said. 'I know people have been hidden there before. I'll take you there and keep you out of harm's way. In the meantime, I'll somehow get word to this Silas man about where you are.'

'Thank you, Yesmin. We'll take you up on your kind offer.'

She smiled reassuringly at him. 'It's the least I can do.' She looked lovingly at her daughter. 'I owe you everything.'

Zander

Zander looked through the bars at the Mute his men had brought in that morning. By any standards, the prisoner was enormous: a broad-shouldered giant with long, greasy black hair that hung halfway down his back in a braid. He was naked from the waist up, not an inch of his true skin colour visible through the tattoos that covered him as he sat, hunched forward, with his huge ham-like forearms resting on his knees. At the sound of their approach, he raised his head to look up at his jailers. Zander was surprised to see the man grinning. One bloodshot brown eye stared back at the politician; the other socket was sightless, containing an orb of tarnished metal that looked like an old ball bearing. Zander idly wondered what might bring a man to choose to wear such a thing instead of an eyepatch. Of course, if he'd been a city dweller he could have had a new eye produced for him using the stem-cell technology that Zander's father's company was famous for.

Zander turned his attention to the ARM officer. 'Please remind me who this charming individual is.'

'Mange,' the caged freak said, getting up and stepping forward. He thrust a filthy hand through the bars for the politician to shake, completely ignoring the shock-rod the guard quickly pulled from his belt and pointed in his direction. 'Steeleye Mange. I run Dump Two. And I have to say, Principal Zander Melk, I don't appreciate unannounced raids like the one your guys sprung on me this morning. That is not the way things have worked for a long time now. You need to ensure these new ARM recruits of yours know that.' He sniffed. 'If I hadn't wanted to talk to you anyway, there could have been a little . . . *contretemps* between your men and mine, if you know what I mean.'

Zander ignored the hand. 'What do you mean, you *wanted* to talk to me?'

Steeleye grinned and rubbed his hand across his face, deliberately pulling down on his left cheek to stretch the lower eyelid and reveal even more of the grotesque metal orb. 'You don't seriously think that I would let this "Agency for the Registration of Mutants" just –'

'Regulation.'

'Huh?'

'It's the Agency for the Regulation, as in control, of Mutants. You said "Registration".'

Steeleye rolled his one eye towards the ceiling. 'Whatever the hell they're called, they gotta know they can't just swan in to my place like that unless I *want* them to, OK?'

'And today you wanted them to?'

'Uh-huh.'

Zander could hardly believe the gall of the man. He also wondered what the jailers here thought was so important that it warranted summoning a member of the Principia. 'Well, if you *wanted* to get yourself arrested and imprisoned, you've succeeded. Congratulations, Mr Mange.'

'Oh, I won't be in here for long.'

'Really?' Zander raised an eyebrow. He didn't like the arrogant grin he received in return.

'Yeah, really. Not only will I be out of here, but all previous charges against me will also be dropped.'

Zander smiled and shook his head. 'You really are quite something, you know that, Mange? What makes you think that I will –'

'I know where the mutant kids are – you know, the ones your men are so keen to find, the ones with the weird powers. At least, I will do very shortly.' He gave Zander that arrogant look again. 'I can give them to you.'

Zander stood as if he'd been frozen. When he spoke next, it was to the ARM agent. 'Open the cell.'

'Sir?'

'Open the cell and escort Mr Mange up to my private suite on the top floor.'

The officer looked in amazement from Principal Melk to Steeleye and back again, then quickly swiped a card in the lock of the steel door, making it swing open.

'I thought my subject matter might pique your interest,' Steeleye said, grinning through mud-coloured teeth at Zander.

It was all Melk Junior could do to hide his revulsion. He gestured for his 'guest' to make himself comfortable on the white leather sofa opposite his own. He would have the furniture destroyed and replaced afterwards. 'Please sit, Mr Mange, or may I call you Steeleye?'

'Sure. It only seems right and proper now we're friends. What'll I call you?'

'Principal Melk will do.'

'Hmmm. You look like your old man, you know that? I mean, you *really* look like him.' He sniffed and took in the opulent surroundings.

'The similarity has been pointed out to me before.'

'Now *that* is one tough cookie. I mean, really, that's a man you do not want to mess with. Must have been something being brought up by a mean old bastard like him. Not that my old man was a saint – you know what I'm saying?'

'I don't really remember him very much. He wasn't around.'

'And now you want to take over from him.' Steeleye leered. '*The president.* Got a nice ring to it, don't it?'

'I guess it does.'

'So where is he, hmm? Rumour has it he's dying or something. Got some disease that's eating him up.'

'You said you had information for me.'

'Not in the mood for chit-chat, huh?'

'Perhaps you'd like some refreshments. Food maybe.'

Mange settled back into the cushions, interlacing his fingers and cracking his knuckles before putting both his feet up on the coffee table in front of him. 'Sure,' he said. 'Whatever you got. And don't be shy with the goodies – I got a big appetite.'

Zander tapped the palm of his left hand with a finger and a series of symbols and motifs in purple light appeared beneath the skin where the tiny communication device was embedded. He was instantly patched through to his secretary, whom he asked to bring 'two steak-with-all-the-trimmings dinners'. He looked across at the massive mutant. 'Make that three,' he said. 'And bring some beers too.' He smiled across at Steeleye.

'You'll like the steak. We've managed to bio-engineer previously extinct cows. Delicious.'

'And there I was, planning to have rat again tonight.'

'Now,' Zander said, the purple lights beneath the skin disappearing as he closed his hand into a fist and turned off the comms device. He leaned towards the one-eyed man. 'You said something about mutant children with special powers?' He raised a quizzical eyebrow.

Steeleye wagged a finger at the principal. 'I knew you had a special interest in them. That's why your ARM boys have set off in all directions, and those that haven't are sniffing about asking questions.'

'What I know and what you think I know might be very different things. Why don't we assume I have no idea what you're talking about, and you can tell me why you're here.'

Mange narrowed his eyes at the politician. 'I'm not really feeling the love here, Principal Melk. I think you might have some trust issues.' Again the wagging finger.

In the short time they'd been alone together, Zander had already radically reassessed his opinion of the mutant; although the man was undoubtedly ruthless and cunning, he'd assumed at first that he was not particularly intelligent, but he was starting to see that beneath the rough exterior was a shrewd mind. It was easy to see how such a man might have risen to a position of power beyond the wall. Nevertheless, Zander reminded himself, he was only a mutant.

Mange gave a resigned shrug and leaned in too. 'Mutes come here from all over. A lot of them are wide-eyed hicks who have never seen any of the cities, let alone the slums. These individuals need a helping hand to establish themselves in such a formidable and daunting place as Muteville. I've taken it upon myself to try and sweep these individuals up before they enter the slums. Take them under my wing, as it were.'

'You don't strike me as a philanthropist, Mr Mange.'

'I'm a facilitator, Principal Melk; that's what I do. I help people to meet their needs. Some of these new arrivals could be an asset to people I know, people who need labourers, workers or . . . female friends.' He gave Melk a lascivious wink. 'I simply facilitate a partnership between two parties and take a small fee for doing so.'

'You're an enterprising individual, Mr Mange.'

Steeleye grinned. 'You don't know the half of it.'

'What does all this have to do with what I'm looking for?'

Steeleye sucked his teeth and fixed Zander with a look before continuing. 'A couple of days ago, my men intercept a pair of Mutes on the edge of the slums. A woman and a girl. They offer them a place to stay for the night and end up bringing 'em back to Dump Two. The woman is real nervous, and as soon as she's there she starts making noises about leaving again.' He stopped and shrugged. 'It happens all the time. I tell her that she's not going anywhere, and she goes loopy; she screams at the kid to run.' Mange looked across at Melk, his good eye boring into the other man's. 'The kid doesn't run, but she does set about my men. This little girl –' he held his hand out, palm down, patting the air in front of him to emphasise his point – 'moves like nothin' you ever seen. Fast doesn't even begin to describe it. One second she's there in front of one of my men, the next he's rolling on the floor holding his balls and crying like a baby. Took two of them out before you could snap your fingers. It might have gone on if I hadn't shot the woman.'

'You shot her?'

'Only with a stunner.' Steeleye waved his hand dismissively. 'But it was enough to put a halt to the kid's shenanigans. I grab the woman and tell the girl that she can earn their freedom by doing a bit of work for me. Somebody that fast can be used in a whole host of ways, but I wanted to start her off easy – a few wallets at the marketplace, you know. I send her out with my lieutenant, and on the very first day she gets snatched.'

'Snatched?'

'Taken by a couple of freaks. At the time I thought it

was a rival gang, you know? But after what happened next, I know that's not the case. No siree.'

Zander had to bite his lip at the effrontery of this man in calling anybody else 'a freak'. 'What *did* happen next?'

'I get a visit from a guy. Two guys, in fact – one regular-looking fellow and a tall, white-skinned dude. They walk into my place as bold as brass. The head man demands I hand over all my stock. Demands it! In my own place! When I tell him where to go, pointing out that there are five of my men in the room with us, he just sighs and gives a little shake of his head. Then he turns and nods to the ghost.'

'Ghost?'

'The skinny pale guy he came with. Albino. There's loads of 'em out in the slums. Anyway, he gives the ghost a nod, and it happened.' Steeleye stopped, puffing out his cheeks and shaking his head at the memory. Zander thought he detected genuine fear on the man's face. 'The two of them turned into monsters: vile, hideous things too dreadful for words. The head guy is this writhing mass of tentacles and teeth, and it moves towards me. I put my hands out in front of me, to protect myself, and as I do so I can see my skin erupting with black worms eating their way out from the inside. Don't misunderstand me here – I don't just *see* them, I can *feel* them too – a huge host of rotten filth that's writhing and squirming inside of me.

I open my mouth and hundreds, thousands of the things fall out, dropping down into my lap, wriggling and twisting about. I'm so scared it takes me a few seconds to realise the howling noise I can hear is the sound of my own screams mixed with those of my men. They were seeing the same thing! Then the tentacled creature asks me if I want it to stop. I screamed something, and then everything was gone, just like that. I looked across at my men. Two of them had pissed their pants and another one was curled up in the corner crying for a mother who's been dead ten years! I'm not ashamed to admit that I wasn't far away from joining him. I had to feel the skin on my own hands and arms to check it was still there. I catch a look at the ghost-kid, who's standing there with a little smile on his lips, and I know it was *him*. He done it.'

'Maybe it was a poison? An airborne gas designed to induce mass hallucinations?'

Steeleye shook his head. 'We all saw the *same thing*. It was the albino; I'm not saying the worms were there, but he put the nightmare into our heads. He did something to make us all see that stuff.'

'Did something?'

Mange gave the politician a hard stare. 'I'm not scared easily, Zander. This wasn't like some hypnotist's stunt. What I saw was as real to me as you sitting there now. I was still shaking when the head guy steps up and asks me how I'd like to experience it all again.'

'So you gave him your "stock"?'

'I'd have given him my good eye if that was what he wanted.'

Zander sat back, taking this in. The men his father had sent out to the locations where the children were supposed to be had been returning empty-handed. Some of the units were still out there, but so far there had been no sightings of the kids they were looking for. And then there was the matter of the bomb incident at the very first raid. Somehow the children, despite being separated by huge distances, had been forewarned that they were in danger. The pair Steeleye had described could only be the man Silas and the albino youngster he'd seen in the picture his father had shown him. And now one of the other hybrids, a girl with incredible speed, had also turned up here. This Silas was drawing them all together, and he was doing so right under the Melks' noses!

But why? That was what Zander couldn't figure out.

He looked across at the mutant. 'Nothing you've told me explains why you're so confident I'll let you go. The individuals you had in your custody have gone, as have the people who rescued them. You have nothing to offer me, Mange.'

'I wouldn't be so sure about that.'

There it was again – that conceited arrogance that rankled so much with him. He waited.

'There are two more in Muteville.'

There was a knock on the door and a young man appeared carrying a huge tray of food.

'Not now!' Zander bellowed, and the waiter quickly backed out of the room. He turned his attention to Mange. 'Go on.'

'I have people everywhere out there.' He gestured towards the windows. 'Inside *and* outside the wall. Oh yeah –' he grinned at the disbelieving look on the politician's face – 'not all of your good Citizens see us as untouchables, especially if there's money to be made. One of my people heard about some strangers who turned up in the slums. One of them magically healed a dying girl and a couple of others. A miracle, by all accounts. In doing so, he himself has become ill and is lying in a ward elder's safe house right now. I'm not one to put two and two together and come up with five, but two Mutes with special powers turning up in Muteville at the same time doesn't seem like a coincidence to me.'

'Where is this healer Mute?'

The finger was wagging again now. The finger accompanied by that infuriating grin that made Zander seethe.

'I reckon you're ready to bargain again, Principal soon-to-be-President Melk. Am I right?'

'What do you want?'

'I want the albino. I want his head on a plate.'

'I think we can do that.'

'And a position in your new force.'

'A what?'

'I think it's time your Agency for the Remonstration of Mutants had a mutant branch.'

'Now wait a minute . . .'

'I know the slums better than anybody. You *need* someone like me.'

'You'd be betraying your own people.'

'They're not my people. They're too weak to be my people.'

Zander frowned, trying to think it all through. 'Is that everything?' he asked.

'No.'

'Somehow I didn't think it was.'

'When I deliver you your freaky kids, I want in.'

'In?'

'That's right. I want to live *inside* the wall.'

'*That* isn't going to happen.'

'Oh, I think you'll find a way to make sure it does, Principal Melk. Maybe you'll need to go and ask your daddy for his help, but one way or another, you'll find a way for Steeleye Mange to be a Citizen of C4.'

Tia

After their initial meeting, Silas and Jax took Tia to the school they ran close to the centre of the slum, in an area known as the White Ward. The slums at C4 contained six such wards, and White was the oldest and most established. As such, the housing and sanitation were better there than elsewhere.

Tia had only been at the school for a short while when there was a knock on the door of the room she had been assigned to. She opened it to discover her host, Silas, on the other side.

'I'm sorry to disturb you, Miss Cowper, but I regret our plan for you to visit some of the children's lessons will have to be postponed.'

'Oh?'

'Jax and I have a rather urgent errand to run.'

There was something about the way he said this that piqued her interest. Normally calm and reserved, Silas appeared to be on edge. He looked up the narrow passage-way towards the entrance to the building.

'Can I help at all?' Tia asked.

'Not this time, I'm afraid. Perhaps we can speak when I return.'

She stood in the doorway, watching him as he walked away. Standing at the end of the corridor was the albino, Jax, and a small girl. Silas stopped, crouching down to her level, and said something that Tia couldn't catch. He nodded to the girl, who returned the gesture. With that, he opened the heavy wooden door and he and Jax were about to leave when Silas paused on the threshold, turning back to the youngster.

'Don't worry, Flea,' he said. 'We'll get her back.'

Tia had gone back to her room to read, only to fall asleep and wake later with the reader on her chest. She powered the device down, scolding herself for being so lazy, and recovered her recording equipment, intent on doing some work and not entirely wasting the day. The school was an ideal backdrop for her journalistic reports. More than anything else, she wanted to show city people that those outside the walls weren't just weird freaks to be visited and gawked at during a day trip, or talked about over dinner as if they were some abstract problem. She wanted to show the human story, film the children as they carried out their day-to-day duties or played in the streets. She planned to cut this footage in among the more unsavoury recordings she had: she already had some video she'd captured of ARM raids and brutality by the agency directed towards people who appeared to have done nothing to deserve it. The story was a powerful one, and she'd decided she was no longer interested in producing a series of individual reports; instead she would produce a full-length documentary that would make people stop and think. What she wanted more than anything was to show them what Melk was really about, demonstrate that by voting for him they'd allowed these things to happen, and that they might go on unabated if they allowed his son Zander into power this time around.

With these thoughts and ideas tumbling through her head, Tia wandered out of her room and went along to the large space down the corridor used as a refectory.

It was simply a long space full of tables and benches, but when she'd arrived at the school it had been a heaving mass of noise and activity. Now though, she had the place to herself. She set up her mobile editing equipment on one of the tables and began to run through her footage, writing notes on a small pad by her side and losing herself in her work.

After a while she felt thirsty. She looked around and spotted a tap set into the wall behind her. Cups were laid out on a table beside it. After saving her work, she stood up and went to fetch herself a drink.

She screamed in fright as she came face to face with the girl she'd seen Silas talking to earlier. Up close, she realised the girl was older than she'd thought – a teenager, in fact. The girl was petite. Reddish blonde hair and blue eyes set into a heart-shaped face gave her an elfin look, and Tia thought her freckles were the cutest thing she'd ever seen. She was no more than an arm's length away.

'Wha . . . ? How did you . . . ?' She looked around her. There was nowhere the girl could have been hiding.

Pulling herself together, Tia let out a little nervous laugh. The girl must have concealed herself somewhere, maybe beneath one of the benches, in such a way that she could not be seen.

'You scared the hell out of me. You really shouldn't creep up on people like that, you know.'

The look of sadness this provoked instantly made Tia feel bad, and she reached out a hand and put it on her arm. She snatched it away again; the heat coming off the girl was incredible. The poor thing must be running a temperature.

Tia made a mental note to tell Silas about this; a virus in a place like this would spread like wildfire.

'Flea, isn't it?' Tia said, remembering the name Silas had called her by.

The girl nodded, a smile briefly touching her lips.

'Are you shy? Is that why you don't speak?'

The girl shook her head.

'You can't speak?'

This question was answered with a tiny shrug.

Tia nodded to the space on the bench next to where she'd been sitting. 'Do you want to join me?' She smiled as Flea plonked herself down on the wooden seat.

'I'll take that as a yes,' Tia said, returning to the small screen and her editing. It was after a few minutes that Tia began to notice something odd: the girl beside her sat unmoving and apparently uninterested in her work except when the reporter was fast-forwarding through a video, trying to find a particular scene or moment. Every time she did this, Flea would lean forward and stare at the screen with interest.

The heat continued to pour off the girl. It was like sitting next to a small heating lamp and it soon made Tia feel uncomfortable. The idea of that cup of cold water appealed again, so she got up and crossed the room to the tap.

She brought back two cups and was about to take her seat again when she realised she'd left her omnipad on the table beside the tap. She sighed. 'Flea, I don't suppose you'd be a sweetheart and fetch my omni–'

There was a brief scraping sound, as if the legs of the bench had shifted against the hard floor, and Tia stared down at the device that had somehow appeared beside her notes. Dumbstruck, she reached out and brushed her fingers over the gadget, as if to assure herself it was really there. Something was terribly wrong. It *definitely* hadn't been there a split second before, and now . . .

She turned to look at the girl beside her who was sitting perfectly still, staring at the screen again.

'Flea . . .' Tia couldn't get her head around what had just occurred. 'Did you just . . . ?'

'Ah, there you are.' Jax's voice made Tia jump. Her heart was still racing wildly. She turned around to see the albino standing in the doorway. He nodded first at her and then at Flea. 'I see you two have met. Has she been bothering you?' he asked.

'Er . . . no. No, she's been fine.'

'Good. Well, I'm afraid to say I'll have to take her away from you now. There's someone who wants to speak to her.' He stared pointedly at the girl. 'Come on, Flea. Lana is here.' He paused before adding, 'She's safe.'

Tia's mind was still racing with ideas and theories about what she'd just experienced. At the same time she was already trying to convince herself that she'd somehow imagined it all. It was easier than accepting the alternative: that Flea was able to disappear and reappear again when she wanted – a sort of teleportation.

Tia shook her head, which was filled with an odd fuzzy sensation. Jax was giving her a strange look.

'Flea has a temperature,' she said, trying to keep the tremor out of her voice.

'She does?'

'She's extremely hot. She must be coming down with something.'

'Your concern is touching, Miss Cowper,' the albino said, 'but Flea is not ill.' He paused, continuing to stare so intently at her that she began to feel a little uncomfortable. 'And she can't teleport exactly. What she is capable of doing is moving at incredible speed. She can only do it in very short bursts – for now at least. That's why she is always so hot; her heart beats at an amazing rate. Silas and I are going to try very hard to help slow the world down for our Flea.'

At the mention of his name, the owner of the school also appeared in the doorway. He smiled at Tia, giving her a nod. 'I think it's time I told you what's going on, Miss Cowper.'

Once Silas had finished telling Tia everything that had happened on that fateful night at the Farm, as well as his efforts to keep the hybrid children safely hidden ever since, Tia sat staring back at him in amazement.

'That's the most terrible thing I've ever heard. Melk is a monster!'

'I thought so too. That's why I acted the way I did. We have little choice but to gather the children together and work out what is best for them.'

Tia thought about this for a moment. 'Why bring them all back here though? Why not somewhere else?'

'Where else can they go? Like you, they're young adults now, and it's not so easy to keep them hidden away. Sure, it was possible when they were very young, but now they have a right to a life where they make their own choices. How would you feel if you were told you could never go anywhere, never properly interact with other people of your age, never explore your talents? No, this moment was always going to come about. Melk's unfortunate discovery has just brought it forward.'

'He won't stop until he finds them,' she said.

'No. Now he knows they're not dead, the president will want his little creations back. He'll want to destroy them and wipe out his historical indiscretions. Either that, or he'll try to use them in some other vile way. Whatever it is, our only hope is to empower them so that that doesn't happen.'

'Empower them? How?'

'Jax rewired parts of their brains after we freed them, suppressed their gifts so they would not be fully realised. But we can reverse that. We think the children's powers might be enhanced by their being together. If Melk Senior really wants to see what he created, I say we give his "progeny" a chance to show him. And maybe change this world just a little while we're at it.'

'That's dangerous talk, Silas.'

'These are dangerous times, Miss Cowper.'

'So where do I come into all of this? You knew the children's existence had been uncovered. It seems to me that the last thing you would want would be a nosy reporter snooping about the place just as you were gathering them all together.'

The older man offered her a resigned smile. 'I want you to meet them. I want their existence, hidden for so long through no fault of their own, to be documented and recorded. If Melk is intent on erasing his grubby little secret to save his and his son's political careers, I want people to know the true story.' He raised an eyebrow. 'I would have thought something like this was every journalist's dream, Miss Cowper. I don't believe in coincidences, and I think your decision to cross the wall when you did happened for a reason. This *is* that reason.'

'Have you really considered what all this might mean? If these children really are as powerful as you say they are – and Melk fails in his attempts to apprehend them – have you thought about what might happen next?'

'Yes, I have. But perhaps you'd be so kind as to tell me what you think?'

'I think there'll be trouble. Big trouble. Maybe even war.' She glanced across at him. 'What?'

'There is a man coming here by wagon with a girl called Anya. The people who know this man call him Tink or Tinker, and he has been a good friend to our hidden children over the years. Tink also has a "gift", although he would describe it as a curse. He has the gift of foresight. He has visions, revelations about possible futures. I asked him once if he'd ever had a vision that involved the children, and he told me he'd had many. He told me that one day they'd be discovered; that they'd be drawn into a conflict; that they'd be at the centre of a fight for freedom.'

'And how did he say the conflict would end?'

'He couldn't, or maybe wouldn't, say.' Silas paused. 'For too long now, the mutant inhabitants of this world have suffered in silence. They have had no choice but to do so – how can you stand up to people who have all that technology and weaponry at their disposal? Maybe a display of what some of *us* are capable of will make them stop and think.'

She smiled, giving a small shake of her head. 'You said "us". You're not even a mutant, Silas.'

'I was referring to all of those who live outside the walls, Miss Cowper. You're one of us too now. I've told you all this in the hope that you can show the city dwellers what has been happening out here, and what their leaders are capable of. None of us wants a war, Tia, but that's exactly where we're heading if we can't put a halt to this madness.' He stood up. 'As soon as you've made your mind up, will you please tell me what you intend to do? I will completely understand if you want to simply go back to your life inside the city.'

It was Tia's turn to smile and shake her head. 'That may not be quite as simple as it sounds. Besides, as you said, this is the journalistic opportunity of a lifetime. I'm staying put. Whatever lies ahead, I'll do my best to see that the people know who was at the heart of it.'

Melk

Zander stood in the hallway, looking through the glass section of the door at his father in the room beyond. It was dark except for a glowing heat panel on the far wall, the light it emitted casting long, fuzzy shadows. In the short time since he'd last seen him, the old man's health appeared to have deteriorated further.

Unaware he was being observed, the former head of Bio-Gen sat hunched in his chair, a shadow of the formidable figure who'd done so much for the Six Cities and their inhabitants. The old man coughed, a nasty sound that carried and made Zander cringe. Pushing the door open, he cleared his own throat to signal his presence.

His father immediately straightened up and turned, beckoning his son to enter and take the seat opposite his own.

'Father.' Zander nodded.

'Junior.' His father knew how much he hated this moniker, and the smirk on his lips said as much. 'To what do I owe this pleasure?'

'I've come to update you on that little matter we spoke of the last time we met.'

'The items that were taken from me, you mean?'

'Yes.'

'So you've found them? They were at the locations I gave you?'

'No.' He watched as the old man's shoulders sank.

'None of them?'

'None of them.' He paused. It was unkind, he knew, but he was enjoying watching the old man squirm. He glanced at his watch. 'However, it seems that our search was not entirely in vain. Despite our failure to reach *them*, your chickens appear to be coming home to roost.'

His father remained still, his brow furrowed as he tried to make sense of his son's words. Always insightful, it took only a few moments for realisation to dawn. His face lit up. 'They're here?'

'In Muteville. Three of them, at least. One, a girl, has joined the man Silas and his albino friend. Two others arrived in the slums this morning and are in Green Ward. They've been put up in what the inhabitants believe to be a safe house.'

'Jax,' the old man said.

'What?'

'The albino. He has telepathic powers, although I had no idea they were powerful enough to communicate across such distances. He's called the children back.'

'Why?'

The old man ignored the question. 'What of the eldest? The one called Brick?'

'The healer?'

'Don't toy with me, Junior.'

'We're pretty certain he's one of the two who arrived today. It seems he has already used his powers to cure a sick mutant. That's why they're still in Green Ward: it appears that in helping cure the sickness, he's left himself weak and unable to travel – for the time being at least.'

'You said there were two?'

'It seems he's travelling with a younger boy – about fourteen years of age – they arrived together.'

'This other one – any indication that he has a special gift?'

'Not that we know of.'

The older man began coughing again, his face going from red to purple as he gasped for air. Eventually he stopped and mopped at his chin with a handkerchief. Unhooking the oxygen mask from the tank by his side, he put the thing over his mouth and turned a lever, releasing the gas in a sharp hiss and taking a few lungfuls before putting it to one side.

'How did you find all this out?'

'I've formed an unlikely alliance with a mutant hood-lum – a man rather appropriately named Steeleye, who has spies everywhere. One of his informers is the cousin of the girl cured by your healer. It seems this family relation has aspirations to take over the running of the ward, and Steeleye has –'

'What are you planning to do?'

'We have three spy drones in the air overhead as we speak.' He looked at his watch again, then got up and crossed the room to the huge screen on the wall across from his father's chair. 'I've arranged for the live feed from the drones to be patched through to here from the command room. A crack squad of my best men is about to raid the place. You and I will have the best seats in the house.' He waved his hand across the front of the device, stepping a little to one side so his father could see the images as they appeared on the screen.

President Melk sat perfectly still. His body might be giving up on him, but his mind was as sharp as ever. He looked up at the images from the unmanned surveillance drones. They were over an area of the slums, the infrared cameras relaying odd green-and-black images that were not always easy to interpret. The live feed switched from one to the next as those in the command room sought to get the best view of proceedings.

'Call them off.'

'What?'

His father gave him a stony look. 'Call them off, Junior.'

'Don't be ridiculous. And don't call me that.'

'You came here today to show me you can be decisive and determined. I admire that, but you haven't thought this through.' He held up his hand when his son started to protest. 'For once, that is not meant as a criticism. Sometimes age and experience allow you to see things more clearly than is the case for those blessed with youth. I may have failed as a father to you, but I have tried to be the best advisor I could.' He paused, briefly lifting the mask to his face before continuing. 'Now, despite the fact that this mess is entirely of my making, *you* are the one having to clean it up. I apologise for that. I can't turn back the clock and undo my mistakes, but I *can* help you make the right decisions regarding them. Clearly it's no coincidence these children have all turned up here together.'

'Of course not.'

'We discovered their whereabouts, and rather than try to hide them again, they're called back here. Why?' The old man sighed, narrowing his eyes, thinking things through. 'Maybe I've misjudged our friend Silas . . . again. I'd always assumed his original rescue of the children from the Farm was nothing more than the man's dislike for what had gone on in that place – an act of compassion and nothing more. But what if he had something else in mind, a plan that was hatched back then but is only coming to term now?'

'That would be far-sighted of him.'

'My brother had a brilliant mind – I've already told you that. Maybe his genius was also Machiavellian in nature.' He paused. 'Do you know what a sleeper cell is?'

Zander rolled his eyes. He hated it when his father lectured him. 'Enlighten me.'

'Back in the days before the Last War, terrorism was rife. Individuals or radical groups struck fear into the hearts of governments and world leaders because they were difficult to trace and apprehend. Some of them were part of the very communities they were to attack – a sleeper cell – remaining dormant until they were activated by a prearranged signal to perform acts of violence. The establishment of these groups required a strategy over a long period of time.' He stared pointedly at his son. 'We discovered Silas's sleeper cell, and because of that he's had to call them into action. The mutants are already revolting – demanding rights and privileges they have no claim to – and now they're ready to take their uprising to a new level. This gathering of the children is an act of aggression against the people of C4 and the other cities. He's been playing the long game, son. Now he's getting ready to make his first big move!'

'You don't know that. You can't just assume –'

'I'm telling you, this is an act of aggression!'

'Then why do you say we should call a halt to the raid on Green Ward?'

'You yourself used the analogy of chickens coming home to roost. Well, we should wait for *all* the chickens to be safely inside the coop before we send the foxes in to do their work.'

'What about your healer?' Zander looked pointedly at the oxygen tank.

'I'll have to hold on for a little longer, won't I?' The old man's face softened. 'Look, I know your pride will be telling you to push on with this. To be a big man and show me what you can do. I understand that. But what if it goes wrong? What if something happens? You won't know where the others are –' he nodded at the screen – 'and you might even lose the ones you *do* know about. Trust me. Call the raid off.'

Zander stood looking back at the man. Try as he might, he couldn't help but feel like a small child again. Everything his father said made perfect sense and he could appreciate that calling off the raid was strategically the right call, but . . . *dammit!* He cursed under his breath and tapped the palm of his hand to activate the embedded comms unit, the purple glow painting his face. He was on the verge of saying the name of the man he'd put in charge of the operation, when he stopped. What was he doing? Caving in again to his bullying and hectoring father – a man who clearly had no respect for him or the decisions he made! He, Zander Melk, was running for president! And a real president called the shots; they didn't kowtow to a sick old man forced to suck air out of a bottle.

He closed his hand, switching off the device. When he spoke again, it was in the formal and clipped manner he used when addressing members of his staff. 'I respect your views, Father, but as of right now I think it better to act on the information we have. Capturing these individuals will give us a bargaining tool with which to flush out the remaining parties.' He turned his back on the man, concentrating his attention on the images showing on the screen.

The father narrowed his eyes in his son's direction. He wanted to say more, but it was clear there was nothing he could do to change Zander's mind. Instead, he held his tongue and turned his face to watch the events unfolding on the monitor.

Steeleye

Steeleye looked down at the gun he'd been given by Zander, turning it over in his hands again.

'Brand new, state-of-the-art,' the younger Melk had said when he unpacked the thing from its crate and handed it to the mutant.

'What does it do?' Steeleye asked, bringing the strange-looking firearm up to his shoulder and sighting down the top of the short, wide barrel at the front.

'It's a non-lethal entrapment weapon. We had it designed especially.'

The Mute slowly lowered the thing from his shoulder and glowered across at the politician. 'Entrapment weapon?' He looked at the other men getting ready in the ARM barracks, all of whom appeared to be packing guns very different to his own. 'Why don't I get one of those PEGs?'

Zander glanced over his shoulder. The regular members of the squad all carried Pulsed Energy Guns. Although these too were supposed to be non-lethal, in accordance with the Principia's weaponry directives, Steeleye knew that the men would have had them customised so they could unofficially be 'dialled up' to kill. They worked by firing a concentrated invisible pulsed beam, creating exploding plasma inside the cells of the body, and he knew from bitter personal experience that, even on their lowest setting, they could leave the target writhing on the floor in a state of agony.

'Because I'm entrusting you, and only you, with this.' Principal Melk had a big grin on his face. 'If these mutant kids try to make a run for it, I want you to employ this to stop them. The rest of the team are under strict instructions not to use the PEGs on them unless it's absolutely necessary; something could go wrong.' He nodded at the gun in Steeleye's hand. 'This one is designed to entrap the target in a rapidly expanding ball of sticky foam that becomes more gluey as the ensnared person struggles.'

'A glue gun?' Mange spat. 'That's what this is? A glue gun?'

'If you like.'

'I don't.'

'You'll also be carrying the hydraulic ram . . . for the door.'

'Let me get this straight. I get a glue gun and a ram?' He glanced across again at the other ARM members who were strapping all kinds of weaponry on to their belts and vests.

'A *hydraulic* ram.' Zander smiled up at the big mutant. 'You said you wanted to join up? Well, this is what the new recruits do until they've completed their training.'

Steeleye opened his mouth to say something else, but decided to bite his tongue instead. He badly wanted to tell Zander Melk where he could shove his glue gun, but even more, he wanted a chance to get his hands on that albino. Matching the politician's goofy smile, he shrugged and walked off, mumbling to himself under his breath.

That had been a little over an hour ago. Now the squad was on the outskirts of the ghetto, waiting for the go-ahead to storm the safe house where the kids were being kept. It was a foul night – the cold blowing in from their backs made the regular men huddle together, huffing into their hands for warmth. In spite of having cut the arms off his ill-fitting uniform, Steeleye stood up straight, apparently immune to the cold.

'How much longer we gonna have to wait?' he called across to the squad commander.

The man turned away, ignoring him. Nobody stood near the mutant. He'd been left alone since it was announced,

to the regulars' collective disbelief, that he would be joining the raid. Not that he cared; as far as he was concerned
the men in the ARM unit were all pussies, and he was
certain he could wipe the floor with each and every one of
them – individually or collectively. But they were his
chance to get these kids and some payback. And if there
was one thing Steeleye liked more than anything else, it
was payback.

Rush

'You should stay away from that window,' Janek, Yesmin's nephew and neighbour, said to Rush. The man had been sent to the safe house by his aunt. He'd been surly with them the entire time, and in the last hour had turned downright hostile.

'It's fine. Nobody can see me; the lights are out.' There wasn't much of a window to look out of anyway. Planks had been nailed across it on the outside, leaving only small gaps to peer through.

'Not *all* the lights,' Janek said, looking across at Brick, who was sitting on the edge of a low pallet, the wind-up torch held in his lap so the beam shone directly up into his face.

'He doesn't like the dark,' Rush said in his friend's defence.

'A great big thing like that, afraid of the dark?'

'Leave him alone.'

Janek grumbled something under his breath, and Rush felt like reminding the ungrateful oaf how Brick had helped save the life of a member of his family, but he couldn't be bothered to argue with him. Instead he returned his attention to the world outside. The safe house was built at the end of a narrow mud lane flanked on both sides by ramshackle houses that leaned forward precariously. From where he stood, Rush could see right up the street. Apart from the large rats making the occasional scurrying run, it was deserted. When Yesmin had first brought them here, he'd been alarmed that there was only one way in or out, until she showed him the hidden door that opened out into an even narrower alleyway at the rear.

'Why is it taking Yesmin so long to get word to Silas we're here?'

'You have no idea how difficult it is finding anybody in the slums. If you think Green is built up, you should see the central wards – the ones nearer the dumps and the old city ruins. Those places are like rabbit warrens, with shacks piled one on top of another. She'll be doing her best.' He stopped at the sound of a dog barking somewhere up the street. With a yawn he got to his feet. 'I'm going out back to use the alley. Call of nature.' He walked off, and Rush heard the door at the rear of the building open and close.

Leaving the window, Rush wandered over to Brick's side. He put his hand on the big man's shoulder, and was immediately rewarded with a broad, lazy smile.

'How are you feeling?'

'Better. It was bad this time. But Brick getting better.'

'You didn't have to help all those people at once.' He looked down at the veins on the back of his friend's hand, relieved to see that they were a slightly lighter shade than they'd been earlier. The black stuff that had filled them immediately after he'd cured the Rot sufferers appeared to be gradually disappearing.

'We'll stay here tonight, but if Yesmin doesn't bring Silas back here by tomorrow we'll –' He stopped as Dotty got to her feet and hurried over to the front of the building, her claws scrabbling on the wooden planks. She stared towards the front door, her body taut. When she made a low rumbling sound, shifting her weight from side to side, he moved towards her.

'What is it, girl?'

Approaching the window, he peered up the street again. It was still empty. No doubt one of those huge rats had come close enough for Dotty to catch its scent. He was about to turn away when a tiny flash overhead caught his attention. He stopped, frowning. There was a high ceiling of cloud tonight, so he was sure it hadn't been a star. Anyway, he thought it had been red. Staying perfectly still, he kept his eyes trained on the sky and saw it again, except this time it had moved a little to the right. A moment later, a second wink of crimson flickered against the dark, then a third. Whatever they were, there were at least three of them up there, hovering high over the street and the safe house, which all of a sudden didn't feel quite so safe. He remembered the small remote-controlled drone the guards in the tower had sent up when he and Brick were on the border of the no-go zone.

He was about to suggest to Brick that maybe they should leave right now, when there was a loud scraping sound outside the back door, as if something was being dragged away from it. There was a muffled *thump*, followed by another, after which the door finally opened again.

'Janek!' Rush hissed. 'There's something flying up in the –'

The person who walked in was not Janek. Instead it was a tall thin young man, dressed from head to toe in black, which made his alabaster skin appear all the more dramatic. To Rush's great surprise, Dotty didn't react how he expected she might towards the stranger; instead of challenging him, she merely gave the albino a quick glance, *hurghed* softly and turned her attention back to whatever was bugging her out in the front alley.

'Who are you?' Rush said. Fear gripped him and he started over in Brick's direction, hesitating as he noticed the big guy's expression turn from anxiety, to confusion, then recognition.

'Jax!' Brick shouted, clapping his hands together and grinning up at the new arrival.

The young man gave a snort, looking genuinely pleased at this greeting. 'You remember me.'

'Jax!' the big man said again, repeatedly jabbing a fat finger in his direction.

'It's good to see you too, Brick.' The albino turned and looked at Rush, who was standing with his mouth open, trying to take everything in. 'And Rush. You've grown an awful lot since I last saw you.'

Rush shook his head. The young man's voice . . .

'You're the one who spoke to me in my dream. You told me to come here to City Four. You told me to go through the wastes and . . .' He frowned, looking over Jax's shoulder at the open door behind him. 'Where's Janek?'

The tall albino made a face and glanced back in the same direction. 'Was that his name? I last saw him running away from here. It would appear that the odious Janek has betrayed you. Before he departed, he lodged two large metal posts across the back door to keep the pair of you from doing likewise.'

Rush gestured towards the window, his unease growing by the second. 'There are things in the sky out there. Things with flashing red lights.'

'They're surveillance drones. We don't have much time. We have to disappear.' The albino stopped, his face turning towards the boarded-up window. 'Damn it!'

Rush, a sense of panic building in him, heard the noise of booted feet running down the lane in their direction.

'We have to go. Now!' Moving quickly, Jax hurried over to the pallet Brick was on. Hooking an arm under the sick mutant's armpit, he proceeded to try to haul him to his feet.

'He's sick,' Rush pointed out. 'He can't move very well.'

'He'll have to do the best he can. We don't have any time. Put that wooden bar across the front of the door and let's get out of here as quickly as possible.'

Rush did as he was bid, sliding the long plank down through the vertical brackets to secure the door.

The heavy footsteps had stopped and there was a moment of quiet outside, as if whoever was there was waiting for something.

'Out the back, quickly, now!' Jax hissed, pulling Brick's arm over his shoulder. 'Lead the way, Rush.'

The boy did so, Dotty instinctively falling in by his side while Jax and Brick brought up the rear. They went out of the door, hurrying down the small, rickety flight of stairs that led to the rear alleyway. As Rush jumped off the bottom step he heard a loud bang behind him.

Jax called to him to keep moving. 'They're using a hydraulic ram. The door won't hold for long.'

Rush went to help him with Brick, but their rescuer shook his head. 'No. Go ahead with your creature. There is a girl with short dark hair waiting at the entrance to the alley. Her name is Anya. Get her and bring her back here.'

'But –'

There was another loud crash, this one accompanied by the sound of splitting wood.

'Go!'

Rush hurried up the narrow alley that curved sharply one way and then the other before straightening out again. Somewhere overhead a window was opened and a bucket of foul-smelling liquid was thrown down into the passage-way, narrowly missing the boy and the rogwan. As he flattened himself against the wall Rush heard a new sound up ahead – a loud rumbling noise that he first imagined to be some kind of engine – maybe an armoured vehicle? He quickly dismissed the idea. There was no way the city authorities could get such a thing through the narrow maze of the slums. Nevertheless, his thoughts turned to that fateful day when the ARM turned up looking for him, and the image of Josuf running out of the farmhouse with the bomb . . .

As if sensing he'd allowed his mind to drift, Dotty banged herself against his leg and *hurghed* up at him. They hurried on, the noise getting louder and changing in quality with each step until it became clear to him that it wasn't mechanical at all. As they rounded one last bend, the end of the alleyway came into view along with the source of the noise. It was people – lots of people – all moving in the same direction. The low murmuring he'd taken to be an engine was in fact the sound of hundreds of voices talking and babbling to each other as they walked along a street that ran perpendicular to the opening of the passageway. Standing in the gap watching them was a dark-haired girl.

'Anya?'

The girl turned. She was attractive. Dark almond eyes took him in, and the hint of a smile touched the sides of her mouth. She had a pair of black studs in one of her ears and the way she wore her dark hair so short gave her an impish, almost boyish look.

'My name is Rush.'

'I know.'

'Jax sent me to get you. He needs help. He's in danger.' He couldn't think of anything else to say, so he turned and started back the way he had come, hoping she would follow.

When he spotted Jax and Brick they were almost at the first bend in the alley, but still in sight of the safe house rear door. The effort of supporting the huge man was clear to see on Jax's face, and Anya hurried past Rush to offer to help him.

The albino shook his head. 'There are three spy drones up there. They look like dark metal balls with a flashing red light underneath. I need them not to be there.'

The girl nodded. Rush let out a cry of alarm as she screeched, her head and shoulders hunching forward and down as if she was going to drop on to all fours. One minute she was there, the next a hideous black creature – half human, half insect – stood in her place. What little light there was reflected off the armoured shell where skin had been seconds before, and a pair of translucent wings unfolded behind her. The thing made a harsh chittering sound with the mandibles at the front of its face, bent its legs and was about to launch itself into the air when Jax put a hand out to stop it. 'After you've taken care of the drones, fly back to Silas and tell him what's happened. We'll be there as soon as we can. Do not come back here, Anya. Do you understand?'

Rush, unable to speak, stared from the hellish chimera to the albino and back again.

The girl-insect thing gave another abrasive chitter and took off, its wings making a deep humming noise as it disappeared into the darkness overhead.

'What was that?' Rush eventually said, unable to believe what he'd just seen.

'That was your sister.'

'Sister? Wh . . . ?' He would have gone on to ask what Jax was on about had he not seen, over the albino's shoulder, the figure of a man filling the doorway. One look at the tattoos that covered every bare bit of skin, plus the glint of metal where one of his eyes should have been, told Rush the man was no regular city dweller. Nevertheless, he was wearing some elements of an ill-fitting ARM uniform.

'Stop right there!' the man bellowed at them, swinging a strange-looking weapon up to his shoulder.

'He's got a gun!' Rush shouted.

Jax didn't hesitate. Still supporting Brick, he surged forward, dragging the big guy along with him and doing his best to get away from the armed man. Rush looked at the distance between the pair and the bend in the alley, knowing if they could make it that far, they might at least be able to –

There was a low *whump!* Rush flinched, turning in time to see an orange ball about the size of a fist shoot from the gun and hurtle in the direction of his fleeing friends. He cried a warning, knowing he was too late: the thing hit Brick in the small of his back, and as soon as it made contact the orange ball began to spread in every direction, a ballooning mass that stuck to everything it touched. From the point of impact it quickly engulfed Brick's upper legs, bringing the man to his knees, from where he had no hope of getting up.

'Brick!' Rush shouted.

The orange stuff continued to expand. Brick, acting on instinct, thrust his hands into it, trying to tear it loose, only to find that he was stuck fast. The big guy, arms now pinioned in the goo, pitched forward, his weight too much for Jax to support. He fell hard, slamming his face into the ground. The foam-glue carried on spreading, and fear gripped Rush at the prospect of it covering Brick's face and suffocating him.

The sound of the tattooed mutant jacking the pump-action at the base of his rifle to load another projectile caused Rush to look back again. Jax also turned at the sound. Rush saw the mutant with the gun grin as he caught sight of the albino, his one eye widening in recognition, and it was clear the pair had met before. That grin widened. Quick as a flash, Steeleye lifted the gun, sighting down the barrel at his prey.

He pulled the trigger.

There was a *click* and nothing more.

Bellowing in rage at the jammed weapon, the mutant smashed at the side of it with his fist, hoping to clear the jam. Without waiting, Rush set off at a run in his direction, dipping low to one side and scooping up a rock from the ground.

Time seemed to slow down. Rush pulled his arm back as far as he could, and then leaped forward, planting one leg and hurling all his weight and momentum into the throw. He didn't worry about the aim. As soon as the missile left his hand, there was never any doubt that it would find its target. At the same time, the one-eyed mutant gave a shout of triumph as he managed to clear the jam. As Steeleye swung the gun up again, the rock caught him flush on the forehead with enough force to snap the huge man's head backwards. Somehow he managed to stay on his feet. A deep, ugly gash opened up over his one good eye, a river of red running down into it and blinding him. The eye rolled back and he burbled something incomprehensible before pitching forward down the stairs.

There was an almighty crash and Rush looked up to see a black-and-silver orb, about the size of a basketball, smash down into the alleyway from the sky above. A moment of silence was broken by a barked command from somewhere inside the safe house. The rest of Steeleye's unit had finally caught up. A hand appeared around the doorframe, hurling a canister into the passageway, where it immediately began to spew a thick, choking smoke. Another quickly followed. Commands were shouted: '*OK, men. Put your masks on and set visor optics to thermal. Let's bag us some freaks!*'

Rush was just reaching down for another rock when Jax grabbed him by the arm and spun him round.

'Give me your hand,' he said.

'What?'

'Your hand!'

With no idea why, Rush slipped his hand between Jax's bone-white fingers, where it was clenched in a vice-like grip. The two turned to face the doorway.

Rush thought nothing could be stranger than what he'd already witnessed, but what happened next blew his mind. The world seemed to swim in and out of focus for a moment and when his vision cleared he found himself occupying *two* minds, his own and Jax's. He looked out through two pairs of eyes and was somehow able to process the information simultaneously. Odder still were the voices. Except they weren't voices; they were thoughts. He could hear the thoughts of everyone around him. Other voices were beyond these, like another layer, but they were tuned out to a low, nonsensical babble so that only the thoughts of the armed men getting ready to launch their offensive from the safehouse came through clearly.

Rush *heard* the ARM squad commander's thoughts. Concerned not to have his men injured like the Mute recruit had been, he was going to launch an all-out assault; pouring through the door in threes, the first men would lay down covering fire for the next wave behind them. He raised a hand and signalled for them to go. As he did this, *his* thoughts were dialled down as Jax/Rush concentrated on those of the men.

They came through the door firing their weapons, and Rush felt his own hand – the one not held by Jax – lift up. Half of the stimulus to perform the action seemed to come from him, half from Jax, whose own thoughts suggested he was helping Rush to do something he'd been suppressing for a long, long time. Palm out as if he was calling a halt to traffic, he shoved at the air in front of him and watched in amazement as the men flew backwards off their feet, slamming into the wall behind them. They were already unconscious before they hit the ground, and Rush noted that he could no longer hear their thoughts.

What the hell is going on? It was the ARM commander again, and to Jax/Rush it was clear his mind was a whirr of ideas and emotions. *This was supposed to be a simple mission!* More of his thoughts bombarded them. The commander had no idea what weapons the Mutes had, but he was damned if he was going to risk the lives of his men just because Zander Melk had ordered him not to use lethal force. He spoke into his communicator, requesting immediate reinforcements and asking what was going on out in the alley. When base told him they were 'almost blind' and that two of the three spy drones appeared to have been deactivated, he swore. His military training kicked in and he addressed his remaining troops. 'All right, men. Switch weapons to full power. It's frying time! Let's give them everything we've got. Go, go, GO!'

Before the men could make it out through the door, Rush/Jax lifted his hand again, this time turning it upward as if he was grasping something invisible. When he pulled the hand down, the entire back section of the house collapsed, falling around the soldiers and blocking their way with rubble and timber from the roof.

Jax let go Rush's hand and the dual world disappeared, along with the cacophony of thoughts. At the same time, all of Rush's strength and energy seemed to evaporate, and he sank to his knees, gasping. Dotty was immediately by his side, nudging him with her snout and looking from him to the collapsed building and back again.

Jax crawled over to Brick. Careful not to touch the

orange substance that enveloped his legs and torso, he tried to get him up off the floor, but it was impossible. There was a crash from behind them as the soldiers began to kick their way through the debris.

Jax straightened up. If the smoke bothered him, he didn't show it as he tried to work out what best to do next. 'We have to go,' he said.

'We can't leave!' Rush coughed. He was still on his knees, his head swimming. 'Brick is stuck in that stuff!'

'We have to. If we don't, we'll all be killed or captured! You, me *and* Brick.' He gestured back towards the safe house. 'You *heard* him! He's called for reinforcements. We can't stay here.'

'I'm not leaving without Brick.' Rush tried to get to his feet and almost fell. Instead he crawled over to his friend.

'Rush go,' Brick said.

'Not without you.'

'GO!' Brick bellowed. 'RUSH HAVE TO GO!' With an effort he craned his neck around to see his young friend and gave him an encouraging nod. 'Go.'

Rush blinked away the tears. 'I'll come for you, Brick. I promised you I'd look after you, remember? We promised each other.'

'Brick and Rush,' the big man said with a sad smile.

'Rush and Brick,' the boy agreed, reaching out for him

and almost putting his hand into the thick orange goo until Jax hooked a hand under his armpit and manhandled him to his feet.

'GO!' Brick shouted.

With that, Jax dragged Rush away just as the ARM commander and his men broke through the rubble in time to see all but one of their quarry were getting away. 'You,' the squad leader barked at two of his men, 'secure the prisoner. The rest of you, after those Mutes with me.' He led the way, stumbling through the debris and down the stairs. 'They're heading for the end of the alleyway,' he barked into his communicator. The final spy drone came smashing down at the man's feet, causing him to cry out in alarm.

As the two mutants approached the junction at the end of the passageway, Rush heard the cacophony of noise again.

'Who are all those people?' he asked.

'Remember how I said we were going to disappear?' Jax replied.

They rounded the last bend to see the tide of mutants moving across the intersection where the end of the passageway met the broader avenue beyond.

'It's a Mute Rights rally, but they're really here for us,' Jax said, pulling the youngster out into the thronging mass, where they were immediately swallowed up and swept along. 'We'll go along with it for a while and then slip away.'

'You arranged all this? So you could get us away?'

'Silas did.'

Rush was having trouble walking. He stumbled, his legs giving way unexpectedly, and he would have fallen had it not been for the young man at his side.

'What the hell happened back there? When you took my hand. What did you do?'

'Thirteen years ago I rewired parts of your brain, made them hard for you to access. It was for the best at the time, and I knew it wouldn't last for ever. Today I gave you a chance to realise some of your potential again. You did those things, Rush, not me. Unfortunately a lack of practice at using your heightened abilities means you're left mentally and physically weak when you do, but it's only temporary, and you're more powerful than you know.'

Rush glared back at him. 'Yeah? Well, if I'm so powerful, why did we leave Brick?' He pulled his arm free, not caring if he fell.

'We had no choice. You know that and Brick knew it too. You heard him yourself.'

They walked on while Rush took this in.

'Where will they take him?'

'Into the city.'

'Will they torture him?'

'Probably.'

Rush swallowed a sob. 'I don't care what it takes – I'm going to get him back.'

'*We're* going to get him back,' Jax replied. 'You're not alone any more, Rush.'

Melk

Zander squirmed in his seat, trying not to meet the eyes of his father, who was staring at him with a mixture of disbelief and anger. Before the botched raid had started the old man had summoned a nurse, demanding she give him 'a shot of juice' to ensure he was alert, and waving away her protests and lecture on the dangerous side effects of the drug. When she'd administered the dose via intravenous tube, the change had been extraordinary. Now faced with a reenergized and angry father, Zander wished he'd insisted Melk Senior listen to the nurse's objections.

The monitor they'd been watching was now wrecked, sporting a jagged, gaping hole where his father had hurled a glass through it. Before this, and despite the loss of visual contact as one by one the drones went down, the two had heard everything relayed between the base and the ARM unit through the speakers.

The unnerving silence stretched out for what seemed like for ever, until his father finally spoke.

'What on Scorched Earth did you think you were doing?' he asked.

'You can't possibly blame me for the unsuccessful outcome of this mission. I was not personally in charge of those men. It's obvious that my officers made –'

'Oh, no, you don't! You chose to do this. You! You don't get to turn round now and foist the blame on anyone else.' He waved away the nurse, who'd been hovering by the door, and waited for her to leave before continuing. 'I told you to call it off. You should have listened to me.'

'You should have made it clearer what we were up against!'

'As if you would have paid any attention.'

Zander bit his lip. 'We captured one of them.'

'If you'd just listened to me, you could have had them all!'

Zander's palm tingled. Holding his finger to his ear he listened to the message relayed to him from the ARM base. When it was finished, he looked across at his father again. He didn't like the expression on the old man's face. It was one he'd seen all too often when he was growing up.

'The prisoner is in custody,' he said. 'I think I should get down there so I can meet up with this creation of yours, don't you?'

The old man struggled up out of his chair, brushing away his son's attempt to help. 'I'm going with you.'

'Don't be ridiculous! You're too unwell. I'll –'

'You'll do as you're told and shut the hell up!' Melk Senior slipped his gown on. 'Assuming it doesn't kill me first, that shot will see me through the next hour or so. Now let's go and see what you've managed to salvage from this train wreck, shall we?'

The Melks observed the prisoner through the one-way mirror. The application of a simple solvent solution had removed the orange foam-glue that had trapped Brick, and he now sat, handcuffed to a metal table in the starkly lit interrogation room. They'd put him in bright yellow overalls which, despite being the largest pair they had, were still far too tight for him. He sat staring down at his hands. There was a cut above his left eye, and his lower lip was horribly swollen. The wounds looked as if they'd been inflicted recently, but if they bothered him he didn't show it. A speaker above the mirror on the observers' side relayed the sounds from the room: the prisoner was humming to himself.

'He's a big one,' Zander said to his father, who grunted something.

'How did he get injured like that?' the older man asked, nodding in the prisoner's direction.

'He resisted when we tried to take this from him.' The guard held out a small plastic torch.

Melk stared at the object before taking it from the guard. 'Open the door. I want to speak to him.'

'I'll come in with you,' his son said.

'*You'll* stay here. If I want you, I'll call for you. I think you've done enough damage for one day.' He coughed for the first time since leaving his hospital room, and once he'd started it was unclear if he'd be able to stop. Bent double, he struggled to breathe until the attack finally abated and he straightened up, wiping his mouth with the back of his hand.

He addressed the guard again. 'Give me the key to his handcuffs.'

'Sir?'

'The key.'

The man looked flustered, but obeyed. Unhooking the key chain from his belt, he handed one over.

'At least let the guard go in with you,' Zander suggested.

'SHUT UP!' the old man barked, rounding on him. Without another word the president gestured towards the security panel beside the door. The guard hurried over and entered the code, and the heavy door slid smoothly aside to provide access to the interrogation room. Melk paused in the entrance, looking back at his son and the guard in turn. 'I don't care what you see or hear in the next few minutes. Once this door closes behind me, neither of you is to come into this room. Is that crystal clear?' He waited for them both to agree before he turned and went inside, shutting the door behind him.

Brick stopped humming and looked up at the man as he entered, his eyes growing wide with fear and recognition.

'I see you remember me,' Melk said, walking over and taking a seat opposite the big man. He waited for the Mute to speak. 'Cat got your tongue?'

Brick looked down at the table again. 'You're the bad man from that bad place.'

'Oh, don't be like that. "Bad man"?' He shook his head. 'Not exactly the welcome a son should give his father, is it?'

'You're not Brick's father.'

'Technically no. But in a way I'm the closest thing to one you'll ever have.' He reached out, giving a little grunt of surprise as the mutant flinched away. Without saying a word he held the little key up between his finger and thumb so the Mute could see it. 'It's a key to the things on your wrists. I'd like to unlock them for you.'

Brick slowly extended his arms and allowed the manacles to be removed.

Melk put the torch on the table. 'Yours, I believe.'

Without a word, Brick shot an arm out and the device disappeared into his meaty hand.

'Where are they?' Melk asked.

'Who?'

'The others. Silas and Jax and the other two.'

'Don't know.'

'You were going to them.'

The hulk shrugged his massive shoulders.

'If you knew where they were, would you tell me?'

The question was met by the same gesture, but this time, instead of looking back down at the table, Brick kept his eyes on the man. He sighed, the edges of his mouth down. 'It's bad. You don't have long.'

'What? What are you talking about?'

'The sickness. I can see it.'

Melk swallowed loudly, the smile faltering on his face for the first time. 'Of course you can. I know that. I also know that you can cure me.' He let the statement hang in the air.

'No.'

The old man sat back in his chair and folded his arms. 'You can't? Or you won't?' He waited.

'Won't.'

'Not even to save the life of your friend? The one you came to Muteville with.'

'They got away.'

Melk made a clucking sound with his tongue and shook his head. 'I'm afraid not. They *did* get away for a while, but the youngest one, well, I think you saw he wasn't too good on his feet. The albino abandoned him, and my men picked him up not far from where they left you. Not exactly loyal, are they, your friends?'

He could see the confused look on the big Mute's face. 'The youngster, the one you were in the safe house with – he's being held in a room like this one as we speak. Unfortunately he's in a bad way. The men he hurt in that house – they were very angry when they got back here, and some of them took their frustration out on him.'

'Rush.'

'What?'

'His name is Rush.'

'That's what you call him, is it? Of course, to me he was always Case Number 3. The telekinetic.' He shook his head, remembering. 'I had big plans for him. It's a shame the damage my men have done to him means those plans will never be realised.'

Brick lowered his head but continued to look up at the man through his eyebrows.

'You have to make a choice, Brick. Make the right one, and I'll let you help your friend. But you have to do something for me first.'

'Take the hurt from you?'

'That's right. Do that, and I promise not to harm anyone else I have here in my custody.'

Brick considered this for a moment. He mumbled under his breath, something that sounded to Melk like, 'Russianbrick.' Then he reached out across the table and grabbed the other man's hands.

Zander watched in horror as his father jolted back and forth in the chair, his face contorted, lips pulled back in a terrible grimace, eyes bulging.

'The code,' he said to the guard.

'Sir?' the guard said, terrified and unsure of what to do for the best in equal measure.

'The code to open the door! What is it?'

The guard dutifully barked the number out to him, and Zander punched it in. But his finger hesitated as he recalled his father's final instruction. He returned to the one-way mirror just in time to see the room's two occupants fly back into their chairs. The Mute stared sightlessly at the ceiling. His father's eyes were closed.

The mutant looked ghastly. His skin was a charcoal grey colour, the veins beneath it black and bulging. Those unseeing eyes were bloody, and Zander saw a small crimson tear trickle down his cheek and splash down on to the front of the yellow overalls. He appeared to be breathing, but only just.

When the son looked at his father, he was surprised to see the hint of a smile on his face. The old man gave a harsh bark and suddenly pushed himself up out of the chair to his feet, opening his eyes and taking in a huge lungful of air that he slowly exhaled as if it was the freshest he'd ever smelt and not the stale, recycled stuff being pumped into the room. He turned to the mirror, knowing his son was observing him, and grinned. It was like being smiled at by a king cobra. The man walked towards the door; his back was ramrod straight now and there was a definite spring in his step. When he came out, he looked at his son.

'Amazing, isn't it?' he said. 'All our technology: the gene therapy, genetic modification, and he can cure me just like that.' He snapped his fingers to emphasise his point. He turned to the guard. 'Put him in the infirmary. We'll move him to the Bio-Gen labs tomorrow.'

'And what are we going to do with him there?' Zander asked.

'Don't be obtuse, Junior. We're going to find out how he does what he does, and isolate it so we can reproduce it.'

'What about the others?'

That flinty smile slipped from his father's face for the first time. 'Let's not spoil the rest of the day, huh? You just leave finding the others up to me.'

'Don't you need to go back to the hospital?'

President Melk laughed. 'What for? I'm cured. Besides, there's work to be done.'

Rush

Even before they'd reached White Ward, Rush's strength had all but returned and he no longer felt the exhaustion that had almost crippled him upon escaping the scene of the ARM ambush. In direct contrast to this, the guilt and sadness he felt at having left Brick behind weighed heavier on him with every step he took. Dotty appeared to feel the same way; she shuffled along by his side, head low to the ground, occasionally pausing to look round as if expecting to see the hulking mutant coming along behind them.

'It's OK, girl,' Rush reassured her, reaching down to pat her. 'We'll get the big guy back.'

Janek had been telling the truth about one thing: the inner wards were even more overcrowded than the outer ones, and large numbers of people filled the streets even at this late hour. Rush pointed this out to Jax, who explained it was even busier during the day, and that they were in the 'between time', when the streets and the people on them changed. 'Most inhabitants of Muteville choose not to venture out after sundown, when the "night people" largely take over.'

Rush glanced about him, trying to identify which of the people around them fell into this category.

'Stick close to me, and try not to make eye contact with anyone if you can help it,' Jax warned him.

Not used to urban living, Rush was more than a little shocked by some of the things he'd already witnessed. Dubious-looking individuals hissed at people from dark alleys, offering various substances for sale, none of which Rush had ever heard of. At one point, two men, who had been arguing over a woman, started to fight, the quarrel quickly turning from pushing and shoving to fists and worse. There was a cry of pain and one man staggered away, holding his abdomen as blood seeped out from between his fingers.

But nobody bothered Jax or Rush.

The longer this went on, the more Rush was convinced that the albino was using some kind of mind trickery to make the two of them look different in some way. It was the way people ahead of them reacted, deliberately moving out of their way and giving them a wide berth.

When he asked, Jax greeted his question with a nod and a wry smile. 'It's not a perfect disguise because I have to transfer the image into so many minds at once, shifting it around as people's attention falls on and off us again. And if anyone should seriously take an interest, we'd quickly be seen for who we really are. But to the casual observer, we appear diseased and dangerous – covered from head to toe in weeping sores: victims of Rot.'

Rush frowned and looked down at his hands. To him, they appeared perfectly normal.

'It's passed on by physical contact. Because of what they perceive us to be, everyone is more than willing to stay out of our way.' He nodded to a man on a street corner who was clearly selling narcotics of some kind. 'He, for instance, is hoping we don't go near him and frighten away his customers. He's also wondering how he can frighten us off if we do.'

Rush thought back to that moment in the alleyway when Jax had taken his hand and he'd briefly experienced the world as the albino did. Hearing all these people's thoughts and feelings all the time? It would be enough to drive anyone mad.

'How can you stand it? All those voices constantly in your head.'

'I don't notice them most of the time. It's like static:

annoying when your attention is drawn to it, but other-wise . . . you just screen it out and pick up on the things you want to.'

Rush walked on in silence, taking this in. After a moment or two his thoughts inevitably turned back to Brick.

'So you knew Brick before?'

'Yes, but a long time ago. And I knew you when you were just a baby.' He stopped outside a gate, undoing the lock with a key he took from his long black coat. The building, like many in the inner wards, was constructed on the ruins of an old pre-war complex, new walls cleverly merging with the remains of older ones which had some-how partially survived the apocalypse. 'This is it. Silas will explain everything to you shortly. Right now, we need to get inside.'

'You're here!'

No sooner had Jax and Rush entered the building than they were greeted by a man who'd clearly been waiting for them. 'I'm so relieved. Anya told me there was trouble.' He hurried over to them and Rush thought the stranger was about to hug him, when he suddenly stopped, frown-ing. 'Where's Brick?'

'There was an ambush. He was captured.'

It was as if the wind had been knocked out of the older

man. He shook his head and looked at the floor. 'I should have come with you.'

'We agreed you should stay here with the others. How could we have known they'd been betrayed?' said Jax.

'Silas?' Rush said, addressing the man, who turned to look at him again. He was about the same age as Josuf, Rush's former guardian, maybe a little older; the grey strands starting to pepper his dark hair matched his eyes, which were steely and intelligent. Rush thought it was a strong face.

'I'm sorry. Forgive me, Rush. Yes, I'm Silas. I've been very much looking forward to meeting you again.' He gave a little shake of his head. 'I was hoping it would be under happier circumstances.'

'We have to go after Brick. I should have stayed with him and fought those men as best I could, and –'

'And then we'd have been launching a rescue for two instead of one.'

'So we are going to rescue him?'

'Of course.'

'When? We should go now.'

Silas sighed. 'I understand how you feel, Rush, I really do. You've come a long way to get here, and no doubt you and Brick have formed a special bond – that was our hope when we sent you out across the Wastes. You see we hoped . . . no, we knew you'd find each other. You're anxious to help him, but to hurry headlong into a rescue attempt without proper planning would be madness.' He smiled kindly at the youngster. 'I'd like you to come inside and meet the others first. Allow me to tell you who you are and why we had to bring you all here. Then –'

'But we're not *all* here, are we?' Rush interrupted.

'You can't get into the city on your own, Rush.'

'These "others". Are they the five Brick spoke about?'

'What has he told you?'

'Not much. Just that there were five of us, and we were all made by the same bad man. I didn't pay him much attention at the time – he says a lot of strange things – but he recognised Jax the minute he walked in the door.'

A sad smile touched Silas's lips. 'There are indeed five of you. Brick is the eldest, then Jax. You and two girls are all the same age. They're here too. You've met Anya already, and I understand you've also had a glimpse of her unique gift.'

'She's some kind of shape-shifter.'

'She prefers the term polymorph, but essentially, yes.' He paused. 'There's somebody else here who's keen to see you.'

'Who?'

'Tinker.'

Despite everything, Rush couldn't help but show his delight. 'Tink's here?'

'He says he told you he would be. Shall I take you to him?'

Rush nodded and Silas led him through to one of the classrooms where, sitting at a table, was Tink. Upon seeing the teenage mutant, the older man put down the small book he'd been reading and stood up.

'I'll leave the pair of you alone,' Silas said, closing the door behind him.

Tink looked tired. He still wore his battered old hat, and he'd pulled it down in an effort to cover up a large cut over his eye that somebody had put six or seven stitches in. The cut, plus the scratches on his cheek and hands, told Rush that Tink's journey, like his own, had not been without incident.

They sat across from each other, neither saying anything for a while, just content to be in each other's company again.

'What happened?' Rush said, gesturing at the wounds.

'Nothing really. Anya and I had a little run-in with some people on the road here. You know how it is. Anyway, I understand you've had a rough old time of it yourself today?'

'Yeah. You could say that.'

The old man nodded. 'I knew you'd make it across the Wastes. Just knew it. And I guess you found what you were supposed to at the trading post.'

'Just about. The place was attacked by cannibals.' Rush gave the man a searching look. 'Why didn't you tell me, Tink? All those times you visited us, and you didn't say anything about the things you knew about me.'

'Would you have felt safer if I had? Would you have grown up happier if I'd revealed that you were actually in hiding out there with Josuf? No. It's better not to know some things, believe me.'

Something about the way he said this made Rush stop and think. 'Are you one of us, Tink? Do you have . . . unusual powers?'

He watched as the man considered this. 'I'm not sure what's usual and what's unusual any more. And I sure as hell don't know what being one of *us* is. There are Mutes out there in places like the Blacklands with strange abilities. Heck, there are probably some right here in the C4 slums. But the five of you are different. When Melk cooked you up in those test tubes of his, he created something that might possibly change this world for ever. Of course, I hope that any change that might occur will be for the better, but that too remains to be seen.'

'You didn't really answer my question.'

'No, I didn't, did I?' He paused, absently stroking his white moustache with the tips of his fingers before continuing. 'I sometimes get visions when I meet people. Like when I first met you. Oh, you were just a little bitty-bob, but I knew you were destined for great things. I sensed you would one day be caught up in a conflict – a fight between right and wrong, if you like – and I knew you'd have to go through a long and painful journey before you could bring an end to that conflict. That journey started when you set out through that tunnel under the farmhouse, and I'm afraid it's far from finished just because you managed to get back here to Silas and Jax. This is yet another start.'

'Do you know what happens to me?'

'No.'

Tink's answer came a little too quickly for Rush's liking. As if aware of this, the old man's face softened and he gave a small shrug. 'No, I do not. I don't see the future, just . . . possibilities. But I have to be careful; anything I say might close off some of those possible outcomes for ever. It's like a game of chess before the first move has been made: there are an almost infinite number of ways the game might be played, but each time a piece is repositioned, that number diminishes slightly, until eventually there's only one ending. I can be sneaky at times and nudge pieces around the board, but I have to be careful that I don't knock any of them over.'

'Is Brick going to be OK?'

Again Tink considered the question before answering. 'I think that will depend on what you do next: on whether you allow yourself to be guided by those who want the best for you both, or if you're governed by your own fear and guilt and hurt.'

There was a long silence while the two of them just looked at each other.

'Thanks, Tink.'

'Hey –' Tink looked around, his attitude completely changing in a heartbeat – 'where's that hideous creature? The rogwan. Did she make it too?'

'You mean Dotty?'

Tink gave Rush a look of disbelief. 'You called that *thing* Dotty?' He let out a laugh and clapped his hands together. 'Why didn't you go the whole hog and name her Petal or Trixiebell?'

'She's outside in the hallway.'

'Well, bring her in! I'd like to see her again.'

Rush opened the door. No sooner had he called her, than Dotty came shuffling and snuffling into the room. 'Look who's here,' Rush said to her, nodding in Tink's direction.

Dotty took one look at the man, let out a less than friendly *hurgh* and walked out again, pausing in the doorway to fart loudly.

'Well, what do you know?' Tink said with a grin. 'The miserable critter still hates me.' The smile faltered and then fell away again. 'What do you say we call Silas in here? Give him a chance to tell you everything he knows about you and the others.'

Rush nodded even though he felt far from sure he was ready to hear some of those things.

'Would you like me to stay?' Tink asked, sensing the boy's unease. 'Stay in here with you and Silas?'

'Yes. Yes, I would.'

'No problem, little friend. No problem.'

Reunited

Rush listened in silence as Silas told the story of how the children had been created at the Farm, and how they'd been freed by him and the members of a mutant resistance movement, one of whom was Tink. After the rescue, they'd asked for volunteers to look after the youngsters, and Josuf had stepped forward for Rush. The man had lost his own son to illness the year before and he saw the toddler as a way to fill the terrible hole the loss had left in his life.

'He was a good father to me,' Rush said.

'We knew he would be,' the man replied with a nod.

Finally Silas described how their existence had been uncovered, how a man named Thorn, an engineer at the facility where Rush was born, had been captured.

'Jax reached out to Thorn with his mind, but the man's thoughts were a scrambled mess. It was clear to us he was being tortured, and we guessed he'd quickly tell them everything he knew. At first we couldn't work out what to do for the best, but eventually we came up with the idea of bringing you all back here.' He noticed the look of alarm on Rush's face. 'Don't worry. Jax has reached out to Brick, and he isn't being tortured. Not yet, at least.'

Tink put a reassuring hand on Rush's shoulder.

There was a quiet knock on the door, and when it opened Jax was standing there. Silas went and joined him. The two spoke together in low voices, then Silas turned and addressed Rush from the doorway. 'I know all this is a lot to take in. If you're feeling up to it, the others are keen to meet you. Should we go and say hello?'

They left the building and walked out into a small quadrangle, hemmed in on all sides by buildings. During the day the place was full of noise as the children under Silas and Jax's care used the space to play in. Although it was now night, the square was still fairly well lit, thanks to a number of arc lights set up around its perimeter. Out of sight, a noisy generator growled. The light was greenish in quality and made the odd array of objects scattered about seem even stranger; there was what appeared to be an ad-hoc assault course laid out around the edge.

Silas ushered Rush forward into the centre of the space,

where three girls stood waiting. All of them appeared to be about the same age as him, but they could not have been more different in appearance and bearing.

The one on the far left was small and clearly very shy, choosing to look down at her feet rather than make eye contact with the new arrival. She had reddish blonde hair that somebody had braided down her back, and her face was speckled with tiny freckles. Next to her was Anya, now a girl again, no hint of the hideous insectile form she'd assumed to disarm the spy drones over the alley. She grinned savagely back at Rush, her arms folded across her chest. But it was the girl on the right he could hardly tear his eyes from. She was tall and beautiful, wearing clothes that could only have come from inside the wall. She moved across to a small device on top of a tripod and pressed a button somewhere on the top. A red light came on.

'Allow me to make the introductions,' Silas said. 'Ladies, this is Rush.' He gestured towards the small girl on the left. 'This is Flea.'

She looked up and gave him the briefest of smiles. When she glanced across at the girl with the camera, she received a nod of encouragement back. Flea swallowed and opened her mouth as if about to speak, only to falter and close it again, little frown lines creasing her forehead. She took another breath, then, in a tentative voice said, 'Hello, Rush.'

It was the tiniest of speeches, but it received a broad smile and a thumbs-up from those around her.

'In the middle is Anya. The two of you have already met, of course. And the young lady filming this historic reunion is Miss Tia Cowper.'

'Nice to meet you,' Tia said. She stepped forward, hand outstretched.

'And you,' he replied. Her hand was soft and warm in his own. For no good reason he felt himself blush, and he silently cursed himself, hoping nobody would notice, but the titter from Anya told him at least one of them had.

Thankfully Silas continued: 'Unfortunately this reunion is incomplete. The young man Rush was travelling with has been captured by the very people we were trying to keep you all from. We have –'

'We have to go and rescue him,' Rush interrupted, unable to maintain his silence any longer. He looked across at Flea and Anya. 'I know you don't know him, and part of you might be wondering why you should risk your own safety to help out a complete stranger, but Silas has told us all who and what we are. Now I don't pretend to have got my head around all of that yet, but Brick is one of us.' Now he'd started talking he found he couldn't stop, and the words tumbled out of him. 'He has a right to expect we will come for him – even though he would never ask that

293

of us. He is . . .' Rush swallowed, fighting back the tears as he tried to describe his friend to these people. 'He's funny and brave and kind, and if it was any one of us in the same situation, Brick wouldn't hesitate for a moment to help us out. We have to rescue him. If you won't come with me, I'll go on my own and I'll –'

'Rush,' Jax broke in, a smile on his face.

'What?'

'I've already spoken to the girls while you were inside with Silas. We've all already agreed that we must rescue Brick. What else would we do? He's our brother, just as you are.'

'Oh.' Rush looked about him at the others, his face flushing red again. *Brother.*

'We just have to work out the best way to do it.'

Silas spoke. 'Perhaps it would help our deliberations if we all knew what our strengths and abilities are.' He turned to Rush. 'That's why I thought it wise to meet out here.'

Anya went first. Even though he had seen her transform before, Rush was still astonished to see the sullen, punkie teenager morph into a series of creatures, each one more hideous than the last, until after six transformations he was within touching distance of a vast, slimy, leech-like creature that reared up over him. The thing smelled horrible. Atop its head were rows of black eyes arranged on both sides of a perfectly round, tooth-lined mouth that was now open so the monster's long, pink tongue waggled in the air inches from his face. It was all Rush could do not to turn and run for his life.

'All right, Anya, I think that's enough, thank you,' Silas said with a smile.

As if the creatures had never existed, Anya appeared in their place again. Thanks to Jax, there was none of the trouble transforming back she'd previously experienced.

'What did you think?' she said to Rush. 'I thought the last one was particularly gruesome, didn't you?'

'Its breath certainly was,' he replied, trying to make light of the situation. 'What are those creatures?'

The self-assurance she'd exuded since he'd first met her slipped away for a moment, and Rush thought he caught a momentary glimpse of the real Anya.

'They're the things that inhabit my dreams,' she said, turning and walking away from him.

'Your turn next, Flea,' Silas said, smiling at the small, taciturn girl. He turned to Rush. 'Jax has been working hard with little Flea so she might, from her perspective at least, speed the world up. Up until now, Flea's view of the world around her has been as if it moved in a terrible slow-motion, and poor Flea, in order not to stand out, has had to force herself to move at the same pace. Imagine wanting to do something and only being able to act at what feels like a snail's pace. When she moves at full speed she's . . . well, very quick.' He pointed to five bells that had been hung on threads at various points on the makeshift assault course surrounding the yard. The little devices were placed at extremes: three were at the top of the highest equipment and could only be reached by climbing the ladders or walls they topped; the other two were down low at the ends of crawl spaces or tubes.

'Flea? Would you be so kind as to go around the course as fast as you can and ring the bells?'

One moment she was standing completely still before him, the next Rush was looking at an empty space.

'Where did she . . . ?'

The first bell, one at the end of a long rectangular tunnel, rang. Rush had no sooner turned his head to look towards the sound when the next bell, this one at the top of a raised section that had to be accessed via a ladder, chimed. There had been a split second between the two sounds. The third, fourth and fifth bells all rang out. Then she was there again, standing in almost the exact same spot as before, except now her chest was rising and falling at a faster rate and she looked a little flushed.

Rush stared from her to the bells and back again.

'She just rang those bells? That wasn't a trick?'

'No tricks here tonight.' Silas smiled back at him. 'Now, you've already had a taste of what Jax is capable of, but he would like your permission to try something else. He wants to reverse some of the things he did to you on that fateful day we rescued you, to allow you access to parts of your brain he made it hard for you to reach.'

The albino, sensing the boy's apprehension, stepped forward. 'The thing we did in the alleyway – when you pushed those men away, and brought those things down on the others? – all I did was piggyback inside your head. I did none of those things; you did. That's what I want to give you back.'

'Why was it taken from me in the first place?'

'You were very young then, Rush. Telekinesis can be extremely dangerous if it is not controlled properly. My concern was that you would not be able to manage your powers.'

Rush felt a spike of anger. 'What gave you the right to make that decision? It doesn't appear to me as if *you've* had to be curbed in any way. Why me?'

'Like I said, you were very young – not much more than a baby. Can you imagine what might have happened if in a fit of temper you'd unleashed your full potential?'

'No. Because I have no idea what my full potential is.'

'Well, it's not my intention for you to explore that tonight, but I think it would be good for you to get an idea of what your gift is really all about.'

'Am I going to feel like crap again after? Like I did when we escaped from the alleyway?'

Jax and Silas exchanged glances before the albino turned back to the teenager.

'Almost certainly,' he said. 'But it'll get better the more you practise, and I think you're going to need your gift if we're going to rescue Brick.'

Rush didn't need to hear any more. He nodded back at the albino. 'Do it,' he said.

Jax placed his hands on either side of the boy's head, his thumbs resting on Rush's temples. When the albino closed his eyes and took a deep breath, Rush's entire body tensed as if he was expecting a bolt of pain or blistering light, neither of which came. Instead Jax simply stepped away, nodding his head slightly.

'Er, I don't know what just happened, but I don't think it worked,' Rush said.

'We'll see,' Jax said, suddenly sounding extremely weary. He gestured towards the corner of the yard nearest to Rush and asked him to stand there. In the opposite corner, about fifty metres away, was a rusty old oil drum standing on its end, atop it a small tin can, no doubt retrieved from one of the dumps. Bending down and picking up two small stones, the albino tossed them to Rush, who caught one in each hand. 'You could hit that target if I asked you to, couldn't you?'

Rush nodded.

Jax started to walk towards the barrel, talking back at the boy over his shoulder as he went. 'And if I asked you to do so a hundred times, you could hit it one hundred times, isn't that right?'

Aware that the three girls were watching all this, Rush shrugged. 'I guess,' he said.

'You guess?'

'OK, yes. I could hit it every time.'

'Demonstrate for the others, would you?'

There was a moment's pause, then with no more than a flick of his wrist, Rush sent one of the stones hurtling out of his hand. It hit the tin can smack in the centre, sending the thing flying.

'Flea?' Jax said, raising an eyebrow in the girl's direction. Rush glanced at the remaining stone in his hand, and when he looked back at the barrel, the tin can was standing on top of it again. He hadn't seen Flea move.

Jax had stopped walking now. He stood almost exactly

halfway between Rush and the barrel, completely obstructing the teenager's view of the target.

'Could you hit the can now?' Jax called out.

'But I can't see it.'

'Is that important?'

'It is if I want to hit it.'

'Why?'

'Because . . .' Rush stopped, realising that he didn't have a good answer. Frowning, he thought hard about how he did what he did – connecting with the missile at some elemental level and using his mind to control its tiniest particles. He was also aware that he 'merged' with the intended target in some way and made a link between the two things. But did he really need to see the target to make that connection?

As if he was aware the teenager had reached this conclusion, Jax grinned at him and gave him a nod. 'Go on, hit it.'

Rush threw the second stone. It shot out like a bullet, grazing the tip of Jax's ear and then swerved viciously to smash into the can again.

Jax led the applause, which was taken up by Silas and the others.

Rush couldn't help but grin back. Maybe Jax *had* unlocked some hidden part of him.

Thinking he was finished, Rush was about to walk away when he noticed Jax was still standing looking at him. The can was back in position on the drum and a slightly breathless Flea had rejoined the others.

'Not bad,' the albino said. 'But now I want you to ask yourself this: why did you bother with the stones?'

'Because you gave them to me. You asked me to hit that thing with them and –'

'No. I asked you to hit the target. I didn't say anything about the stones.'

Rush looked down at his now empty hands.

'Hit the target, Rush,' Jax said, standing a little taller in anticipation.

'What . . . ?'

Remember what happened in the alley when the men came through the door. Jax's voice was right inside his head. Rush looked up again to see the intent look on the young albino's face. *Don't think, just do it!*

Rush raised his hand, palm up, as he had during the ambush. Something built up within him, some invisible force that felt both alien and familiar at the same time. When he could hardly hold on to it any more he let it go, willing it to hit the can.

Jax flew backwards off his feet as if he'd been hit by a car, arms and legs out before him, head down, back arched.

When he hit the oil drum the front of the thing caved in from the force. The crumpled figure of the albino lay in an unmoving heap.

With cries of dismay everyone ran across the yard, swarming around Jax until Silas demanded they step back and give him some room. The man crouched down and placed two fingers on the side of the albino's neck, feeling for a pulse.

'Is he dead?' Anya asked.

'No, he is not dead,' Silas said, shooting her a withering stare. He was about to tell them to go and fetch the medical supplies when Jax groaned and stirred, his eyes flickering once before opening and looking about him in a daze.

'Stay still,' Silas urged, but Jax gently pushed his hand aside, nodding that he was OK and slowly getting himself into a sitting position. He shook his head as if to clear it, and looked up at Rush, who had been terrified he might have killed him.

'We might need to work on that a bit,' he said, before passing out again.

Tia

A short while later, after they'd got Jax comfortable – the albino waving away Rush's repeated apologies – Tia found Rush standing outside the front door of the school, head tipped back, taking in some air. She stopped short of calling out to him straight away, observing him for a moment instead. He seemed lost in thought, no doubt trying to get his head around everything that had happened to him since arriving at this place. It was hardly surprising. She herself found it almost impossible to believe some of the things she'd seen and heard. Inside the city wall there had always been rumours about mutants with gifts, but these had always been dismissed as fairy tales or anti-Mute sentiment.

Like the others that Melk had created from the stolen embryos, the boy was handsome and unblemished in a way that marked him out from most other mutants. Of course, he wasn't strictly a mutant, not in the true sense of the word. He was . . . he was something else. They all were: Rush, Jax, Anya, Flea and Brick. None of them could be easily pigeon-holed; they were neither one thing nor the other. Outsiders. Perhaps that was why she'd come to feel so passionate about their plight. Because she too was an outsider, caught between two worlds. She'd never felt she belonged inside the city, and now she was outside she felt equally adrift.

She followed his line of sight. He was looking up, past the rooftops of the buildings in this part of the ward, out beyond the slums to the highest floors of the tower complexes of C4 in the distance. Bright light shone out from these places, even at this late hour.

She saw him tense a little, as if becoming aware that he was not alone.

'It's a nice evening,' she said.

'Yeah, I guess.' He continued to look at the towers.

'I was sent to find you. The others were worried when you walked out.'

Silas had called a meeting to try to formulate a plan.

'There's too much talking and not enough doing! Brick is in that place –' he nodded in the direction of the city – 'and despite what he says, Silas doesn't seem in much of a hurry to get him out.'

'I think that's unfair. He's pulling his hair out trying to come up with a plan that doesn't get everyone killed.'

They stood in silence for a moment.

'What's it like?' he asked.

'What?'

'In there. Inside the wall. What's it like?'

She thought for a second before answering. 'Unkind.'

'In what way?'

'City dwellers have so much; they have the technology and science to enable them to do so much good, and they choose to use it in such frivolous ways. They genetically, chemically and cosmetically alter themselves and their pets and their children in some vain effort to achieve "flawlessness".' She huffed and shook her head. 'It's as if, having abandoned the dream of creating a perfect world from the ashes of the last one, they strive to perfect themselves instead. It all looks beautiful, but inside it's as ugly, if not uglier, than anything you'd ever see out here.'

'And you?'

'I'm not sure I understand . . .'

'What do you hope to achieve by being *out here*, with us?'

She heard the accusation in his voice and stiffened a little. 'I want to expose that ugliness. I want to show them that the real monsters are inside, not outside, the walls.'

'Don't they already know?'

'They pretend not to.'

She gestured towards the building behind her. 'They need you inside.'

The first thing Silas did was to ask Tia to give the group an account of the security measures inside and around the metropolis.

She did so, pointing out the passive and active systems they could expect to encounter. 'Without a CivisChip you can't go through any of the entrances. The wall wardens are instructed to use lethal force on anyone failing to stop should their entry set off a checkpoint alarm.'

'I could fly over the wall,' Anya pointed out. 'All I'd need to do is avoid being seen by the guards and the drones.'

'You could, but you'd be alone.' Tia held up her hand as the other girl started to protest. 'As freaking awesome as you are, Anya, you can't possibly do this by yourself. Besides, getting inside the wall is just the start of things. Every building inside the city is set up in the same way: internal and external doorways will, at the very least, alarm if you pass through them unchipped, and the most important places – government buildings, for instance, including the ARM headquarters – are rigged to send a deadly electrical charge through anybody attempting unauthorised entry. You walk through a doorway you have no right to . . . you die.'

They sat in silence, taking this in.

'So there's absolutely no way in without one of these things in your leg?' Rush said in a low whisper.

'Brick doesn't have a chip,' Tia said, a sly smile playing about her lips. She waited.

'Yeah, but he was . . .' Rush stopped when he realised what she was suggesting. 'We give ourselves up?' He stared at her in disbelief. 'That's your plan? We just offer ourselves up to the ARM and Melk?'

'Not quite.'

The vehicle carrying the two ARM officers was making a routine patrol of the fence perimeter when the driver shouted out in alarm. One second the way ahead had been clear; the next a young Mute kid – a cute, freckle-faced girl – was standing right in front of them. There was no look of fear on her face. She just stood there, in the beam of the headlights, staring in through the windscreen at them. The driver wrenched on the steering wheel, knowing even as he did there was no way to avoid hitting her. The thump of the impact was followed by the unmistakable sound of what could only be a body rolling beneath the vehicle's chassis. Both men cried out in dismay.

'Where the hell did *she* come from?' the driver asked as soon as they'd come to a halt.

'Damned if I know. Just seemed to appear out of thin air.' If anything, the officer in the passenger's seat seemed even more shaken than his colleague.

Both men opened their doors and climbed out, forgetting the protocol that stated one patrol member was to remain inside at all times. They walked around the back of the vehicle and stared down at the figure on the ground. The stitched seams that had held its right arm and leg in place had been ripped open so straw stuffing spewed out, but the dummy's crudely drawn face smiled vacantly back at them.

'What the . . . ?'

There was a loud bang as a surveillance drone crashed to the ground no more than a stone's throw away. The thing rolled over, but the glass eye that hung beneath it was already blinded.

The officer who had been the passenger was first to react, his hand instinctively dropping to his belt to where his shock-rod ought to be, only for his fingers to close around nothing but air.

'Looking for this?'

Both men spun round to see a tall, white-skinned mutant smiling calmly back at them. Their nerves were already shot to pieces, and the sight of their shock-rods in the weirdo's hands did nothing to make them feel any better. Standing at the pale figure's side was the small redhead they thought they'd hit with the car.

The albino stepped forward and shoved the devices at the officers' chests, watching as they crumpled to the floor, where they jerked a few times before becoming quite still. Just before he'd rendered them unconscious, Jax had dipped into the men's minds and retrieved the information he needed.

Tia turned the wheel, steering the vehicle down the gently sloping ramp, nodding nonchalantly at an armed guard standing on one side. The jumpsuit she'd taken from the driver was ill-fitting, but the helmet sat well enough now she'd tucked all her hair up inside it, and with the visor pulled down, something that was not uncommon when driving out of the darkness into the brightly lit areas around the vehicle entrance, she thought she wouldn't draw any unwanted attention. Rush, in the other man's uniform, was sitting in the passenger seat. Separating the front seats from the rear of the car was a clear plaziglas divider, behind which the two ARM officers were slumped unconscious on the back seat.

The metal shutters to the entrance began to rise,

revealing the stark, brightly lit space beyond. Another set of shutters, these still closed, lay at the other end. Tia slowly drove the car into the holding zone, stopping it within the brightly coloured hatched markings as indicated. There was a camera in every corner, and hanging down from the ceiling in front of them was a large screen displaying instructions. The shutter behind them descended noisily and eventually shut with a loud, jarring bang.

The HALT! instruction flashing on the screen was replaced by a prompt for Tia to lower her window. As she did so, a voice spoke from a small panel set into the wall.

'Identification and pass-key.'

Rush leaned over and spoke through Tia's window, trying his best to make his voice sound as gruff as possible. 'Lacroix and Masters. Today's pass-key is "humble237".' He knew the scanners buried somewhere in the floor beneath the vehicle had already identified the unconscious men's Civischips, and Jax had provided the rest of the information they needed. He thought of the albino curled up in the boot of the car, and couldn't help but wonder how uncomfortable it must be for somebody of his height. 'We've brought in a couple of Mutes we found hanging around the perimeter. Masters got punched in the throat by one of the goons and needs to go straight to the infirmary. Poor bastard can hardly talk.'

Tia croaked and pointed to her throat.

'Why didn't you call for backup?'

'No need. We took care of them, and when we get them into the cells we're going to take care of them again.'

There was a brief pause and then the voice instructed, 'Come on through.'

The metal shutter in front of them rose. The noise was almost deafening inside the enclosed space, and Tia used it as an excuse to shut her window again. They both stared out at the long tunnel slowly being revealed. Illuminated at regular intervals by orange lights, the road sloped gently downwards.

'It leads to the underground garages below the agency's headquarters,' Tia pointed out. She softly depressed the pedal, and they set off.

Silas approached the entrance gate. It felt strange to be in city clothing after all this time, and he secretly relished the feel of the soft material against his skin. He was next in line, and as he stepped forward into the free-standing frame that was the scanner, he felt the waft of a draught flash past his left cheek. It was all he could do not to smile. If the wall wardens felt it too, they didn't react.

The scanner made a loud howling noise and two armed men levelled their weapons at him.

'Stop right there!' the first man said, looking down at the monitor. He frowned, swiped his hand across the screen and refreshed the data. When he turned to his colleague he looked even more confused. 'He came in alone, right?' He received a nod. 'Then this damned scanner is on the blink again!' He kicked the frame with his steel-toed boot. 'According to this –' the man gestured at the screen – '*two* people just came through that portal, and *this* one is dead.'

'I can assure you both, wardens, I'm not deceased. I am, however, President Melk's brother and the uncle of Principal Zander Melk who shortly hopes to accede to that role.' He smiled at the astonished looks on the men's faces. 'I'm sure they'll both be very interested in seeing me.' He held out his arms, hands together so the men could easily cuff him. 'Take me to your leaders.'

Tia pulled to a stop in the underground car park, choosing a corner space away where the shadows were deepest.

Rush opened the boot and looked down at Jax, who grimaced up at him. 'Comfortable journey?' he asked, offering the albino a hand.

'You have no idea,' Jax said, wincing as he straightened up to his full height. He reached into the boot and retrieved Rush's usual clothes, handing them to him and looking away while the youngster slipped out of his jumpsuit and put them on.

Tia had already pressed the button to call the elevator, so the doors were open by the time Jax and Rush approached.

'The custody suite and the cells are all on the third floor,' Jax said, pressing the appropriate button.

'How do you know that?'

'I didn't, but Messrs Lacroix and Masters did. I took the liberty of delving into their heads while I was in the boot. They don't know where Brick is being held, so we'll have to find that out when we get upstairs.'

'What if they come round before we get out of here?' Tia asked as the lift rose.

'They won't,' Jax said in a tone that left her in no doubt.

The elevator doors opened. Directly in front of them was an extremely tall counter that stretched the full width of the room. An overweight man sitting behind the desk glanced up and beckoned them forward. Behind him, in a large open-plan office, at least ten uniformed men and women went about their work.

'Who have we got here?' he asked, his attention only half on the newcomers.

'Two Mutes that were hanging around the perimeter fence.'

'I was referring to you. You new?'

'Yes, sergeant,' Tia said, spotting the insignia on the man's shirt. 'I was assigned to the ARM only this week.' The agency had been fervently recruiting recently, and Tia hoped her story would sound plausible.

'Are these Lacroix and Masters' mutants?' the man asked, looking at his screen.

'That's right.'

'Then why aren't *they* booking them in?'

'They're in the infirmary. Masters got hurt during the arrest.'

He glanced across at Jax and Rush. Thanks to the albino, the custody sergeant saw two bloodied individuals who'd clearly been roughed up during their apprehension. He raised an eyebrow. 'I see Lacroix has been up to his usual tricks. Never one to miss a chance to beat up on a resident of Muteville, that one.'

The man gave Tia his full attention for the first time. 'Now listen up, rookie. I don't care *who* asks you – in the future, somebody asks you to book their prisoners in? You tell them to go to hell. Those two officers are taking advantage of you.' He sighed and heaved himself out of his chair, nodding towards a door on Tia's right. 'Bring them through to the cells,' he said.

Tia, Rush and Jax waited until the custody sergeant

pressed a button to open the entrance from his side. Stepping through, they found themselves in a narrow corridor, the right-hand side of which was taken up by a row of metal and plaziglas doors. The custody sergeant beckoned for them to follow him as he waddled off towards the cells.

'Busy?' Tia asked.

'Not really. Just a couple of freaks in.'

'I heard you had a special guest. One of the Mutes that Melk has been looking for?'

'The big guy? Yeah, he's in Cell 4. But not for much longer.'

'No? Why's that?'

'Melk wants him moved to the Bio-Gen labs. The transportation team is on its way over here now.'

Tia watched as the man approached one of the cell doors and pressed a button on the small pad on the wall beside it. When he pushed his palm – fingers splayed – against the pad, there was a loud *clunk!* as the locks slid open.

'Put your guys in here. I'll –'

The man slumped to the ground.

Holstering her shock-rod, Tia glanced up the corridor before turning to Rush and Jax. 'Well, that went a lot more smoothly than I thought it would.'

Rush was already hurrying towards the cell numbered 4. Through the plaziglas viewing window he could see Brick sitting on a low bench, hunched over, his massive forearms resting on his thighs. At the far side of the cell was a large mirror and another door. Even from where he stood, it was clear to Rush that Brick was even more sick now than he had been at the safe house. With a bunched fist, Rush banged on the door to get the big guy's attention.

Rush struggled to contain his emotions when his friend slowly raised his head; on Brick's face was a bewildered look that turned to recognition, swiftly replaced by joy. Brick clapped his hands together and pointed back in Rush's direction, shouting loudly until Rush, glancing behind him, gestured for him to be quiet.

Jax and Tia had dragged the custody sergeant over to the door so his hand could be pressed to the pad. As soon as the door was released, Rush pushed his way inside, hurrying over to Brick, where he was enveloped in the big guy's arms.

'I said I'd come for you,' he said.

'Good to see you again, Brick,' Jax said from the entrance. 'This is Tia; she's helping us.' He closed his eyes and small frown lines appeared on his forehead. 'Silas is with Melk. Let's get out of here.'

Silas

'You've got some gall, coming here like this,' the president said, glaring across at his brother, who was standing with his back to the floor-to-ceiling windows that made up one wall of the penthouse. The two men were alone, Melk having sent his guards out of the room and locked the door.

'What? No hugs? No tears of joy at our fraternal reunion?'

'When they said you just walked in through the gates, I assumed you must have lost your mind. But you don't sound like a jabbering lunatic.'

'If I could have come carrying a white flag, I would have.'

The two men stared at each other.

'Why?' Melk asked eventually.

It was only a single word, but Silas knew exactly what his brother meant.

'Because what you were doing was wrong. That place . . . "the Farm"? That was wrong. What you're doing now is wrong.'

'I want my property back.'

'They're not your property. They're living human beings.'

'Mutant hybrids! Not one thing or another. They're aberrations. Freaks.'

'If they are, it's because you made them that way! Call them what you want. You can't escape the fact that they have a right to life – a life that has meaning and purpose, and not just so you can experiment on them, clone them and discard them when they're no longer of any use.'

'Who said anything about cloning?'

'Don't insult my intelligence. We both know what you were planning.' Silas stopped. A shouting match with his older sibling was not what he had come here for. 'I heard you were ill. You don't look it. I wonder why that might be.'

'Maybe I have a fairy godmother and used up one of my wishes.'

'If you let him go, all this can end peacefully.'

The president stared back at him in disbelief. 'You really are something, you know that? Let me just see if I've got this right – *you* are threatening *me*?'

'Do you have any idea what it's like to live out there?' Silas gestured over his shoulder towards the slums beyond the wall. 'Poor health, poor hygiene, not enough food, freezing in the winter, roasting in the summer, no lights at night, no hot water in the morning.' He looked across at his brother's sneering face. 'I could go on, but I see that I'm in danger of breaking your bleeding heart. The mutant people have had enough. At the rallies the talk is of uprisings and revolution. Your Agency for the Regulation of Mutants is doing nothing to help the situation – they're mindless thugs. Nothing more than a big stick you're using to stir up the beehive.'

'You,' Melk said, jabbing a finger back at his brother, 'and the likes of you, are the reason there is such discontent out there. People like you, telling the Mutes that they have rights to the same things we city dwellers have.'

'Where's my nephew?' Silas stared stonily back. 'Except he *isn't* really my nephew, is he? Oh, I guess you had his face altered a bit when he was very young so the similarity isn't quite so striking, but even so, I'm amazed that nobody else seems to have worked it out. I caught one look at him on a news broadcast and I instantly knew what you'd done.'

'I don't know what you're on about,' the president said in a small voice.

'You never could resist flouting the rules, could you? Neither state laws nor those of nature mean anything to you. What did you think? That a clone of you would somehow fulfil all the dreams you were unable to? That you could achieve some kind of immortality if you reproduced yourself and shoehorned that individual into the position you had to vacate? What memories did you give the poor thing? Does it think it's really your son?'

'Shut up.'

'What do you think the people of the Six Cities would have to say about that, hmm? How do you think they'd react if they found out the man standing as the next president is nothing more than a clone of the former one – a pitiful puppet whose very memories have been implanted by the man pulling the strings!'

'It's stupid to limit a man – a man with the dreams and aspirations I had for my people – to no more than three terms! That isn't long enough!'

'What you've done is illegal and immoral. And despite all that's bad about the vast majority of the people inside the city wall, it is something that even *they* will not stand for.'

Another long silence stretched out between the two men. 'You always were too clever for your own good,' Melk muttered, walking over to his desk and opening a drawer. He regarded the gun in his hand for a moment before turning it on his brother. 'I have to say, it's an interesting theory, brother. But even if it's true, nobody will ever have the chance to hear it. You walked into this building as a dead man, and now you're going to be carried out as one.'

Silas's gaze didn't waiver. 'It doesn't have to end like this. All you have to do is give Brick back to me, and this can end. For now, at least. You can take that as your final warning.'

'The fact that I'm the one holding the gun doesn't seem to have registered with you. You're in no position to issue warnings.'

'I take it you won't let him go then?' Silas let out a weary sigh. Behind his back he pressed the button on the small torch device he held in his palm. A red light blinked on and off repeatedly. 'You disappoint me.'

Melk raised the gun, aiming at his brother. 'Save it for somebody who gives a damn.'

The first explosion was a low, rumbling boom from somewhere deep beneath the earth. Despite this, the building Melk and Silas were standing in shook, as if trembling with fright.

'What was that?' Melk asked.

'That was either the underground tunnels that lead to the dumps or . . .'

There were two more resonant explosions, one after another. These too were clearly underground, but seemed a little nearer. 'No, I think *that* was the tunnels. The first would have been the pumping systems for the water and sewage.'

Melk lowered his weapon a fraction, staring disbelievingly at the man across from him.

Silas gave him a brief, sad smile. 'Do you remember how I asked you just now if you had any idea what it was like to live out there beyond the wall?' He tipped his head back, regarding the other man. 'Well, you and the people of C4 are about to find out.'

The next three explosions were all above ground. They went off within seconds of each other. The last one was by far the biggest, and both men flinched at the monstrous noise and power unleashed.

The lights in every building in City Four went out all at the same time.

'Ah, those must have been the electrical substations,' Silas commented as the meagre emergency backup lighting winked on overhead.

There was a violent banging on the door to the office, the guards pounding and shouting the name of the president.

Melk watched as his brother, silhouetted against the

glass wall, lifted a finger, as if waiting for something. There was a pause and then one last, smaller explosion could be heard. Silas lowered the raised digit.

'I wanted to bring down the Bio-Gen building, but I didn't have enough explosives. That last one was the communication centre. I had to be very careful with that one because I knew people might still be working there, even at this time of night, and I didn't want to risk the loss of lives. Every one of those explosions was carefully placed so as to destroy infrastructure but not people. Two of your "creations" – Anya and Flea – put them in place, but if anybody was unfortunate enough to be hurt, the blame is all mine, not theirs.'

'What have you done?'

'I tried to warn you. I told you what you were doing was wrong.' Silas turned and pushed a small device, no bigger than his thumb, on to the glass. 'I'd stand well back and cover your eyes if I were you,' he said over his shoulder as he hurried to one side and crouched down behind a column, turning to look back at his brother one last time. 'Now.'

Melk staggered back and managed to get his arm up in front of his face as the glass wall exploded outwards, raining deadly daggers down the side of the building on to the ground below. The cold night air blew in through the ragged hole, quickly lowering the temperature of the dark interior. The banging on the door was louder than ever, as if something very heavy was being used to break it in. In addition to this, a new voice had joined the other men – this one calling out to his father. The noise hardly registered with Melk. He was transfixed by the sight of his brother hurrying over to the destroyed window. Silas stood on the edge, squinting against the wind, which blew and buffeted him. He looked up for a moment, nodded once and jumped, his arms held straight out, perpendicular to his sides.

Melk cried out in shock as two massive tentacles snatched Silas in mid-air and grasped him by the armpits.

The huge foul-looking creature hissed for a moment as it dropped alarmingly with the extra weight, but it quickly recovered, beating its leathery wings frantically and carrying the man off into the darkness.

The door finally gave way under the assault of the hydraulic ram. Zander and two guards half stumbled into the room, staring wildly about them. When the president turned to look at them he had a bewildered expression on his face. The uncharacteristic look quickly passed. Melk lifted the gun and shot the two soldiers dead.

When he turned the gun on his son, the look on the younger man's face was priceless.

'Father –'

'I'm not your father. You're just another version of me – a weak, feeble, disappointing translation, but a version of me nonetheless.'

'What?'

'You're a clone, a copy, a . . . facsimile. Nothing more. I had high hopes for you, but I have to say, you've been a disappointment. You've served your purpose, Junior, and now it's time to let the real Melk take over again.' He pulled the trigger.

Rush

'Stop,' said Jax, halting in front of the door that led back into the foyer of the custody suite. His hand hovered over the round button as he turned and looked back at the others, the expression on his face unreadable.

'What are we waiting for?' Rush asked.

The building shook as the first bomb went off. There was a moment of silence and then the scrape of chair legs against the floor as the ARM officers hurried over to the windows, all talking and shouting at once.

'That,' Jax said, and pressed the door release.

Rush gently grabbed Tia by the elbow as she went to call the elevator. He shook his head. 'We're taking the stairs, remember? If we're in that thing, we'll get stuck when the power goes out.'

They might have escaped undetected had one of the

men in the office not turned around and spotted them at the very moment they passed through the doorway leading to the fire escape. They didn't wait to hear the shouted warnings for them to stop.

There was another low booming noise.

'Hurry,' Tia urged. A loud, blaring klaxon sounded, the pitch and volume of it painful enough to make the four of them hunch their shoulders and wince.

They took the stairs as quickly as they could, helping and encouraging each other on the way down. At least one of them was always by Brick's side, supporting the giant as best they could. When, somewhere overhead, loud voices ordered them to halt or be fired at, they ignored the warnings, but the threat was enough to spur them onward with even greater urgency. They reached the bottom of the stairwell and the exit to the underground parking facility just as the main lights went out and insipid emergency auxiliary lighting took their place. Annoyingly, the klaxon was still blaring out from big speakers all around.

Three men were waiting for them, standing at the far end of the car park with small masks over their mouths and noses. There were no shouted warnings, no orders to put up their hands. The man in the centre simply stepped forward, aimed a strange-looking gun at the mutants and fired.

'Rush!' Jax shouted out.

The small canister with greenish-grey smoke spewing from it was almost on top of them when Rush lifted his hand. The gas grenade stopped, hanging in the air, shaking as if still trying to push its way past the invisible force that had halted it. Then it suddenly went into reverse, hurtling back with even greater speed towards the men who'd fired it, hitting the ground at their feet and discharging its contents into the air around them. Rush flicked the fingers of his hand downwards, swiping at the air like a cat pawing an invisible fly, and the men's masks flew from their faces. They began to choke and cough, grasping at their throats, tears pouring from their eyes. All three of them collapsed to the ground.

Jax shouted out again as the door behind him flew open. Rush spun around and caught a glimpse of men on the other side before he slammed it shut again with his mind. It was clear to the others that Rush was having to expend enormous effort to keep the door barred as the men battered against it from the other side, and he physically flinched and winced as they bodily threw themselves against it.

'Hurry up,' he said through gritted teeth.

Tia was already approaching the vehicle they'd arrived in, when Jax stopped her. 'Not that one,' he said. She turned to look at the albino and inwardly shuddered at the wicked grin on his face. He indicated another vehicle: an armoured personnel carrier with a large gun turret on top. '*That* one.'

As soon as everyone was safely inside the vehicle, Rush finally relaxed his control on the door. The look on the men's faces as they poured through and saw the smiling albino pointing the powerful cannon in their direction was incomparable. With a cry of dismay they turned on their heels and scrambled back in the direction they'd come, just as Jax fired round after round of explosive bullets into the concrete walls. He had no intention of hitting the men, but the sound of the gunfire in the enclosed, underground space was deafening. Large hunks of masonry shattered, filling the air with a thick, impenetrable dust, and when he had finished his barrage there was an eerie silence, broken only by the odd lump of concrete tearing loose and crashing down.

Tia drove them out of the car park and up the tunnel.

This time there was no halting in front of the metal shutters. Jax shot the housings at the top to bits and Tia burst through unchecked.

The escapees sat in silence. There was no whooping or shouts of triumph when they finally emerged into the night air. Even before they had set out to rescue Brick, they all knew what the consequences of their actions might mean for the population of Muteville. They'd discussed it, talking long into the night about what the Principia's response was likely to be, and how they could best avoid unnecessary bloodshed and suffering.

'Are you all right, Brick?' Rush asked his friend as the two bounced around together in the back.

The big guy simply nodded and returned his attention to the world beyond the bulletproof glass, as if he too was aware of the potential price of his freedom.

Tia steered the vehicle towards the agreed rendezvous.

Melk

An emergency assembly of the Principia was called, Melk despatching security agents to personally escort the ruling elite to the great hall where the meeting was to be held. In addition, a series of announcements was made by men standing in the streets to tell the Citizens what was going on. With no power, the meeting would not be broadcast on the large screens outside the parliament building as it usually was. Instead, the vast doors at the front of the building were left wide open so that anybody who wanted to could see and hear what was happening. They came in their droves. The residents of City Four – most of whom had taken to the streets in fear and terror as the sequence of explosions stripped them of light, heat and communications – were drawn to the building they recognised as their centre of power. The first to arrive were treated to a view of their president atop a hastily constructed dais. Lit by glaring arc lights powered by generators, Melk was a stark and shocking testament to the events of terror that had taken place that night.

Wrapped in bloody bandages where he'd had pieces of broken glass removed from his arm, neck and face, the man stood looking out at the principals as they hurriedly took their places. The forum was designed so the members sat in a horseshoe, an arrangement designed to maximise debate. By placing himself in the centre-front of this array, Melk guaranteed that he was the focus of their attention.

The hall was already packed beyond its capacity, and when the last principal was seated Melk tapped the microphone in front of him, pleased when he found the thing to be working. He began to speak.

'When our ancestors emerged from the Arks and finally made their way back to the surface of Scorched Earth, they were shocked that anything up here had survived. The creatures they encountered were hideous and terrible. Stricken with disease and disfigurement, they were an aberration of the natural order of things. It has been argued that wiping them out might have been the kindest thing; to eradicate them from this planet, so their miserable mutated genetic material would not be perpetuated. But the mass extinctions of the Last War were still too raw in our ancestors' minds, and the Mutes were allowed to survive. Not only did they endure, but they thrived. And *we* –' he looked about him, not just at the dignitaries but also at the multitude of people crammed into the auditorium, many of whom were relaying his words to those in the streets beyond – '*we* ignored the threat living on our doorstep. *We* are to blame for what has happened here tonight.'

He let the noise of the discontented voices wash over him for a few moments before lifting his hand for quiet.

'Out there –' he pointed, holding out his arm so the bloodstained dressings could be fully appreciated – 'is a race of people who have done nothing to build this world back up again. And yet, despite that, they believe they are somehow entitled to the privileges we have worked so hard for. They resent us. THEY HATE US! And tonight they have committed an act of war against the Citizens of City Four and all the cities of Scorched Earth, to prove just how much they hate us!'

There were loud cries and shouts.

'Our weakness in the face of this enemy has finally been exploited. Our unwillingness to deal with this scourge has come back to bite us!'

He allowed the shouts and cries to rise and then slowly die away. Eventually he leaned in to the microphone, and when he spoke again it was in a low, bleak tone.

'I have terrible news for you all,' he said, lowering his head and shaking it. To everyone in the auditorium he appeared like a man only just in control of himself, struggling for composure. When he looked up again, there were tears on his cheeks. 'My son – a man I hoped might take my place as your proud leader – was . . . assassinated tonight!'

There was a tumult of gasps and cries as people turned to look at each other in shock. The news must have quickly spread because more expressions of dismay could be heard from outside in the streets.

Melk carried on, his voice slowly rising in pitch and volume. 'He was killed trying to save me from the mutants who broke into the city with the express wish of ending not just my life but the lives of so many others with their bombs and wanton destruction. He was killed defending the people of City Four, defending them in the way the Melks have done for generations. He was killed defending the rights of the people he loved. And before he died in my arms, he demanded something of me. He demanded that I continue in the role I've had the honour of holding for so long now. He demanded that I avenge his death. He demanded that this act of terrorism not go unpunished. HE DEMANDED JUSTICE!'

The noise in the hall was deafening now, the crowd

whipped into a frenzy by the news, delivered in Melk's fervent oratorical style.

'Now I know this is not the way this parliament is run. I know that there are procedures and processes. But desperate times require desperate measures, and I say we don't have time for niceties! I want the Principia to vote. In fact, not just the Principia. I want all of you here tonight to vote, to give me your mandate. I want you to tell me, this very night, that you will let me lead you in ridding ourselves of the mutants for good!'

An ocean of noise broke over him. It seemed as if every voice was shouting out in support of his proposal. He'd played his hand very well.

As planned, he left the podium, nodding to his right for the speaker of the forum, who just happened to be one of his oldest friends, to take his place.

The man addressed the audience, asking them for a show of hands if they were willing to allow Melk to continue as president for an unprecedented fourth term. There were few dissenters. And those who did try to make their voices heard were quickly shouted down. Even so, Melk made a careful note of who they were, not in the least surprised to see Towsin Cowper among them.

Nodding his head, Melk left the great hall wearing a grim expression. It was only once he'd passed through the door at the rear, and was safely in one of the ante-chambers, that he allowed his features to break out into a satisfied smile. Waiting for him was General Razko. The assembled crowds didn't know it yet, but these two men together would become an all too familiar sight in the coming months.

The military man turned to his president, raising one bushy eyebrow in a characteristic gesture. 'That went surprisingly well. I must say, sir, I expected more resistance from the members of the council.'

'I didn't. They're soft. They proved that when they stifled so many of my bold plans in the last few years. I can assure you, general, they will not do so again. There are one or two that may prove troublesome, but I'll deal with them.'

'When do we strike back at the mutants?'

'Not yet. I want our response to be decisive and brutal. That requires a full assessment of what military forces and armaments we have at our disposal. Things have been allowed to slip a little in that regard, I'm led to believe.'

'The Principia *has* made a number of cuts in recent years, sir. We're horribly undermanned and under-resourced.'

'Then you and I will have to put that right, won't we?' Melk gave the other man a searching look. 'Tell me, Razko, what happened to Project C-27?'

'The cyborg programme?'

'Yes.'

The general paused, considering his response. 'Officially it was scrapped.'

'And unofficially?'

'I had it put on ice.'

'Then I think it's time it was thawed. And I believe I have the perfect candidate to use as our first test case.'

Steeleye

There was a jolt – a flash of blinding light and pain that made him grunt and jerk on the cold, flat surface. As his faculties slowly returned, he became aware that he was not alone in the room.

Steeleye Mange lay on his back. He opened his eyes, one of which had not worked for a very long time, but now, amazingly, appeared to be relaying data: facts and figures about the visual input signal as well as information regarding the current status of various systems operating within him. He paused and shook his head. *Systems?*

Without any idea how, he knew the images and data he was receiving came via his HUD, or Heads-Up Display, and that it had been installed in his right eye socket where the ball bearing had been. He turned his head to look in

338

the direction of the people his perimeter scanners told him were occupying the room with him.

The two men and the woman were wearing white coats. The information in his HUD told him the one staring back at him was called Dr Arnak. The other two – Drs Svenson and Levitt – were too engrossed in the analytical data displayed on their omnipads to pay him any attention. Their identities had already been programmed into his information database. He frowned and shook his head again, a wave of terrible nausea washing over him. *Information database? What the hell was going on?*

'We have lift-off,' Arnak informed his colleagues, a dry smile ghosting across his lips. He turned his attention to Steeleye again. 'Welcome back, Commander Mange. Now, things are going to feel rather strange to you for a while. The reorientation of your organic body to your bionic augmentations will take a little time to get used to; that's perfectly normal and as expected. We'd like to run a few diagnostic tests on you before you have the chance to meet the person responsible for your . . . rebirth. Would that be OK with you?'

Commander Mange?

Steeleye sat up and, ignoring the doctors' pleas, swung his legs round.

The first thing he noticed was the high-pitched whine

of the servo-motors as his motorised legs sprang into action. The feedback in one part of his HUD was a stream of data about the orientation and speed of the limbs, but he completely ignored it and concentrated on getting upright. His stomach rolled, making him feel as if he might throw up, and he felt light-headed. The solid *clunk!* noise as his feet made contact with the floor was like two bowling balls being dropped. He had no idea how much he weighed, but it must have been one heck of a lot.

'Well, that was very impressive, but I suggest you –'

'What the hell have you done to me?' Steeleye asked, raising first his human right arm, complete with its covering of tattoos, then the matt steel one in place where his left one had once been. 'Where are my legs? And my arm?'

'As I say, I suggest you –'

'ANSWER ME, DAMN IT!'

'We've . . . enhanced you.' Arnak shot his colleague Dr Levitt a glance. 'Get Melk and Razko.'

On one wall was a series of viewing panels, designed so that observers could see what was going on inside. Right now, the observation area was empty and dark, transforming the glass panes into black mirrors.

Steeleye approached, staring at himself.

One side of his face remained, along with his nose and mouth. On the other side, from the back of his jaw, up his cheek and through the centre of his forehead, a metallic skull looked back at him. Wherever the two interfaced was an ugly ridge of puckered flesh that appeared to be riveted to the metal beneath. Bloody tissue still lined these borders and would clearly take more time to heal. His natural eye took in its domed plaziglas partner. Despite the lens being tinted, mechanical parts could be seen moving behind it as the optical device constantly adjusted focus. He lifted the arm again, this time holding the hand out before his face and flexing the articulated metal fingers. He could sense the power in the thing. Everything he did was accompanied by a flow of information streamed right into his brain.

He turned to the doctors again, his look unreadable. He was amazed at how calm they were, considering they were shut in a room with a huge half-man, half-metal monster.

'You made me into a 'borg?'

'As I said, all will be explained to you when –'

With a roar Steeleye threw himself at them, his robotic arm pulled back, ready to pulverise them all into bloody little pieces.

'SVENSON!' Arnak barked, and the woman jabbed at a button on the omnipad she was holding.

Steeleye froze.

His organic self was still fully operational – he could breathe and feel his heart beating. But his mouth wouldn't work, and he guessed that, despite leaving the soft tissue of his lips and tongue in place so he could talk, they'd mechanised his jaw. He was still able to move his eyes, and information streamed across his vision, in the centre of which flashed the words EXTREMITY MOTOR FREEZE.

As if on cue, two men appeared in the doorway. Steeleye's HUD identified them both: President Melk and General Razko.

The older man, the politician, entered, taking in the situation. He turned to the scientists. 'Why's he frozen like that?'

'He was getting a little . . . excited,' Svenson said.

'I see. Can he hear me?' Melk looked to Dr Arnak for confirmation before stepping forward and narrowing his eyes at Steeleye. 'Well, it suits my purpose to have his undivided attention right now.' He pointed a finger at the mutant cyborg. 'I'm guessing that the last thing you remember is the botched raid on the mutant safe house. The one my son allowed you to be part of. Would that be right? The Mute kid hitting you with the rock. *Bam!*' He smacked a clenched fist into his other palm. 'Straight in the middle of your head – like David slaying Goliath!' He sighed and shook his head. 'Well, that blow caused a huge amount of harm. Even with a thick skull like the one you had, the doctors tell me the impact resulted in untold damage to your brain.' He paused for a moment before going on. 'Bad things have happened since then. My son is dead, and I'm now back in charge.

'Before his death I was made aware of the deal you two struck – that you wanted to join our forces for a chance to get revenge on these troublesome Mutes we'd been looking for. The very same Mutes that tried to kill you during the raid.' He locked eyes with Steeleye, letting this sink in. 'And I thought you deserved a second chance. I said to myself, in honour of my son, I will give this man that second chance. Now, if I get these good people behind me to unfreeze you, are you going to behave yourself? Hmm?'

Steeleye grunted something that sounded vaguely like agreement, and Melk nodded at the scientists.

There was a whirr of motors coming back to life and Steeleye was able to move again. He lowered his arm and straightened up to his full height.

'Do you still want your revenge, Mange?'

'What do I have to do?'

'All you have to do is find them.'

'And when I do?'

'They're all yours.'

Epilogue

Escape had been straightforward. But the knowledge of what they were leaving behind weighed heavily on all of them. The children at Silas's school were collected, many of them fast asleep, and along with Dotty were put aboard the stolen vehicle or Tink's wagon. Silas got word out to ward leaders and other mutant heads that trouble was coming to Muteville and that everyone who could should leave. There was little else he could do. No doubt Melk's revenge would be terrible, and those left behind in the slums would be made to suffer, but Silas and those he was directly responsible for knew they could not stay; they had to get away, and hope others heeded their warnings to do likewise.

They headed north, always looking over their shoulders for pursuers that didn't appear. When they eventually stopped, it was at a fishing community established at the edge of a huge lake. Silas knew the people there, and the fisherfolk agreed to give the group shelter in a large outbuilding they used to build boats. It was only a temporary arrangement for the adults and teenagers; not so for the younger members of the band. The young orphans would stay behind when the others moved on. Despite the tears and upset this arrangement caused, everyone knew it was for the best.

'What'll happen now?' Rush asked Tink that first night. They'd all eaten a meal of fresh fish, and the pair had volunteered to do the washing-up down at the waterfront.

'I don't know.'

'You don't know, or you won't say?'

Tink gave a sigh. 'Things'll get bad for mutants – all mutants. But they'll be worst for this group. You'll be hunted, and you'll have to fight to stay alive.'

'Will we all make it?'

'Now that I really do not know. What I do know is you're far stronger together than you are apart. Nobody needs a vision to tell them that.'

They finished up and went back to rejoin the others. When they were all together again, bellies full, Silas stood and addressed them.

'For a long time now, I've fought for mutants to have rights. Nothing special, nothing unreasonable – rights you'd think everyone was entitled to in a world where man cares for his fellow man. But these things have not been granted to us, so now it's up to us to try and take them. What we did back at City Four, rescuing Brick like that, was the right thing to do. But President Melk will turn it into something else. We're outlaws now, and he'll do whatever he can to bring us to justice, at least that's how *he'll* see it.

'For now, we have no choice but to run. But we won't run for ever. We owe it to ourselves and to all mutants to see that *true* justice is done. It's time the Mutes made a stand. It's time we said no to the tyranny we've been made to suffer for so long. It's time for a mutant rising!'

Acknowledgements

Stories can be belligerent so-and-sos, and at times it seems they are doing their utmost not to be told. When this happens, an author needs a strong team behind him to make sure the tale he wants to tell can come about. For this book there is a special trinity who need a big 'thank you':

My agent, Catherine Pellegrino, and I had a brief parting of ways before I realised that, although there are others out there, none of them 'get me' like she does. I'm glad to have her back and grateful she found this book such a great home at Bloomsbury Publishing.

My editor and I were also reunited after a brief sojourn. The brilliant Rebecca McNally is responsible for whipping this book into shape, rejigging chapters and events with great craft to make it 'work'. It's always a pleasure to work with Rebecca and I look forward to doing so on the rest of the books in the series.

The final person in this Big Three is my wife, Zoe. It's not easy being a writer's partner, but she's still clinging on to the bars of the rollercoaster cart, screaming at the top of her lungs and waiting for the next big dip or loop-the-loop. Thanks for holding my hand and riding along with me.

I'd like to thank everyone at Bloomsbury for all the hard work they've done in getting this book to market. Although this is my first project with them, I already feel that I'm in the right place, with the right people.

Finally, I'd like to thank my fans for all the emails and terrific support on social network sites like Facebook and Twitter. You've all been very patient waiting for this book to come about. When I'm at my lowest and the words won't come, you guys pick me up, dust me off and get me back on the horse. Yee-haa!

SF

TAKE THE QUIZ

TO FIND OUT IF

YOU

ARE A MUTANT

OVER AT

www.mutantcitybook.com

THE TRUTH BEHIND MUTANT CITY

Mutant City **sprang out of my love of sci-fi/fantasy books and comics.** When I was a teenager, I devoured everything in this genre I could get my hands on. Thanks to my wonderful local library, I was able to transport myself to an alternative world filled with characters like Elric, the albino prince with his soul-drinking sword; Slippery Jim, the Stainless Steel Rat; Judge Dredd; Professor Xavier and his X-Men and many more. I don't pretend that some of these works haven't heavily influenced this book – it would be really weird if they hadn't.

I set out to write the type of story I loved then, and still love now.

Scorched Earth is a world of two disparate societies: the haves and the have-nots, the technologically rich and the poor, the Pures and the Mutes. As I began to write it, I became aware of how many of these themes still ring true in our own world, and how the mistakes of the past could so easily be repeated in the future.

Always a backer of the underdog, I wanted to create a group of young characters who, despite being 'born' on the wrong side of the walls, had the capability to really shake this world up.

And what better way to do that than to give them superpowers? Hell, what kid in the world hasn't dreamt of having a superpower?

It's been a blast writing this book – and things have only just started! Our mutant heroes have a long and arduous road ahead of them. Melk is not the sort of man to take the attack on City Four lying down. The battle lines are being drawn, and neither side can afford to back down now. If you enjoyed *Mutant City*, look out for the next book in the series, **Mutant Rising**.

Steve Feasey

LOOK OUT FOR

MUTANT RISING

COMING 2015

F FEA